The Kiss
of the
Unborn

AND OTHER STORIES

The Kiss of the Unborn

AND OTHER STORIES

by Fedor Sologub

Translated and with an Introduction by
MURL G. BARKER

THE UNIVERSITY OF TENNESSEE PRESS
KNOXVILLE

Library of Congress Cataloging in Publication Data

Teternikov, Fedor Kuz'mich, 1863–1927.
The kiss of the unborn, and other stories.
CONTENTS: The wall and the shadows.—The worm.—
The hoop. [etc.]
I. Title.
PZ3.T292Ki5 [PG3470.T4]   891.7′3′3   76–27836
ISBN 0–87049–202–0

for J.B., N.B., *and* R.M.

Preface

Fedor Sologub (1863–1927) has yet to find the appreciative audience of readers and critics that his works deserve. Misinterpreted and virtually banned in his own country, he is also relatively unknown to Western readers. Yet it was Sologub who was praised by some of his contemporaries as being a second Gogol and whose poetry was compared to Pushkin's. One British admirer predicted, in 1920, that Sologub would some day rank along with Tolstoy; more recently an American critic suggested that the ever growing numbers of Nabokov *aficionados* might well look to Sologub as an influence on that writer. Others, quite to the contrary, feel that Sologub's themes and devices are monotonous; they view him as a solipsist, whose decadent preoccupations are too extravagant and have but a limited appeal. In the final assessment, I have no doubt that Sologub will be recognized as an important contributor to Russian symbolism. While he may not keep company with the giants, he nonetheless will emerge as a writer of great significance in the history of Russian literature.

Sologub's works are both timely and timeless. He shares with his predecessors an intense concern for man and the world created by him. At the core of his philosophy is a rejection of reality, a reality he depicts as bestial; for it is the creation of those dark forces, the demonic in man. But at the same time, Sologub exalts the energy within each individual, one's creative will, which is capable of creating escapist worlds of beauty, legends, and miracles.

Looking to the recent past, I can see interesting parallels between Sologub and our now wilted flower children of the sixties: rejection of rigid rules of conformity; reaction against stifling establishments; a horror of wanton violence; experimen-

tation in and expansion of life styles; and a charmingly naïve
striving for an impossible dream. His works are a testimony to this
quest: to transform Aldonsa into Dulcinea. And the key word in
describing this journey is *creating*. He sees himself as the artist-
creator; as such, he takes the reader with him in the process of
creating through the artistic mediums of poetry, drama, novels,
and here—the short story.

It was a difficult task to decide which stories should be included
in this selection from the myriad volumes in Russian. My first
thought was to translate only those stories which had never been
put into English, but that would have been unfair both to the
reader and to Sologub. Obviously, his earlier translators had
chosen from the best examples of the author's work in the genre.
Eight of these stories have been translated, some by John Cournos, others by Stephen Graham: "The Wall and the Shadows,"
"Hide-and-Seek," "The Hoop," "The Youth Linus," "The
Search," "The Kiss of the Unborn," "The Lady in Bonds," and
"She Wore a Crown." The translations are dated, often inaccu-
rate, and are difficult, if not impossible, to find now in libraries.

Originally I had intended to follow one theme in order to tie
the stories together. The most obvious, to me, was children. (As
it happened, eight of the fifteen in this selection do revolve
around children.) However, that idea appeared to be too limiting, and I decided to choose those stories which I felt were most re-
presentative of Sologub in theme and style and to arrange them
chronologically. The stories range from six pages in length to
over forty pages, and they cover the period from 1894 to 1913. My
decision will be open to criticism because the last story here, "She
Wore A Crown," is dated 1913; and in 1916 seventeen new stories,
united by the central theme of World War I, were published
under the title *The Violent Year*. Running as a thread throughout
this volume is a shift in Sologub's attitude toward religion: now he
writes about his faith and a belief in God. But I feel that these
stories suffer from an exaggerated jingoism and a certain maw-
kishness. In 1921, a collection called *Numbered Days* was pub-

lished; it consisted of three stories and a drama. I feel that they, too, are artistically inferior. Just as Sologub was capable of writing shoddy novels, the same may be said about these two volumes of short stories.

Sologub has been called one of the foremost stylists of the Russian language. Much is lost in translating, but my aim here is to be accurate to the content and follow Sologub as closely as possible. Even in translation, the reader is able to draw some conclusions about Sologub's style. The abundance of negatives reminds one of Gogol and of course emphasizes Sologub's rejection of reality. A study of the author's lexical nucleus, those words most often repeated in all of his works, reveals a preponderance of negative concepts and words of evil. His vocabulary is divided into the two opposing worlds of negation of life and affirmation of art, but the negatives appear to predominate.

Stylistically, Sologub shuttles the reader between two antithetical extremes, which is in harmony with his world view. The reader is lulled into realism by an even tempo, repetition of words or phrases, and an abundance of realistic detail. Then suddenly there will be a shift to dreamlike fantasy where the prose becomes heavy and heady, soaring away into symbolic poetry, or thickening into a purple patch. Of course alliteration and rhythm are lost in translation. There are passages in the Russian where the reader is struck by sentences falling into perfect iambs, plus an alliteration that transports the prose into poetry. This, unfortunately, I have not been able to approximate in English. Also, the reader will notice a shift in tense: from narrative past tense to active present. I have followed this shift in English because I feel that it is important to note the shuttling of the narrator with regard to his realistic-symbolic positioning.

One difficulty which every translator encounters is dialogue, particularly when a character is illiterate or speaking in dialect. Sologub's peasants and servants often use archaic forms, dialect, and substandard Russian, and one runs the risk of making them sound like American cowboys or plantation blacks when bringing them into English. His children speak like adults, but that fact says much more about their symbolic role than it does about their vocabulary.

Sologub is often criticized for his unorthodox word order. While Russian is an inflected language and in most cases allows great freedom in the placement of words, there are limits. And Sologub strains those limits. Sometimes euphony, or poeticizing the prose, influences the placement of words. It may be the assertion of Sologub's creative will. It may stem from his love for lexical tomfoolery. Often there is an intellectual or symbolic motivation behind the arrangement. For example, the sentence from "The Wall and the Shadows" translated as "A faint shadow was running from the little spoon to the saucer and to the tablecloth and dissolved in the tea," reads in Russian: "From the little spoon to the saucer and to the tablecloth was running a faint, dissolved in the tea, shadow." Here the unconventional word order functions symbolically. The elusiveness of the shadow, its mobile quality, its ability to place itself, despite the logic of grammar, at the end of the sentence, is symbolic of the reversal of order within the story where the shadows no longer need to be created, but take over reality.

In spite of what may be lost in translation, Sologub stands as an original, somewhat bizarre, but thoroughly fascinating writer. I hope that these fifteen stories will spark an interest in the reader who is unfamiliar with Sologub in English and who cannot enjoy him in Russian.

MURL G. BARKER

Philadelphia, Pennsylvania
July, 1976

Contents

Introduction

A Silver Age of Russian literature was destined to light up the horizon where the Golden Age was setting. Russia had witnessed an outpouring of literary masterpieces unparalleled in world literature during the nineteenth century. Beginning with Pushkin, the Golden Age dawned through poetry; then, for the next fifty years, the giants of prose—Gogol, Turgenev, Goncharov, Tolstoy, and Dostoevsky—dominated the scene with a veritable deluge of works destined to become classics. It was in the eighties when the uneasiness set in. Not only was the century coming to an end, but there was the unavoidable fact that the geniuses of Russian letters were dying along with it. Dostoevsky died in 1881, Turgenev in 1883, and Tolstoy had condemned all of his previous works and was involved in an inner struggle, grappling with a soul sickness, his spiritual crisis. Would they be replaced? Could they be replaced? Chekhov was not a writer who could continue the panorama of Tolstoy nor the violent and probing psychological conflicts of Dostoevsky. But what he did do was to evoke the mood of those uneasy times with a piercing fragment, a poignant short story, or a gently humorous play where the unspoken was often weightier than dialogue. Lines were blurred; there was an inclination toward introspection and retrospection. It was a period of suspense and suspension.

This mood was *fin de siècle*: the dying out and drying up of great men and ideas. The individual was in an emotional turmoil: he was depressed to see greatness fading, yet he was excited by the possibilities of what a new century might hold; it could mean a fresh start. If his feeling of impotence did not make him passive, then he was reacting against the positivism and rationalism of the nineteenth century. The haze hanging over Russia left by the setting sun of a Golden Age was dispersed under the moon of another, shorter-lived and less dazzling, but equally precious, Silver Age.

The heyday of Russian symbolism occurred during the period between 1890 and 1910. It was in the nineties that a kind of revolt developed: writers were searching for a means of expressing their impatience with the civic priorities of the second half of the nineteenth century. There was a search for new forms of poetic expression to follow a great age of prose. It was an interest in French symbolism that triggered the explosion. Verlaine, Mallarmé, Baudelaire, Rimbaud, Leconte de Lisle, and others were discussed, read, and translated. With the example of the French masters as an impetus, the first generation of Russian symbolists was born.

Critics and literary historians have a tendency to seek neat boundaries separating the two trends of Russian symbolism: geographical (the Moscow v. the Petersburg groups), philosophical (oriented toward German philosophy as opposed to French aesthetic), political (those who accepted the October Revolution, and those who did not). On the one side, there is the first generation: Valery Bryusov, Konstantin Balmont, Zinaida Gippius, Dmitry Merezhkovsky, and Fedor Sologub, who were influenced primarily by the French and represented both an aesthetic trend and the excesses of decadence. The second group, Alexandr Blok, Andrey Bely, and Vyacheslav Ivanov were drawn to German philosophy; and they were most immediately influenced by the Russian poet-philosopher, Vladimir Solovyev. However, geographical and idealogical lines were crossed: Bryusov and Balmont, for example, were in Moscow along with Blok and Bely; Bryusov, Bely, and Blok, accepted, at least partially, the October Revolution.

The first generation, to which Sologub belonged, were called decadents because of their preoccupation with death, decay, and perversions. They were out to shock the Philistine, they threw themselves into excesses in order to experience new sensations, they refined the refinements. They were criticized for being bizarre and gaudy, shocking and too dramatic, and indeed, they often slid into the melodramatic as their art became a testament to their Bohemianism. They were establishing, among other things, a cult of beauty where words were used for their phonic effect in order to approximate music in verse. Previous limits of poetic forms were expanded or done away with entirely: experimentation was as important to their art as it was to their lives. Much of their mysticism was derived from this musicality as well as from the individual word which was to connote rather than denote, and from the symbol, which was to allude to a whole realm of possibilities in the artist's vision.

Yet in spite of the flurry of excitement inherent in any revolutionary about-face, and in spite of the music and the color and the joy of creating their myths, they could not escape the sense of impending doom. Not that the artists did not take themselves seriously; that was part of the problem. They often took themselves far too seriously, and it was then but a step to disillusionment and deflation and, finally, destruction. Merezhkovsky, in a poem titled "Children of the Night (Before the Dawn)," characterized this awareness when he wrote that they were the "Premature forerunners of a too slow Spring." These "children of gloom," waiting for the sun would ". . .see the light and, like shadows, we will die in its rays." The symbolists did burn themselves out and up. The acmeists, who followed them, dethroned these high priests of vagueness.

So, Bryusov will be remembered as the superbly educated, true European, whose controlled, eloquent verses echoed the themes of eroticism, classical antiquity, and the modern city. There is the legacy of Balmont's heady, impressionistic poetry, so lush with its density of musical phonics. Merezhkovsky, with his wife Gippius, was instrumental in founding the Religious and Philosophical Society with the aim of inspiring a mystical spiritualism among the intelligentsia. His political and philosophical essays, along with his historical novels, and her brilliant poetry and criticism, testify to their importance in the movement. The wave crested with the second generation and their philosophical, theoretical, and lyrical intensity: Bely, who was a wizard of rhythmic prose, an eccentric memoirist, astute critic, and impressive poet; Ivanov, one of symbolism's greatest thinkers and most scholarly poets; and Alexandr Blok, who was the luminary of them all—twentieth-century Russia's greatest poet. In the midst of this furious flurry of light and sound stands a figure incongruous to his times: a schoolteacher, bald head, pince-nez glasses, severe and aloof, reserved and secretive—Fedor Sologub.

He was born Fedor Kuzmich Teternikov on February 17, 1863, in St. Petersburg. The son of a poor tailor who died when the boy was four, he lived with his younger sister in the Agapov household, where his mother worked as a domestic. The Agapov family were cultured; they encouraged the boy to develop his interests in music and books, and he was often taken along with them to the theater. He completed the course at the teacher's institute in 1882 and moved to the little town of Krestcy in Novgorod province, where he taught for three years. The atmosphere was one of stifling provinciality, but the young teacher had his family (his sister Olga and his mother) and writing as diversions.

The editor of the journal, *Northern Messenger*, felt that Teternikov was unsuitable as a name for a poet, so he happened on Sologub as a nom de plume for the first verses submitted by the young poet. There is no record of Teternikov's reaction, but he was Sologub from then on. Sologub was writing verses as early as 1875 and his first printed poem appeared in 1884. He was moving about to various teaching positions, each one more stultifying than the former, but he continued to write and he began to translate French authors, particularly Verlaine. Finally, in 1892, he was transferred to St. Petersburg where he settled permanently. Although he was made a district school inspector in 1899, Sologub was becoming more and more involved in the literary life of the capital, attending meetings and soirees with the leading writers of the day.

Sologub and Olga were living together at the time; their mother had died in 1894. It was a strange duo, as testified to in the memoirs of writers who frequented their apartment. Olga was a shadow-like figure: thin, always dressed in black, and suffering from "bronchitis" (later diagnosed as tuberculosis). Gippius remarked that the order and cleanliness in their household was reminiscent of a monastery, and that there was even something monklike about Olga.

Sologub himself was very much the schoolmaster: reserved, silent, speaking in a monotone. It appeared that he had never been young; he seemed to remain one age all his life. He avoided large gatherings, and he was very reluctant to talk about himself. But it was clear to everyone that brother and sister were absolutely devoted to one another and to an unusually intense degree.

Sologub's writings were appearing in various journals and newspapers, and by 1902 he had published four books of poetry. Two years later a collection of short stories came out. Following the 1905 Revolution, which he supported, he published a volume of poetry; and in 1906 two volumes of tales and a play (he wrote a total of fifteen plays) were published.

The year 1907 was an eventful one for Sologub, both in his personal life and in his literary career. His beloved Olga died from consumption, and Sologub was inconsolable at her death. But that same year he achieved literary fame with the publication of his novel *The Petty Demon*. Finally, after twenty-five years of service, he was eligible for a pension, and he retired from education to devote himself to literature.

In the fall of 1908, Sologub married Anastasia Chebotarevskaya. The intense loyalty and absolute devotion he had felt for his sister were now directed to his new wife. Her personality was dramatically different from the retiring Olga: she had studied in France and was working as a translator. She was a nervous chain smoker, hysterical, and paranoid. Sologub's career became her whole life: a larger apartment was rented and decorated, invitations sent out indiscriminately (Sologub sometimes did not even know his guests), and the silent, stern-looking husband obligingly submitted to his wife's frenzy of alterations by shaving his beard. Sologub defended Anastasia at every turn and even quarreled with old friends because of her when they were alienated or irritated by her behavior. But no one ever really penetrated their bond, which was founded on true love and mutual respect.

The couple visited Paris in 1909 and went abroad again in 1914, to Paris and Berlin. They traveled frequently to Finland, and the revolutionary years were spent between Petersburg and the town of Kostroma.

Sologub's reputation became firmly established with the continued success of *The Petty Demon*; there were five editions by 1909. Other works appeared in rapid succession: volumes of short stories and poetry; dramas; reviews and articles in journals and newspapers; and in addition, both he and Anastasia were translating French and German authors. Sologub's collected works were published from 1909 to 1914 and numbered twenty volumes. From 1915 to 1923 more short stories and poetry, as well as a novel, appeared; but after 1923 he could not publish because the Soviets considered him to be "outmoded" and "counter-revolutionary."

Sologub did not accept the 1917 Revolution. Unlike some of his contemporaries who saw it as a catharsis, or a great mystical event, Sologub believed it to be the destruction of Russia. But then he was not disillusioned as many were either. He did not allude to the new regime in his printed verse, thereby condemning it with his silence. However, there are reputed to be many overtly anti-Soviet poems among his unpublished works.

In the spring of 1921, the Sologubs, both ill, applied for permission to go to Paris. The Bloks, too, had made application to leave the country. The Soviets gave the Sologubs permission, but denied the Bloks. An uproar ensued when it became known that an enemy of the proletariat had been favored over the poet of the Revolution, and the Politburo reversed its decision. With

Gorky's help, Sologub had a passport in the fall, but it was recalled and then reissued.

Blok's death that year (ironically, he was never to use his visa)
and the cat-and-mouse tactics of the regime with the passports,
intensified Anastasia's periods of deep melancholy and nervous-
ness. On September 23, just days before their planned departure,
she committed suicide by throwing herself into the freezing Neva.
Although there was at least one eyewitness to the suicide, Sologub refused to believe what had happened. He felt she had gone
off to collect herself and that when she was calmer, she would
return. Her place at the table was set each evening. When the ice
broke up the following May, her body was washed ashore and
Sologub had to accept her death as fact.

Sologub was plunged into grief, he was alone, he could not
publish. He was supplementing his income by translating and
editing. His aloofness and strength of will saved him. But he was
enigmatic to the end: there was the one Sologub who appeared to
be a loyal citizen of the new regime, the permanent chairman of
the Writer's Union; and there was the private Sologub who had
an intense hatred for all that was going on around him and was
hoping for a miracle that would overthrow the government so
odious to him.

Sologub presaged his death in one of his poems ("Death Will
Destroy Me in December") and in a conversation once when he
told a friend that he would die from "Decemberitis" and went on
to explain that it is the illness from which one dies in December.
During his last two years he was ill and indeed, he did die on
December 5, 1927. His papers, which include manuscripts, letters, and unpublished works, were collected and catalogued, but
these archives are unavailable to Western scholars.

Sologub is highly regarded as a poet by critics and readers alike.
While not particularly innovative, his poetry is nevertheless impressive with its clarity, precision, and economy; it has been
called Mozartian. However, his prose is somewhat uneven.
There is no question about *The Petty Demon*'s claim to rank

among the classics. Written in the years 1892 to 1902, it was serialized in a journal *Questions of Life* in 1905 and appeared in book form in 1907. The story centers around a provincial school-teacher, Peredonov, who is determined to become the district inspector of schools. The novel is a realistic portrayal of his increasing paranoia, it is a satire on the vulgarity of provincial life, and it is a symbolic dramatization of the author's world view: at one pole there exist the Peredonovs who are ugly, vulgar, mean and petty, and who define reality. At the other extreme are Sasha and Ludmila. (Ludmila is a young woman who leads the pre-pubic Sasha through a maze of titillating and perverted experiences using costumes and perfumes.) Her cult of beauty and creative will offer an alternative to, and escape from, the rampant Peredonovism.

Sologub's first novel, *Bad Dreams*, took some eleven years to write and first appeared in 1895. Confusing and heavy-handed, it is a kind of finger exercise for *The Petty Demon*. The hero, Login, is a schoolteacher who has vague dreams and plans for a better society, but he achieves nothing in his stifling provincial town except to win the love of a young neighbor.

Two other novels are so dismal that it is difficult to imagine they were written by the author of *The Petty Demon*. *Sweeter Than Poison*, which appeared in 1912, is the history of a tiresome love affair. The melodrama and tedium make this work an endurance test for the most zealous of Sologub fans. The author's last novel, *The Snake Charmer*, published in 1921, recounts the struggle of Vera (the charmer of the title) to lure Gorelov into turning over his factories to her for the benefit of the workers. The novel is so stilted and downright silly that it might be assumed that Sologub, whose austere demeanor hid a lively wit and razor sharp tongue, was, in reality, condemning the revolution by killing off Vera (which means "belief" in Russian) and reflecting his attitude through this parody of a Socialist realist work. Neither of these novels has been translated into English as yet.

Sologub's trilogy, which appeared between the years 1907 and

1909, is a fascinating mishmash of realism, symbolism, history, and science fiction with language that is archaic, journalistic, riddled with clichés, poetic, and banal. The first volume is titled *Drops of Blood*; the second, *Queen Ortruda*; and the third, *Smoke and Ashes*. (Only the first volume has been translated into English, by John Cournos, under the title, *The Created Legend*.) The hero, Trirodov, who lives in Russia during the time of the 1905 Revolution, is a kind of sorcerer who conducts bizarre experiments in order to expand the boundaries of experience and to alter reality. He is not just the Sologubian dreamer, yearning for a utopia; he is actively involved in achieving it. Queen Ortruda (of the United Islands, located in the tropics) has been duped by her husband and throws herself into excesses of sensuality as an escape. She suffocates when a volcano erupts and the islands are in revolutionary chaos. The third volume brings the two narratives together with a parallel account of the two strifetorn lands. In the end, Trirodov, along with his fiancée, Elisaveta (who experiences Ortruda's life while unconscious), and his son from his first marriage, along with some of his followers, fly off in a greenhouse-turned-spaceship to the United Islands, where he is to reign as King George in this perfect setting for his utopia. There are numerous subplots and countless characters and situations that have nothing to do directly with the main story line. The trilogy is known under the general title of "Tvorimaya legenda" in Russian which, accurately translated, means: "a legend in the process of being created." This is a clue to the work's charm and ultimate failure: the reader tends to become lost in the legend, both through the hero's maze of experiments and the author's numerous and whimsical digressions.

Critics, in attempting to assess Sologub as an important figure in the modernist movement, have named him Russia's only true decadent, Russia's Baudelaire, Russia's Marquis de Sade. Being labeled a decadent in the symbolist movement was usually not much more than a question of thematic emphasis; and while the themes of death, sex, and perversions predominate in the author's symbolic world, a closer look at his aesthetics reveals his kinship to many of the basic tenets of other symbolists. He believed that the movement was a liberating force, that when an artistic image is extended to the limit and the one who perceives it experiences a multitude of sensations, then the represented subject becomes a symbol, and myths are produced by contact with various experiences.

In an article published in 1914, Sologub explained that in his view, there are three variants of symbolism: cosmic, individual, and democratic. Cosmic symbolism he sees as reflection on the world, life in the world and the One Will which rules the world. The individual symbolism is rooted in the consciousness of separate individuals. It is when the individual becomes concerned and identifies with the universal that symbolism enters the third phase and becomes democratic. It is at this period where, according to Sologub, there exists a dictum to "love life." And if one does not love life, because contemporary life is not worthy of love, then life must be transformed through the creative will. And this view is at the basis of three adjectives applied to Sologub's philosophy: Manichean, escapist, and solipsistic.

Manicheism is a religious philosophy that was taught from the third to the seventh centuries A.D. by the Persian Manes, or Manicheus, and his followers. The doctrine is dualistic: good is light, God, the soul; and evil is equated with darkness, Satan, and the body. Sologub's symbolic world also falls into two opposing categories, emphasizing the writer's affinity to this system of oppositions. Culling the most outstanding and recurring images from his works, the reader can define the positive, light world in Sologub: I, Yes, Dulcinea, Moon, Dream, Art, and Beauty. Standing in the contrast are: Non-I, No, Aldonsa, Sun, Reality, Life, and Vulgarity.

It is because Sologub cannot "love life" that he seeks an escape. It is through the creative will, the all-powerful "I," or ego, that he creates legends which transform coarse reality into an ideal beauty. The trilogy is introduced by an incantation which explains his intent in art: "I take a piece of life, coarse and poor, and I create out of it a delightful legend, for I am—a poet. Whether you, life, dim and everyday, stagnate in gloom or rage in a furious fire—I, the poet, will erect above you a legend created by me about the charming and the beautiful." Sologub's rejection of the real world echoes Nietzsche's statement, "We have Art that we may not perish from Truth." The truth that Sologub sees surrounding him is the vulgarity, coarseness, stupidity, meanness, pettiness, and the banality of reality (all of these negative qualities are nicely summed up in one Russian word which names the concept, but, as Nabokov contends, is virtually untranslatable: *poshlost*).

In *The Petty Demon*, Ludmila defines herself as a pagan who worships the bare body. Her dalliance with Sasha is a legend of her making, using the artifices of perfumes, costumes, and sweets. The "affair" cannot be consummated (we assume), and to do so would defile the ideal. The titillation is enhanced by overt sadism and masochism on the heroine's part. This is true also of another favorite "legend" of the author's: a nude, female body, dancing in the style of Isadora Duncan before an audience—ideally elevating the observers into the realm of pure beauty without inciting lust. These are "constructive" escapes. When reality cannot be transformed through a creative process, then the escape is through madness or death, and particularly the latter. It is not surprising that Sologub was condemned for his morbid tone when the reader, over and again, comes across the question "Why live?" asked most often by children.

The controlling force in this legend-making, that which praises madness and courts death, is the author's "I." It is an oversimplification to label Sologub a solipsist, for it was not merely a preoccupation with the self that he was condoning. Sologub sees his inner world, the "I," or ego, as a dynamic force, an entity of reserve energy, capable of creating new worlds to escape the evils inherent in the existing order of things. And Sologub even defended the solipsist by asserting that seeing the world through one's own experiences puts the responsibility for what happens in the world on the individual. And in this way, man strives for that merging of the self with the One Will. This world of Sologub's unfolds through his short stories and indeed, he was a prolific writer in the genre: there are nine volumes in his published works. The strictures of the short story curtail the author's tendency to become diffuse as he often does in his less successful novels. The combination of realistic detail with symbolism is both startling and haunting. The fifteen stories presented here were chosen in order to bring the reader into this decadent, solipsistic, erotic, Manichean, escapist world of Sologub's.

The first story of the collection, "The Wall and the Shadows" is a masterpiece of the genre. Published in 1894, it is a chilling combination of realism (the study of madness) and symbolism (a testament to the author's view of reality and his inherent escapism). Volodya is a typical portrait in the Sologubian gallery: being twelve years old, he stands at the abyss of maturity, where he can comprehend the evil raging around him. This is particularly true of the school, a setting Sologub will return to over and over again to dramatize the suffering of innocent children. It is a microcosm of the real world, where Gogol's hierarchy of Very Important Personages sets up a chain reaction of brutality ending with the children who become the real victims. Ivan Karamazov's question about the injustice of innocent childrens' suffering is immediately brought to mind.

Volodya's physical appearance is lightly sketched by the author and suggests his vulnerability. The boy's paleness is also symbolic: he has not been touched by the "Dragon" or "Serpent," Sologub's symbolic reference to the sun which incites destructive passions. And those large eyes are significant, for they are the receptors through which the boy is burdened by the truths of reality.

The emotional relationship between Volodya and his mother borders on the perverse. Their vexations and fears and the intense affection they share, plus the fact that Volodya speaks like an adult, force the boy into the role of a surrogate husband. The shadows evolve into a symbolic world starting with the funny girl in a peaked hat and developing into the image of a helpless and homeless old man being felled by hostile elements. At first the shadows seem to offer Volodya an escape from a reality which is defined as repulsive through the scenes at school and the descriptions of nature. But the shadows gradually gain control over Volodya and become his master. And since Sologub has stated, through Volodya, that man is trapped by walls, then the only escape is madness or death. In this early story, death is not courted by Sologub. Here, the legend-making does not result in beauty, but rather Volodya, and later, his mother, create legends on those symbolic walls, legends which control their creators and drive them mad.

Religion, another possibility for escape, is rejected in "The Wall and the Shadows." Sologub's attitude toward organized religion will change with time, but here, the mother's prayers are ineffectual and the icons and church appear alien and offer no consolation. One shadow is likened to an angel that is flying off to heaven from a "depraved and grieving world." There is a heaven then, and there are angels, but Volodya and his mother are isolated and trapped within the walls of reality. Sologub asks, "Isn't there something significant, yet scorned, being carried away from the world in the gentle hands of the angel?" Perhaps it is Volodya's (and his mother's) innocence, or their creative will. But while the angel is able to soar above those symbolic walls, Volodya and his mother turn to them for their escape which is shadow-making. But their ultimate escape from reality is madness.

"The Worm," written two years later, in 1896, again has a victimized child as the central figure. At the realistic level, the story may be read as the history of a girl suffering from tuberculosis who experiences a trauma which hastens an already impending death. Symbolically, it is a dramatization of the de-

structive forces in Wanda's world: her boring classes, the other
girls who tease her, but primarily the hateful Rubonosov family
(Anna and Vladimir) where she boards. Sologub characterizes
Anna Rubonosov's sister who lives with them as resembling her
older sister "the way a frog resembles an older one." Anna herself
hisses, turns green and shows her yellow fangs. Her husband is
constantly roaring and turning purple with rage. They are de-
scendents from Gogol's human zoo where the borderline between animal and human becomes blurred. The beasts raging
behind the mask of civilization are unleashed in a frenzy of
sadistic torment directed against the helpless girl.

Wanda's escape from the oppressiveness surrounding her is
the memory of her distant homeland. The snowy expanses and
cold weather she recalls are a respite from the inferno of her
suffering. But like Volodya, she, too, is trapped: her memories are
not a "legend" arising from her creative will. Rather, she creates a
destructive myth by concentrating on the activities of the worm
which she believes was put in her mouth by Rubonosov after she
accidentally broke his favorite cup. Sologub reflects the triumph
of evil over innocence stylistically: Wanda's dreams of her loved
ones and the countryside emerge only three times in compact
scenes of a few lines. While these sequences are alive (they are
related in the present tense) with love for Wanda's family and
nature, most pages of the story are saturated with negative words
that add to the dismal tone: "terror," "grief," "melancholy,"
"yearning," and "torment" crowd the text. Everything man-
made surrounding the girl is a threat: the city with its walls; the
ceiling in her room that seems to suffocate her; the iron beds that
smell like something unpleasant in a jail or hospital. Even nature,
which was so attractive at home turns against her in the form of a
howling wind.

As in "The Wall and the Shadow," prayers offer no relief or
solace for the girl. And again, Sologub returns to the image of an
angel in this story: after praying, Wanda senses something fluttering nearby. "The meek angel flies above her toward the happy

and the meek—and will not press close to her." Abandoned by man and God, Wanda's only salvation is the ultimate escape: death.

There are many parallels between "Hide-and-Seek" written in 1898 and "The Wall and the Shadows": the doting mother, a shared game between child and mother, and the threat of death and madness. "Hide-and-Seek" brings the last two themes together with the child, Lelechka, evading reality in death; her mother, in madness. Praskovya, the servant in "The Wall and the Shadows," was a rather insignificant character. Here the servants play a much more active role. In "Hide-and-Seek," they pose a threat to their masters' stable world. It is their superstition and cunning that brings terror to the mother's heart. Serafima Aleksandrovna's madness is not the blessed madness of escape from an evil reality, but rather an escape from her isolation brought on by her grief.

Lelechka, just before dying, sees her mother as a "white mama." A character's whiteness or paleness places him in the author's positive symbolic system. It connotes innocence, virginity, or purity. The reference to a white mama is obviously connected to a story written in the same year as "Hide-and-Seek" called "The White Mama." In this story, an abandoned boy refers to his wicked stepmother as "black mama," but he remembers that at one time he had had a "white mama," and she symbolized all that was good and loving. Thus a parallel may be made in "Hide-and-Seek": Lelechka's vision of her mother being white is symbolic of the dying child's intuitive knowledge of her mother's suffering and goodness. The irony of the child's insight is further emphasized by her mother's mad efforts to recapture their legend of hide-and-seek with her dead daughter.

"Beauty," written in the following year, 1899, combines Sologubian decadence with a philosophic statement. In these pages there is madness (paranoia and manic depression), narcissism, hints at masturbation and lesbianism, voyeurism and suicide. But Sologub's credo is clear: through artifice and adulation of the naked body, an escape from "boring conventionality" is possible. Elena is an example of the Sologubian ideal: virginal, with virginal thoughts, she rejoices in her body's movements as a true disciple of Isadora Duncan. She is a sister in spirit and belief with *The Petty Demon*'s Ludmila and the trilogy's Queen Ortruda.

Sologub defines his theory of beauty here, but the legend still does not have the power to overcome reality: it is impossible for the "I" of a lover of beauty (Elena) to merge with the "I's" of those surrounding her, for they are blind to the enchantments of her myth of pure beauty. In spite of the fact that she tries to isolate herself, she cannot deny her part in the community of mankind, the sharing of the world and her tie to the One Will. So conventionality, banality, and vulgarity triumph over her efforts at creating a legend; and death is her only escape.

In "The Hoop," written in 1902, Sologub again returns to the themes of innocent children and a created legend. The hero, an old man, remains nameless, but he symbolizes the old person who had suffered cruel mistreatment in his youth and whose present reality consists of being trapped within the four walls of the mechanized hell of his factory. He escapes by reverting to a recreated childhood and the hoop is his magic wand to transform reality. The story stands in vivid contrast with "Beauty": the crude workman and his rusty hoop achieve a transformation of the ugly into the beautiful more successfully than Elena did with her elaborate rituals; his death is more incidental than pivotal in the story.

"The Beloved Page," written in 1906, is a blueprint for Sologub's drama "Vanka the Servant and Jean the Page," which was written in 1908 and is generally considered to be the author's best play. The drama is really two plays shown side by side: one is set in sixteenth-century Russia and the other in sixteenth-century France. Both servants apply to the court for positions and soon become lovers of the countesses. Both boys reveal their secrets and are sentenced to death. Jean is flogged and Vanka escapes, thanks to the countess's intercession and in the end, both royal couples are reunited. The drama is structured on the antithesis of the crude, ignorant, and slapstick Russian scenes as opposed to the refined, poetic French surroundings. While the ending of the play is basically comic, the short story is playful in tone only up until the dramatic denouement, where the page is literally sacrificed. His loyalty to his master and his heroic efforts to preserve his innocence fail. He is used by the countess to satisfy her lust and by the obviously impotent count to impregnate his wife so that the "noble" lineage might be continued.

The eroticism in the story is structured on the juxtaposition of the page Adelstan's beauty with that of his mistress. While Edwiga is described in an abstract, almost clichéd manner, the youth's attractiveness is savored by the author. Adoration of a boy's bare legs occurs over and over again in Sologubian eroticism. Edwiga's lust and will to destroy the beauty she cannot conquer drive her to sadistic excess: by stabbing the boy and licking the blood from the blade of her knife, she emerges as a unique figure—something of a nymphomaniacal vampire. (The theme of a young boy's seduction by an older woman occurs frequently in Sologub's prose, particularly in the trilogy's *Queen Ortruda*.) The story reads as an indictment against the adult world that strives to satisfy its bestial lust at the expense of youth's innocence and beauty.

The gloomy drama of a youth destroyed in a historical setting is found in the next story, "The Youth Linus." It was first published in 1906 under the title "The Miracle of the Youth Linus," and, in fact, the story is a realistic account of a miraculous event: the resurrection of the slain Linus, an innocent victim of ruthless brute force and savage slaughter, who comes back again and again to haunt the troops with his blood-stained body as a symbol of their wanton destructiveness. Linus belongs to the same genus as the suffering child who figures so prominently in the works of Dostoevsky. Linus is a child in age only; he possesses a wisdom far beyond his years. The boy is catapulted into the adult world by his recognition of the evil which the Roman soldiers represent. The adult perception of the child is reflected in his speech: he addresses the old centurion in a linguistically mature style; and the content of his address strains for credulity when the reader remembers that a youth is speaking. His speech symbolically addresses a far wider audience than the group of soldiers: Linus is speaking for all of the insulted and injured who have been victims of destructive forces.

"The Youth Linus" is an example of Sologub at his most pessimistic. There is no light-hearted or even sardonic character (like the wizard, for example, in "The Beloved Page") to relieve the all-pervading gloom. The syntax is complicated, the prose heavy, the repetitions monotonous. The heavy tread of the horses' hoofs pounding down on a despairing earth, and the evil Dragon-Serpent inflaming the man-beast with the desire for blood allow for no escape: the natural world, the animal world, and the human world unite into one repulsive and horrifying image. The reappearances of Linus do not offer the antithetical escape which is usually found in Sologub. The story presents no alternative to the brutality. The miracle of Linus's appearance is no escape, and death is no escape. No one is triumphant; the reader is left only with a sense of all-pervading horror.

"Death by Advertisement," 1907, contains a bit of Sologubian self-debunking. In this story, the author mixes the highest form of abstract symbolism with Gogolian humor. Some of Sologub's critics were appalled at his "decadent" preoccupation with death, and this story might be interpreted as the author's parodying his purported attitude towards the theme when the hero, Rezanov, advertises for someone to play the role of his Death.

Here are the blurred edges so favored by the symbolists: there is a "someone" who talks to Rezanov; and the whole mood of a dreamlike reality and the hallucinations (when he does not know whether or not he is speaking or thinking). The dialogue between Rezanov and Death is loaded with symbolic overtones and undercurrents: the repetition of such words as "melancholy," "pining," "sadness," "yearning," "torment," and the abundance of exclamation points parody the symbolists' significant preoccupations. And Death herself ("death" has a feminine gender in Russian) mocks the symbolists' myths with her vision of their ruler sprinkling the stars with a mixture made from Rezanov's soul juices and her quiet tears.

What is particularly bizarre in this story is Death's death. In his rather sly twist of events at the end, was Sologub symbolically killing off his preoccupation with death? Perhaps the author meant to imply that he was releasing himself from symbolism's obtuse legends and the decadents' handmaiden of finality.

The characters Rezanov observes in the post office are true Gogolian types. Their behavior depresses the hero and intensifies his desire for death. In this scene, Sologub piles up insignificant detail about inconsequential persons and the result is a study of the grotesque. A perfect example is the woman with the wart who is not only characterized by that wart, but also is fated to carry a ridiculous and hilarious name. (Ruslan is the hero of Pushkin's poetic fairy tale "Ruslan and Ludmila." "Zvonareva" might be translated as "trumpeter." She stands isolated from equally bizarre caricatures by a wart and an absurd name.

The longest story in the collection, "In The Crowd," written in 1907, is an entirely different matter. The story is based on fact: on May 18, 1896, some three thousand people perished and many more were injured in a crush on the Khodynka field near Moscow. The occasion was the ascension of Nicholas II to the throne, and the populace had been promised presents of kerchiefs and a cup. An estimated three hundred thousand people gathered, but owing to the ineptitude of the authorities, the distribution turned into utter chaos and tragedy.

"In The Crowd" is an excellent example of Sologub's complete control over the genre of the short story: it is a forceful blending of realism and symbolism, and its cohesiveness in content and form is impressive. The narrator plays an active role in the story from the very beginning where, as he is matter-of-factly describing the events in Mstislavl, he adds a judiciously wry comment or outright condemnation of human folly. There is that Gogolian stratification of society when we are presented with a picture of very important people who are as petty and vulgar as the lowliest peasant. The Udoev children are somewhere in the middle: not only do they represent the innocence of youth, but they also stand in the middle as a kind of collective Everyman. Their individual personalities are rather sketchily presented; it is their innocence, naïveté, and good will that are important.

The nightmare is built up gradually. The metaphysical horror keeps pace with the physical. Sologub utilizes opposites again to develop the tension: the expanse of the heavens in contrast to the crowd, darkness versus daylight, children against adults, coolness and heat.

It is through the children that the reader views the metamorphosis of man-beast into man-devil. The cohesion which existed at the beginning is fragmented into a bedlam, which is reflected in the author's style: from conventional descriptive prose and the narrator's tone of indulgent irony, the style changes to elusive, elliptical sentences and the expressions "it seemed" and "for some reason" describe the chaos. As the story develops, realistic detail gives way to symbolic constructions by the narrator. And at the end, the title takes on a more symbolic than realistic denotation: Sologub has dramatized here the fact that by the individual being in a crowd, he is, as Volodya said in "The Wall and the Shadows," surrounded by walls from which one cannot escape. Here they are human walls—oppressive , repulsive, and deadly.

The narrator addresses his readers directly in the next story, but the tone is far from serious. Sologub's penchant for the bizarre and his unorthodox wit make "The Queen of Kisses," published in 1907, a delightfully piquant tale. While the nymphomania, murder, and necrophilia may have startled some readers, the fundamentally jocular tone of the work should not be overlooked (certainly Mafalda's story is not "an allegory to the fate of Russia" as one sober critic has judged it to be). From the beginning, Sologub, tongue-in-cheek, is wagging a playful finger at the wiles of women; and his story ends with the author himself stepping forward to offer some advice to his readers. It is a frivolous, original, and amusing anecdote full of mock sympathy, mock horror, and mock seriousness.

The story "The Search," 1908, is a succinct, realistic account of an incident in a young schoolboy's life that has far wider and more serious implications when viewed in context with Sologub's other works. We have the familiar Sologubian situation of a devoted mother and her son. The hateful routine of school with its boring curriculum is a theme that predominates from Sologub's earliest prose works. Volodya, in "The Wall and the Shadows," is repelled by his lessons and the teacher. The school system in which Login of *Bad Dreams* finds himself, is a gathering of beasts: the officials and teachers are corrupt, cruel, ignorant, and sadistic; and those traits apply equally to Peredonov and his cohorts in *The Petty Demon*. In "The Search," the behavior of Sergey Ivanovich, the inspector, is openly malicious and sadistic; Shura stands as yet another example of innocence wronged and tormented when he is zealously searched after being accused of theft. But here, as in numerous other scenes in Sologub's prose, there are hints of homosexuality. There is no evidence to prove that Sologub was a bisexual; indeed biographical information is so sparse that to make such an assumption would be grossly unjust to the author. Because of his preoccupation with expanding the limitations imposed on experiencing new sensations in life and his "decadent" emphasis on the perverse, this theme comes as no surprise to the reader.

In *Bad Dreams*, Login "adopts" a runaway orphan boy and acknowledges his sexual attraction to him. In *The Petty Demon*, Peredonov's limited imagination is sparked by rumors that Sasha is a girl, but he dreams of the boy beckoning him into a dark alley. And he makes nighttime visits to the schoolboys in order to torment them (and, one might assume, to punish them for their attractiveness). A story, "The Cavalry Guardsman," written in 1907, is an account of Pereyashin, a school inspector in charge of a dorm who has Valya, a young charge, brought to him from bed, naked, and whips him. He later resigns in order to join the Cossacks and lead raids where his sadism will be condoned. In the trilogy's *Queen Ortruda*, the queen enters into a lesbian relationship after being abandoned by her husband and seducing a young boy. The homosexuality is never explicitly detailed. This is an important aspect of Sologub's eroticism: physical abuse often exists as a substitute for the sex act, be it heterosexual or homosexual. This, of course, serves a twofold function: it is punishment of the desired object and it is release from sexual frustration. For in Sologub's view, to consummate an attraction sexually is to put the participants on the lowest bestial level. It is in the creating, the process, of the (sexual) legend that one derives pleasure. The agony of temptation is a major ingredient of the ecstasy.

Sologub's attitudes toward death and religion vacillated between attraction and revulsion. Certainly death offers the ultimate escape from a dark and evil world. Religion—or at least Christianity, with its ritual, fine trappings, and mystery—holds some allure (and Christ on the cross delights Ludmila, who sees the suffering through eyes that seek out the sadistic). But in story after story, religion appears as a mechanical response and prayers go unanswered. There is no spiritual solace in blind faith. However, in the story "The Red-Lipped Guest" written in 1909, we see a curious reversal in Sologub's treatment of the theme.

The myth of Lilith is much favored by Sologub and he uses her extensively in his works. Lilith, according to Semitic belief, was Adam's first wife before Eve. Rather than submit to him, she became a female demon, belonging to the night. Traditionally, this evil spirit is especially dangerous to children. In Sologub's symbolic world, however, Lilith is generally regarded as a positive symbol: she belongs to the moon and the night; she is in that lyrical company where Dulcinea also reposes. Lydia Rothstein, who is the Lilith in "The Red-Lipped Guest," reverses Sologub's usual treatment of the myths; here she takes on her traditionally evil personality. A certain tension in her person is evident from the outset when her physical appearance is described by Vargolsky's servant, Victor, in his clumsy attempts at eloquence: she is compared to both a Greek statue (Tanagra) and a French courtesan of the turn of the century (Cleo de Mérode). Thus she is primarily a woman of the flesh, and while she promises a legend for escape, it must be paid for by physical sacrifice.

Many of Sologub's later stories show that the author ultimately did profess a belief in God. And "The Red-Lipped Guest" dramatizes the possible appeal of religion for him. The antithetical myth presented here by the Youth of the spirit and protector of life underscores the Bible's "wise and simple stories" as opposed to the destructive complexities of the Lilith symbol. (Equally appealing to Sologub's aesthetics is the victory of a beautiful, innocent boy over the destructiveness of a demanding woman.)

Another miracle occurs in "The Kiss of the Unborn," written in 1911. The story of Seryozha's suicide brings another portrait of youth catapulted into adulthood by the realization that life is a nightmare. Seryozha is obviously referring to Tolstoy when he talks to his Aunt Nadya about "the best of all people," who, as an old man, ran away from his home and died because he "glimpsed the terror in which we all live and could not bear it." This is an oversimplification of the spiritual crisis, involving moral, aesthetic, philosophic, and religious questions that compelled Tolstoy to leave his home, Yasnaya Polyana. Tolstoy was not seeking out death as the ultimate escape, but this is what Seryozha does by his act of suicide. One reason that Seryozha is so drawn to the mid-nineteenth-century poet Nekrasov is because the writer had great compassion for suffering. (The other writers he mentions are Nadson, a poet of the late nineteenth century and Balmont, the symbolist, who are polar opposites: the former was a civic poet, socially conscious; the latter, concerned with the impression of sounds in his poetry more than the ideas behind them—and neither answers the boy's needs.)

The miracle in "The Kiss of the Unborn" occurs at the end of the story when Nadya sits on the stairs before going in to comfort her sister (Seryozha's mother). Nadya had had an abortion some years before, but she has been visited by the image of her son over the years. While he would sometimes press his lips to her cheeks, he had never kissed her on the lips. At the end of the story, her child appears to her again and this time he does kiss her and forgives her for depriving him of life. ("I don't want to live" he assures her.) Seryozha's death brings about this resurrection of love, a symbolic "birth" of Nadya's son. Seryozha's death is a rejection of reality; her unborn son is an affirmation of the dream, and a reaffirmation of the rejection of life and reality.

The last two stories of the collection provide final examples of Sologub's decadence and symbolism. "The Lady in Bonds," 1912, is a study of sadism and masochism. Here is another legend, but a perverted one (a bound woman who incites a guest to torture her). The heroine, Irina Omezhina, has been victimized by her cruel husband earlier, but her guilt over her husband's death is a thin veil concealing her desire for torture. The nighttime setting connects her in the reader's mind with Lilith. But unlike Lydia Rothstein, another perverted Lilith, Omezhina does not want a man's blood to accomplish her legend. Physical torture is equally gratifying to her.

"She Wore a Crown," 1913, depicts a legend totally antithetical in tone to "The Lady in Bonds." Here the heroine believes that she has been crowned the queen of the forest princesses. Perhaps the story suffers from sentimentality, but it concludes this selection of short stories by emphasizing Sologub's view that "man is the ruler of the earth." Once more the heroine is an Elena; but unlike Elena in "Beauty," this heroine creates a legend and lives it within herself because she has utilized that magical force, the "I." All of Sologub's works emphasize this point: while rejection is at the core of his philosophy, what saves man, the way man can survive, what separates man from the blind beast, is that precious, all-powerful creative force, his "I."

The Kiss
of the
Unborn

AND OTHER STORIES

The Wall
and the Shadows

Volodya Lovlev, a slender, pale boy about twelve years old, had just returned from school and was waiting for dinner. He was standing in the living room by the piano looking through the latest issue of the magazine *Niva* which had arrived in the morning mail.

A little booklet printed on thin gray paper fell out of the newspaper which was lying there too, covering up a page of *Niva*. It was an advertisement for an illustrated magazine. In the booklet the publisher listed some fifty well-known literary names—the future contributors—and then went on with verbose praise for the magazine as a whole and for its highly diverse sections. Included was a small sample of illustrations.

Volodya absent-mindedly began to leaf through the little gray booklet, looking at the tiny pictures. The large eyes in his pale face moved wearily.

One page suddenly caught the boy's attention and caused his wide eyes to open even wider. Printed down the page was a series of six drawings, showing various hand positions whose shadows, thrown on a white wall, formed dark silhouettes: the head of a girl in a funny peaked hat, the heads of a donkey and a bull, a squirrel in a sitting position, and things of that kind.

Smiling, Volodya became more absorbed in looking at the sketches. This was a game that was familiar to him: he himself could arrange the fingers of one hand so as to make a rabbit's head appear on the wall. But here were some things Volodya had never seen before and above all, these were more complicated figures involving both hands.

Volodya wanted to reproduce these shadows. But of course now, in the diffused light of the late autumn day, nothing would come out well.

"I'll just have to keep this booklet," he thought. "I'm sure it isn't important."

Just then he heard the approaching footsteps and voice of his mother in the next room. For some reason he blushed, and quickly thrusting the booklet into his pocket he moved away from the piano to meet his mother. She came in, smiling tenderly, so much like him, with the very same wide eyes in her pale, beautiful face.

She asked, as she usually did, "So what's new today?"

"Nothing's new," Volodya said sullenly.

But immediately it seemed to him that he was speaking rudely to his mother, and he was ashamed because of it. He smiled tenderly and began to recall what had happened at school, but in so doing, he felt the vexation even more clearly.

"Pruzhinin distinguished himself again," and he began to tell about his teacher who was disliked by the students because of his crudeness. "Leontev was reciting the lesson and he got mixed up. Pruzhinin said, 'That's enough. Sit down! Blockhead!'"

"You notice everything right away," his mother said, smiling.

"He's always awful crude."

Volodya was silent for a moment, then he sighed and began to speak in a complaining voice:

"And they're always in a rush."

"Who?" asked his mother.

"I mean the teachers. Every one of them wants to finish up the course as soon as possible and to review for the exams. If you ask a question, they probably think: here's a student who's showing off to kill time until the bell rings, so he won't be quizzed."

"Then speak to them after class."

"Yes, but after classes they're in a rush too, to get home or to go to lessons at the girls' school. And everything is done in such a hurry—no sooner are you done with geometry, then you have to study Greek!"

"It keeps you on your toes!"

"It keeps me on my toes all right! I'm like a squirrel in a cage. Really, it irritates me."

His mother smiled gently.

II

After dinner, Volodya went off to his room to study. His mother had taken pains to see that Volodya was comfortable—and his room had everything he might need. No one bothered him there and even his mother did not come to him then. A little later, she would come to help Volodya if he needed it.

Volodya was a conscientious and, as they say, able boy. But today it was difficult for him to study. No matter which lesson he took up, he was reminded of something unpleasant—each subject brought to mind that teacher's passing remarks which were either sarcastic or crude and went straight to the depths of the sensitive boy's soul.

For some reason it happened that many of his recent lessons had been unsuccessful: the teachers seemed dissatisfied and things were not going well with them. Their ill temper was communicated to Volodya and now a gloomy, vague uneasiness was transmitted to him from his books and notebooks.

He went hurriedly from one lesson to another, then to a third; and this haste to complete trivial tasks so that the next day he would not be the one to be called a blockhead, this incoherent and unnecessary haste, irritated him. He even began to yawn from boredom and vexation, impatiently dangling his legs and squirming about in his chair.

But he knew very well that he had to learn all these lessons without fail, that it was very important, that his whole future depended on it, and so he conscientiously went on with the task so boring for him.

Volodya had made a small ink spot on his notebook and he put his pen aside. After examining it carefully, he decided it could be removed with his penknife. He was happy for the distraction. His knife was not on the table. Volodya put his hand in his pocket and rummaged about there. In the midst of all the litter and junk small boys habitually have crammed into their pockets, he caught hold of his knife and pulled it out together with some sort of booklet.

He did not know yet what the paper in his hand was, but as he was fishing it out, he suddenly remembered that it was the booklet with the shadows—and all at once he grew cheerful and animated.

Yes, there it was—that same booklet which he had already forgotten while doing his lessons.

He jumped nimbly off his chair, moved the lamp closer to the wall, cast a look cautiously at the closed door—to see that no one should enter—and, having turned the booklet to the familiar page, began to examine the first drawing carefully and to arrange his fingers according to the drawing. At first the shadow came out awkwardly, not at all as it should have—Volodya moved the lamp this way and that, bent and stretched out his fingers—and finally, on the white wallpaper of his room, he achieved the little head of a woman in a peaked hat.

Volodya grew cheerful. He bent his hands and moved his fingers slightly—the little head bowed, smiled, and made funny faces.

Volodya went on to the second figure, then to the next ones. At first, they all came out wrong, but Volodya eventually managed with them.

He spent about a half an hour with this pastime and forgot all about his lessons, about school, about everything in the world.

Suddenly he heard familiar steps behind the door, Volodya

blushed, shoved the booklet in his pocket, quickly moved the lamp back into place, nearly overturning it in the process—and sat down, bending over his notebook. His mother entered.

"Let's have some tea, Volodya dear," she said.

Volodya pretended that he was looking at the ink spot and was about to open his penknife. His mother tenderly put her hands on his head—Volodya threw down his knife and pressed his blushing face against his mother. Apparently his mother noticed nothing and this made Volodya glad. But he was still ashamed, it was as though he had been caught at some stupid prank.

III

On the round table in the middle of the dining room the samovar was quietly humming its cooing song. The hanging lamp was shedding a drowsy feeling along the white tablecloth and the dark wallpaper.

Volodya's mother was pondering something, leaning her beautiful pale face over the table. Volodya had his arm on the table and was stirring the spoon in his glass. Sweet little streams from the sugar were running through the tea, thin bubbles were rising to the top. The silver spoon was jangling quietly.

The boiling water sputtered out of the samovar's spigot into his mother's cup.

A faint shadow was running from the little spoon onto the saucer and to the tablecloth and dissolved in the tea. Volodya scrutinized it: among the shadows cast by the sweet streams and bubbles of air, it was reminiscent of something—what exactly, Volodya could not decide. He inclined and twirled the little spoon, ran his fingers over it, but nothing emerged.

"Still and all," he thought stubbornly, "it's not just with fingers that shadows can be made. Anything can be used, you need only adapt yourself."

And Volodya began to scrutinize the shadows of the samovar, of the chairs, of his mother's head and the shadows thrown on

the table by the dishes—and he tried to catch a resemblance to
something in all of these shadows. His mother was saying something—Volodya was listening inattentively.

"How is Lesha Sitnikov doing in school now?" his mother
asked.

Meanwhile, Volodya was observing the shadow of the milk
pitcher. He roused himself and answered hastily:

"Like a tomcat."

"Volodya, you are sound asleep," his mother said with surprise. "What tomcat?"

Volodya blushed.

"I don't know what I meant," he said. "I'm sorry, mama, I
didn't catch what you were saying."

IV

The next evening before tea, Volodya again thought of the
shadows and once more he busied himself with them. One of his
shadows kept coming out poorly no matter how he held or bent
his fingers.

Volodya was so engrossed that he did not notice his mother
approaching. When he heard the scrape of the door opening, he
thrust the booklet into his pocket and turned away from the wall,
embarrassed. But his mother was already looking at his hands
and a fearful uneasiness flashed in her wide eyes.

"What are you doing, Volodya? What have you hidden?"

"No, oh–nothing," muttered Volodya, blushing and shifting
awkwardly.

His mother imagined for some reason that Volodya wanted to
smoke and was hiding a cigarette.

"Volodya, show me at once what you are hiding," she said in a
frightened voice.

"Really, mama . . . . "

She took Volodya by the elbow.

"All right then, shall I look in your pocket myself?"

Volodya grew even redder and pulled the booklet out of his pocket.

"Here," he said, handing it over to his mother.

"Just what is it?"

"Well, you see," explained Volodya, "here are some little drawings—of shadows. Well, I was making them on the wall, but I really didn't have much success."

"So what was there to hide then!" his mother said, having put her mind at rest. "Just what kind of shadows are they? Show me!"

Volodya felt ashamed, but obediently began to show his mother the shadows.

"Here's one—a bald man's head. And this is a rabbit's head."

"So!" his mother said, "This is how you prepare your lessons!"

"But I only do it for a little while, mother."

"So, just a little while! Then why are you blushing so, my dear? Never mind. I know very well that you will do everything you are supposed to."

His mother ruffled Volodya's short hair, and Volodya began to laugh and hid his burning face under his mother's elbows.

His mother left—but Volodya still felt awkward and ashamed. His mother had caught him doing something that he himself would have ridiculed had he found a friend at it.

Volodya knew that he was an intelligent child, and he considered himself to be serious, but this was really a game fit for gatherings of little girls.

He thrust the booklet with the shadows a little farther back in the table drawer and did not take it out for more than a week; indeed, during that whole week he gave very little thought to the shadows. Only sometimes in the evening, while going from one lesson to another, he would smile when he happened to think of the woman's little head in the peaked hat—sometimes, he even poked about in the drawer after the booklet, but he would remember at once how his mother had caught him, and he would feel ashamed and go about his work even more quickly.

V

Volodya and his mother, Eugenia Stepanovna, lived in her house on the outskirts of a provincial town. Eugenia Stepanovna had been a widow for nine years. She was now thirty-five, still young and pretty, and Volodya loved her tenderly. She lived solely for her son; she studied ancient languages for his sake, and suffered over all his anxieties about school. A quiet and affectionate person, she viewed the world somewhat timidly through her wide eyes which glimmered meekly in her pale face.

They lived with one servant. Praskovya, a sullen, middle-class widow, was strong and vigorous; she was about forty-five years old, but because of her stern taciturnity, she looked like a hundred-year-old woman.

When Volodya looked at her gloomy, stonelike face, he often wanted to find out what she was thinking about during the long winter evenings in her kitchen, as her cold knitting needles, clicking, moved rhythmically in her bony hands, and her dried-up lips kept count soundlessly. Is she recalling her drunken husband? Or her children who died prematurely? Or does her lonely and homeless old age loom before her?

Her stony face is hopelessly despondent and severe.

VI

It is a long, autumn evening. On the other side of the wall are both wind and rain.

How tiresomely, how indifferently the lamp burns!

Volodya leaned on his elbow, bending completely over the table to the left and looked at the white wall and the white window blinds.

The pale flowers of the wallpaper are not visible. . . . There is the boring, white color. . . .

The white lampshade partially diverts the lamp's rays. The whole upper half of the room is in half-light.

Volodya stretched his right arm upward. Along the wall shaded by the lampshade, a long shadow stretched; it was blurry in outline, vague. . . .

It is the shadow of an angel, flying off to heaven away from a depraved and grieving world; it is a transparent shadow with widespread wings and with its head bowed sorrowfully on its high breast.

Isn't there something significant, yet scorned, being carried away from the world in the gentle hands of the angel?

Volodya drew a heavy breath; his arm dropped lazily. He turned his bored eyes back to his books.

It is a long, autumn evening . . . . There is the boring white color . . . . Beyond the wall, something cries and murmurs . . . .

VII

Volodya's mother caught him a second time with the shadows.

This time he had been very successful in making the bull's head and he was admiring it, making the bull stretch its neck and bellow.

But his mother was displeased.

"So, this is how you study!" she said reproachfully.

"But I've just been at it for a little while, mother," Volodya whispered, embarrassed.

"You could do that during your spare time," his mother continued. "You aren't a little boy any longer—you should be ashamed to waste your time on such foolishness!"

"I won't do it any more, mama."

But it was difficult for Volodya to keep his promise. He liked to make shadows very much, and the desire to do so often overcame him during an uninteresting lesson.

Some evenings this mischief took up a great deal of his time and prevented him from preparing his homework well. Then he had to make up for it and lose some sleep. But how could he give up his fun?

Volodya succeeded in inventing several new figures by using things other than his fingers, and these figures lived on the wall and it sometimes seemed to Volodya that they carried on entertaining conversations with him.

But Volodya had always been a great one to daydream.

VIII

It is night. Volodya's room is dark. Volodya had gone to bed, but he cannot sleep. He is lying on his back, looking at the ceiling.

Someone is walking along the street with a lantern. His shadow moves across the ceiling among the red spots of light from the lantern. It is apparent that the lantern is swinging in the hands of the passer-by—the shadow wavers and flickers unevenly.

For some reason Volodya becomes terrified. Quickly he pulls the covers over his head and, trembling all over from haste, he hurriedly turns on his right side and begins to daydream.

He feels warmed and soothed. The sweet, naïve dreams which visit him before sleep begin to take shape in his head.

Often, when he goes to bed, he suddenly feels terrified, it seems he is becoming smaller and weaker—and he hides in his pillows, forgets this childishness and feels tender and affectionate, and he wants to embrace his mother and cover her with kisses.

IX

The gray twilight grew thicker. Shadows merged. Volodya felt melancholy.

But there was the lamp. Its light spilled over the green tablecloth and the vague, beloved shadows stole along the wall.

Volodya felt a rush of joy and animation and he made haste to take out the gray booklet.

The bull is bellowing . . . . The woman is laughing loudly. . . . What evil, round eyes this bald man is making!

Then he begins to make up his own figures.

It is steppe country. There is a wanderer with a knapsack. It seems one can hear the sad, drawn-out song of the road . . . . Volodya is happy and melancholy.

X

"Volodya, this is the third time I've seen you with that little book. What do you do—spend the whole evening admiring your fingers?"

Volodya was standing awkwardly by the table, like a naughty boy who had been caught, and he turned the little book in his burning fingers.

"Give it to me!" his mother said.

Abashed, Volodya handed over the little book. His mother took it, and left without speaking—Volodya sat down to his schoolwork.

He was ashamed that he had brought himself to this. He felt very awkward and his annoyance with his mother tormented him: he was ashamed at being angry with her, but he could not help being angry. And because it was shameful to get angry, he became even angrier.

"So let her take it away," he thought finally, "I'll manage somehow."

And, indeed, Volodya already knew the figures by heart and had used the booklet only for checking them.

XI

His mother took the booklet with the drawings of the shadows to her room and opened it—and was plunged into thought. "He really is a bright, good boy—and suddenly he is carried away by such nonsense!"

"No, it must not be just nonsense."

"What is it then?" she asked herself insistently.

A strange fear was born in her, a kind of hostile, timid feeling towards these black drawings.

She rose and lit the candle. With the little gray book in her hands, she went to the wall and paused in fearful anguish.

"Yes, finally I must find out what this is all about," she decided—and she began to make the shadows, from the first to the last.

Persistently and carefully she arranged her fingers and bent her hands until she had succeeded in making the figures she wanted. A vague, apprehensive feeling stirred within her. She tried to overcome it. But her fear grew and captivated her. Her hands were trembling, but her thought, intimidated by life's twilight, ran head on toward the threatening sorrows.

Suddenly, she heard her son's footsteps. She shuddered, hid the little book, and put out the candle.

Volodya entered and stopped at the threshold; he was confused by his mother's stern look and her awkward, strange stance near the wall.

"What do you want?" his mother asked in a severe, uneven voice.

A vague conjecture flitted through Volodya's mind, but Volodya quickly dismissed it and began to talk with his mother.

XII

Volodya had left.

His mother paced around the room several times. She noticed that her shadow was moving behind her on the floor and—strange as it was—for the first time in her life, her shadow made her feel awkward. The thought that it was indeed a shadow was constantly in her mind, but for some reason, Eugenia Stepanovna was afraid of this thought, and she even tried to avoid looking at her shadow.

But the shadow crawled along after her and taunted her. Eugenia Stepanovna tried to think about something else—in vain.

Suddenly she stopped—pale, agitated.

"But it's a shadow, a shadow!" she exclaimed aloud with a

strange irritation, stamping her foot. "So what of it? What, indeed?"

And at once she realized that it was stupid to cry out so and stamp her foot, and she became quiet.

She went up to the mirror. Her face was paler than usual, and her lips quivered with frightened anger.

"It's nerves," she thought. "I must take myself in hand."

XIII

Twilight was falling. Volodya was daydreaming.

"Come, let's go for a walk, Volodya," his mother said.

But on the street, too, there were shadows everywhere—nocturnal, mysterious, elusive—and they were whispering to Volodya something familiar and infinitely sad.

In the hazy sky two or three stars peeped out, they were distant and foreign both to Volodya and the shadows surrounding him. But Volodya, in order to please his mother, began to think about those stars: they alone were foreign to the shadows.

"Mama," he said, not noticing that he had interrupted her as she was telling him something, "What a pity that it is impossible to reach those stars."

His mother glanced at the sky and answered:

"It isn't necessary. Things go well for us only on earth; there it is quite different."

"But how faintly they shine! Anyway, that's all for the better."

"Why?"

"Because if they shone more strongly, then they would create shadows."

"Oh, Volodya, why is it you think only about shadows?"

"I didn't mean to, mama," Volodya said in a penitent voice.

XIV

Volodya tried harder to prepare his lessons better; he was afraid of grieving his mother with his laziness. But in the evenings he used the full power of his imagination to cover the table with a pile of objects which would cast a new and fantastic shadow. He arranged this way and that everything that come to hand, and he rejoiced when definable shapes took form on the white wall. These shadowy outlines became near and dear to him. They were not dumb, for they spoke—and Volodya understood their murmuring language.

He understood what that despondent passerby was grumbling about as he wandered along the great road into the autumnal mire with a crutch in his trembling hands and a knapsack on his bowed back.

He understood why the snow-covered woods, grieving in the wintry calm, complained with the frosty crackle of dry branches, why the lingering raven was cawing in the gnarled oak, and why the bustling squirrel was lamenting over its deserted hollow.

He understood why the old beggar women, decrepit and homeless, cried in the mournful, autumnal wind, shivering in their threadbare rags among the rickety crosses and hopelessly black tombs of the crowded graveyard.

Self-forgetfulness and agonizing sadness!

XV

His mother had noticed that Volodya was continuing to misbehave.

At dinner she said:

"Volodya, you should get interested in something else."

"But what?"

"You could read."

"Yes, but when you begin to read, the shadows still beg to be made."

"See if you can't think of another pastime—like blowing soap bubbles."

Volodya smiled sadly.

"Yes, the bubbles will fly off and there will be shadows behind them on the wall."

"Volodya, you'll end up ruining your nerves this way. I can see that you have even lost weight because of all this."

"Mama, you exaggerate!"

"Not at all! I do know that you have started sleeping poorly at night and sometimes you are even delirious. Just imagine if you were to be taken ill!"

"What an idea!"

"God forbid that you should go insane or die. What grief that would be for me!"

Volodya began to laugh and threw himself on his mother's neck.

"Mama, I won't die. And I won't do it anymore."

His mother saw that already Volodya was crying.

"Now that's enough," she said, "God is merciful. There, you see how nervous you have become? You're laughing and crying at the same time!"

XVI

Volodya's mother observed him intently and fearfully. Every trifle disturbed her now.

She noticed that Volodya's head was somewhat asymmetrical: one ear was higher than the other and his chin was slightly off center. His mother looked in the mirror and noticed that Volodya was like her in this respect.

"Perhaps," she thought, "this is one of the signs of bad heredity—of degeneration. And in whom was this seed of evil? Is it I, who am so unbalanced? Or was it his father?"

Eugenia Stepanovna recalled her late husband. He was one of the kindest and dearest of people, but weak-willed and given to senseless impulses—now enthusiastic, now mystical in mood. He envisioned a better social order and went among the people—and he had been drinking heavily during the last years of his life.

He was young when he died—only thirty-five.

His mother even took Volodya to a doctor to whom she described the illness. The doctor, a cheerful young man, heard her out, and laughing a bit, gave her some advice about the boy's diet and way of life, accompanied by some witty remarks; he cheerfully scribbled a prescription and added playfully, clapping Volodya on the back:

"The very best medicine would be a spanking."

Volodya's mother was deeply offended for her son, but she carried out all the other instructions exactly.

XVII

Volodya was sitting in class. He was bored. He was listening inattentively.

He raised his eyes. A shadow moved on the ceiling next to the entry. Volodya noticed that it came in from the first window. In the beginning, it stretched from the window to the middle of the room, but then it stole forward quickly past Volodya—obviously someone was walking on the street under the window. While this shadow was still moving, another shadow appeared from the second window; it too began at the back wall, then quickly moved forward to the entry. And so it went with the third and fourth windows—the shadows appeared in the classroom on the ceiling and depending on how much the passerby moved forward, they stretched out backward.

"Yes," thought Volodya, "this is not the same as in an open space where the shadow stretches out behind the person; in here, when the person walks forward, the shadow slides backward and still other shadows meet him up in front."

Volodya turned his eyes to the dried-up figure of the teacher. The teacher's cold, yellow face irritates Volodya. Volodya looks for his shadow and finds it on the wall, behind the teacher's chair. The deformed shadow bends and sways, but it does not have the yellow face and caustic grin, and Volodya enjoys watching it. His thoughts run off somewhere far away, and he no longer hears anything.

"Lovlev!" his teacher calls him.

Volodya rises as usual and stands, looking stupidly at the teacher. He has such a vacant look that his comrades laugh, but the teacher make a reproachful face.

Then Volodya hears the teacher jeering at him in his polite and malicious way. Volodya is shaking from mortification and from weakness. The teacher announces that he is giving him an "F" for his ignorance and inattention; and he invites him to sit down.

Volodya smiles stupidly and tries to imagine just what has happened to him.

XVIII

This "F" is the first in Volodya's life!

How strange this was for Volodya!

"Lovlev!" his comrades tease him, laughing and jostling about, "got a big 'F.' Congratulations!"

Volodya feels awkward. He does not know how to behave in these circumstances.

"So I got an 'F'," he says angrily, "what business is it of yours!"

"Lovlev!" the lazy Snegirev yells to him, "Our forces have increased!"

His first "F"! And he had to show it to his mother.

It was embarrassing and demeaning. Volodya felt a strange heaviness and awkwardness in the knapsack on his back: the "F" was stuck most uncomfortably in his consciousness and was connected in no way with anything else in his mind.

An "F"!

He could not get used to the idea of an "F," and yet he could not think of anything else. When the policeman near the school looked at him severely as he usually did, Volodya, for some reason, thought:

"But if only you knew that I got an 'F'!"

It was totally awkward and unusual—Volodya did not know how he should hold his head or where to put his hands—there was an awkwardness throughout his whole body.

And still, he had to put on a carefree look for his friends and talk about something else.

His friends! Volodya was convinced that they were all terribly happy about his "F."

XIX

His mother looked at the "F" and turned her uncomprehending eyes on Volodya, glanced once more at the mark and quietly exclaimed:

"Volodya!"

Volodya was standing before her, crushed. He was looking at the folds of his mother's dress, at his mother's pale hands and he felt her frightened glances on his trembling eyelids.

"What's this?" she asked.

"Well what of it, mama?" Volodya began to speak suddenly, "After all, this is my first 'F'!"

"Your first!"

"But it could happen to anyone. And really, it was an accident."

"Oh, Volodya, Volodya!"

Volodya began to cry, rubbing the tears across his cheeks with the palm of his hand like a child.

"Mommy, don't be angry," he whispered.

"There, it's those shadows of yours!" his mother said.

Volodya detected tears in her voice. It wrung his heart. He glanced at his mother. She was crying. He threw himself to her.

"Mama, mama," he repeated, kissing her hands, "I'll give up those shadows. Really I will."

XX

Volodya made an enormous effort of will and did not get involved with the shadows, no matter how drawn he was to them. He tried to make up for what he had skipped from his lessons.

But the shadows appeared persistently before him. Though he

did not summon them by manipulating his fingers, or pile up objects so that their shadows would appear on the wall, still the troublesome, relentless shadows clustered themselves about him.

Soon objects were no longer entertaining for Volodya, he almost ceased to see them—his whole attention was directed to their shadows.

When he was walking home, and the sun happened to peep through the autumn clouds as if through a smoke-colored icon frame—he was glad, because there were shadows running about everywhere.

The shadows from the lamp gathered around him when he was at home in the evening.

The shadows are everywhere around—sharp shadows from flames, dim ones from the waning light of day—they all crowded toward Volodya, crisscrossing and enveloping him in an indissoluble net.

Some of the shadows were incomprehensible, mysterious; others hinted at, reminded him of something—out there were also the beloved shadows, intimate and familiar—it was these that Volodya himself, however casually, sought out and detected everywhere in the confused flashing of the alien shadows.

But these beloved and familiar shadows were sad.

Whenever Volodya noticed that he was seeking out these shadows, his conscience bothered him and he went to confess to his mother.

Once it happened that Volodya did not overcome this temptation, and he moved close to the wall and began to make a shadow of a calf. His mother caught him.

"Again!" she exclaimed angrily. "I'm going to ask the director to give you a seat in the punishment room after all."

Volodya blushed from vexation and answered morosely,

"There's a wall there, too. Walls are everywhere."

"Volodya!" his mother exclaimed mournfully, "what are you saying!"

But Volodya already repented his rudeness and was crying. "Mama, I don't know myself what's happening to me."

XXI

But still his mother is unable to overcome her superstitious fear of shadows. She begins more often to think that, like Volodya, she too will become lost in the contemplation of shadows, but she tries to comfort herself.

"What stupid thoughts!" she tells herself. "God grant that everything will turn out fine; he will misbehave, but then he will stop."

But a secret terror grips her heart and her thoughts, frightened in the face of life, persistently rush off to meet future sorrows.

In the melancholy moments of early morning she examines her soul, recalls her life—and sees its emptiness, uselessness, aimlessness. There is nothing but the senseless flashing of shadows, merging in the thickening twilight.

"Why have I lived?" she asks herself, "For my son? But for what? That he, too, should become the prey to shadows, a maniac with a narrow horizon—chained to his illusions, to senseless reflections on a lifeless wall?"

"And he, too, will enter into life and give his life to a series of existences as illusory and unnecessary as a dream."

She sits down in an armchair by the window and thinks and thinks.

Her thoughts are bitter, drawn-out.

She begins, in her grief, to wring her beautiful, white hands.

Her thoughts are scattered. She looks at her contorted hands and begins to imagine what kind of shadow figures she could make out of them. She catches herself and jumps up in fright.

"My God!" she exclaims, "Why, this is—madness!"

XXII

At dinner, she watches Volodya.

"He has grown pale and thin since he came upon that unfortunate booklet. He has changed completely—in character, in everything."

"They say that one's character changes before death. What if he were to die?"

"No, no, God forbid!"

The spoon began to tremble in her hand. She raised her fear-filled eyes to the icon.

"Volodya, why didn't you finish your soup?" she asks in a frightened voice.

"I don't want it, mama."

"Volodya, don't be difficult, my dear; it's bad for you not to eat your soup."

Volodya smiles lazily and slowly finishes his soup. His mother has poured the bowl too full. He leans back in his chair and wants to say, from annoyance, that the soup did not taste good. But his mother has such a worried look that Volodya cannot mention it, and he smiles faintly.

"I'm full now," he says.

"But Volodya, I have all your favorites today."

Volodya sighs sadly: he knows that when his mother speaks about his favorite dishes, it means she will stuff him. He also guesses that just like yesterday, his mother will force him to eat some meat after tea.

XXIII

In the evening Volodya's mother says to him:

"Volodya dear, you will be carried away again; perhaps you had better not close the door!"

"I just can't work this way," he shouts, pushing back his chair noisily. "I can't study when the door is open."

"Volodya, why are you shouting?" his mother reproaches him tenderly.

Volodya is already repentant and he is crying. His mother caresses him and tries to persuade him.

"But Volodya dearest, I look after you in order to help you cope with your distractions."

"Mama, sit here a while," begs Volodya.

His mother takes a book and sits by Volodya's table. Volodya works calmly for a few minutes. But little by little, his mother's figure begins to irritate him.

"It's as if she were watching over a sick person," he thinks maliciously.

His thoughts are interrupted; he moves forward with vexation and bites his lips. Finally his mother notices this and leaves the room.

But Volodya feels no relief. He is tormented by regret at having shown his impatience. He tries to study—but he cannot. Finally, he goes to his mother.

"Mama, why did you leave?" he asks timidly.

XXIV

It is the eve of a holiday. The little lamps are burning in front of the icons.

It is late and quiet. Volodya's mother is not asleep. In the mysterious darkness of her bedroom, she gets down on her knees and prays and cries, sobbing like a child.

Her braids fall on her white dress, her shoulders are shaking. With an imploring movement, she raises her hands to her breast and with tear-filled eyes, looks at the icon. The little lamp moves imperceptibly on its chains from her ardent breathing. Shadows flit, crowding into the corners, stirring behind the icon case, and they murmur mysteriously. There is a hopeless yearning in their murmurings, an inexplicable melancholy in their slowly wavering movements.

She stands up, pale, with wide, strange eyes, and she sways on her unsteady legs.

She goes in quietly to Volodya. The shadows cluster around her, rustling softly behind her back, crawling around her feet;

light as a spiderweb they fall onto her shoulders and, looking into her wide eyes, they murmur something incomprehensible.

She approaches her son's bed cautiously. His face is pale in the light of the icon-lamp. Sharp, strange shadows lie on him. His breathing is inaudible—he sleeps so quietly that his mother is terrified.

She stands, surrounded by vague shadows, fanned by vague fears.

XXV

The high vaults of the church are dark and mysterious. The vespers rise up to these vaults and resound there with exultant sadness. The dark icons, illuminated by the yellow flames of wax candles, appear enigmatic and stern. The warm breathing of wax and incense fills the air with a majestic sorrow.

Eugenia Stepanovna placed a candle in front of the icon of the Holy Virgin and got down on her knees. But her prayer is distraught. She looks at her candle. Its flame surges. The shadows from the candles fall on Eugenia Stepanovna's black dress and onto the floor and waver adversely.

The shadows hover about the walls of the church and become lost up in those dark vaults where the solemn, sorrowful songs resound.

XXVI

It is another night.

Volodya awakened. The darkness has surrounded him and it moves without a sound.

Volodya has freed and raised his hands and begins to move them, fixing his eyes on them. He does not see them in the darkness, but it seems to him that dark shapes are moving before his eyes . . . .

They are black, mysterious, and they bear in them sorrow and the murmuring of lonely grief . . . .

His mother also does not sleep—anguish torments her.

She lights a candle and walks quietly to her son's room, to see how he is sleeping.

She opened the door soundlessly and looked timidly at Volodya's bed.

A ray of yellow light trembled on the wall, cutting across Volodya's red blanket. The boy reaches his hands towards the light, and with a beating heart, watches the shadows. He does not even question where the light comes from.

He is completely immersed in the shadows. His eyes, riveted to the wall, are completely mad.

The strip of light grows wider; the shadows are running, morose and hunched, like homeless women wanderers hurrying to carry off someplace their decrepit belongings which burden their shoulders.

Volodya's mother, shaking from terror, approached his bed, and softly called to her son:

"Volodya!"

Volodya came to himself. For half a minute he looked at his mother with wide eyes, then began to tremble all over, he jumped out of bed and fell at his mother's feet, embracing her knees and sobbing.

"What dreams you do dream, Volodya!" his mother exclaimed sorrowfully.

XXVII

"Volodya," his mother said at morning tea, "you can't go on this way, my dear. You will be completely exhausted if you make shadows during the night, too!"

The pale boy hung his head morosely. His lips twitched nervously.

"You know what we will do?" his mother continued. "Perhaps we had better play a little while together with the shadows each evening and then sit down to homework. Shall we?"

Volodya grew a bit more lively.

"Mama, you are a dear!" he said shyly.

XXVIII

On the street Volodya felt sleepy and fearful. The fog was spreading; it was cold, dismal, The silhouettes of houses looked strange in the fog. The gloomy human figures moved in the foggy mist like ominous, unfriendly shadows. Everything seemed immensely unusual. The coachman's horse, dozing at the intersection, appeared in the fog like an enormous, unknown beast.

The policeman gave Volodya a hostile look. A crow on a low roof presaged sorrow to Volodya. But sorrow was already in his heart—he felt sad to see how everything was hostile to him.

A little dog with mangy fur began to yap at him from a gateway, and Volodya felt strangely offended.

And it seemed that the little street urchins wanted to insult and make fun of Volodya. In the past, he would have boldly made short work of them, but now fear gripped his breast and left his hands powerless.

When Volodya returned home, Praskovya opened the door for him and greeted him with a sullen, hostile look. It made Volodya uncomfortable. He went inside quickly and did not raise his eyes to Praskovya's cheerless face.

XXIX

His mother was sitting alone in her room. It was twilight—and it was boring.

Somewhere a light flashed.

Volodya ran in, animated, happy, with wide, somewhat wild eyes.

"Mama, the lamp is burning; let's play a little."

She smiles, and follows Volodya.

"Mama, I've thought up a new figure," Volodya says excitedly, positioning the lamp. "Watch . . . there, you see? This is the steppe, covered with snow, and it is snowing—a real snowstorm."

Volodya raises his hands and arranges them.

"Now, there—you see? It's an old man, a wanderer, up to his knees in snow. It's difficult to walk. He is alone. Just the open field. The village is far away. He is tired, cold, frightened. He is completely bent over—he's such an old man."

His mother rearranges Volodya's fingers.

"Oh, oh!" Volodya exclaims excitedly. "The wind tears his hat off, blows his hair about, buries him in the snow. The snowdrifts get higher and higher. Mama, mama, do you hear?"

"It's a blizzard."

"And he?"

"The old man?"

"Do you hear, he's moaning?"

"Help me!"

Both are pale, they are looking at the wall. Volodya's hands shake—the old man falls.

His mother was the first to come to herself.

"It's time to get down to business," she says.

XXX

It is morning. Volodya's mother is home alone. Immersed in incoherent, melancholy thoughts, she is walking from room to room.

Her shadow was outlined on the white door, dimly in the scattered rays of the fog-bound sun. She stopped by the door and raised her hand in a wide, strange movement. The shadow on the door wavered and began to whisper about something familiar and sad. A strange feeling of comfort spread through Eugenia Stepanovna's soul and she moved both hands, standing in front of the door, smiling a wild smile as she followed the flashing shadows.

Praskovya's steps sounded, and Eugenia Stepanovna realized she was doing something absurd.

Once more she feels terrified and melancholy.

"We must move," she thinks. "Go anywhere far away, where everything will be new."

"We must run away from here, run!"

And suddenly she remembers Volodya's words:

"There will be a wall there, too. There are walls everywhere."

"There is no place to run!"

In her despair she wrings her pale, beautiful hands.

XXXI

It is evening.

The lighted lamp stands on the floor in Volodya's room. Volodya and his mother are sitting on the floor behind it, near the wall. They are looking at the wall and making strange movements with their hands.

The shadows are running and surging along the wall.

Volodya and his mother understand them. They smile sadly and say agonizing and impossible things to one another. Their faces are peaceful and their visions are clear; their joy is hopelessly sorrowful and their sorrow is wildly joyful.

Madness shines in their eyes, blessed madness.

Night is falling over them.

The Worm

I

Wanda, a dark-complexioned, strapping girl of twelve, had returned from school, ruddy from the frost and cheerful. She ran noisily through the rooms, shoving and pushing her girl friends about. They tried to calm her down, cautiously, but they themselves were infected with her gaiety and ran after her. However, they stopped timidly when Anna Grigorevna Rubonosova walked by. She was the teacher from whom the girls took rooms. Anna Grigorevna grumbled angrily, rushing busily from the kitchen to the dining room and back. She was displeased both because dinner was still not ready even though Vladimir Ivanovich, Anna Grigorevna's husband, was due home from work and because Wanda was misbehaving.

"No," Anna Grigorevna was saying with annoyance, "this is the last year I will keep you. I am fed up with you at school, and I have trouble with you here, too. No, I have had it with you."

Anna Grigorevna's greenish face took on a malicious expression; her yellow, canine teeth jutted out from under her upper lip; and she gave Wanda's arm a painful pinch as she passed. Wanda was not quiet for long—the girls were afraid of Anna Grigorevna—but soon the rooms in the Rubonosovs' house again resounded with laughter and noisy running about.

The Rubonosovs owned their own home, a wooden, one-story house which they had recently built and took great pride in. Vladimir Ivanovich worked in a provincial government office, Anna Grigorevna worked in the girls' school. They had no children, and perhaps that was why Anna Grigorevna often wore a malicious and irritated expression. She loved to pinch. And she had people to pinch: each year the Rubonosovs rented rooms to several new girls in the school, and Anna Grigorevna's sister, Zhenya, lived with them. She was a girl of thirteen, small and thin, with bony shoulders and large, cold lips which were pale raspberry in color; she resembled her older sister the way a young frog resembles an old one. At present, besides Zhenya, four girls were living at the Rubonosovs': Wanda Tamulevich, the daughter of a forester from the distant regions of Lubyansk province, a cheerful little girl with large eyes, who secretly longed for home and always, towards the end of winter (this was her third year at Rubonosovs') grew noticeably sickly because of this; Katya Ramneva, the oldest and cleverest of the girls; dark-eyed Sasha Epifanova, who was easily given to laughter; and the lazy, brown-haired beauty, Dunya Khvastunovskaya, the last two about thirteen.

Wanda had a reason to celebrate: today she had received an "A" in her most difficult subject. Wanda always found it difficult and boring to prepare lessons which involved memorization. Often while memorizing something uninteresting, her thoughts strayed and her daydreams would carry her off into the mysteriously quiet, snow-covered forest where she used to ride in a light sleigh with her father. There were gloomy, silent firs there with snow-laden branches that bent over her and the brisk, frosty air poured into her breast in such cheerful, sharp spurts. Wanda would daydream, the hours would fly by, and the lesson would remain unlearned; and in the morning, Wanda would read it through quickly and, if called upon, answer somehow, getting a "C."

But yesterday evening had been successful; Wanda did not once think about the distant forest of her homeland. Today she had answered the old priest word for word from the textbook. The priest who taught "Divine Law" held to the old method by which he himself had been taught forty years earlier. The old priest had praised her, called her "a fine girl," and had given her an "A."

That was why now Wanda was rushing about the rooms in an uproar, teasing Nero the sullen dog, who, by the way, treated her prankish escapades with condescending pomposity. She laughed, and pestered her girl friends. Her rapid movements took her breath away, but her joy revived her and started off her frenzy anew. In running about, Wanda bumped into the fussy servant girl, Malanya, and knocked a plate out of her hand; but she caught it adroitly in midair.

"Damn you, you crazy thing," Malanya shouted angrily at her.

"Wanda, will you stop fooling around!" Anna Grigorevna also shouted at her. "You'll break something."

"I won't break anything," Wanda cried gaily, "I'm nimble." She began to spin about on her heels, waving her arms, and knocked against Vladimir Ivanovich's favorite cup, which stood on the edge of the dining table, and she froze with terror. The sound of breaking china was mercilessly clear and cheerful; the multi-colored pieces of the broken cup rolled on the floor. Wanda stood over the fragments, clasping her hands to her breast; her black, alert eyes became mad with fright; and her swarthy, full cheeks suddenly paled. The girls grew quiet and gathered around Wanda, casting frightened glances at the fragments.

"You've gone too far with your fooling around," Zhenya said didactically.

"Vladimir Ivanovich will give it to you," Katya noted.

Suddenly it struck Sasha Epifanova as funny; she snorted and covered her mouth with her hand, as she always did to keep from laughing aloud. Anna Grigorevna, having heard the noise, ran in from the kitchen exclaiming:

"What's going on here?"

The girls remained silent. Wanda began to tremble. Anna Grigorevna caught sight of the fragments.

"That's all I needed!" she exclaimed, and her malicious little eyes flashed dimly. "Who did this? Speak up, at once! Is this one of your tricks, Wanda?"

Wanda was silent. Zhenya answered for her:

"She was jumping and spinning around right by the table, waving her arms; she hit the cup and it broke. And all of us were trying to calm her down so she wouldn't fool around."

"So that's it! Thanks a lot!" Anna Grigorevna began to hiss, turning green and threatening Wanda with her yellow fangs.

Wanda threw herself impetuously at Anna Grigorevna, clasping her shoulders with shaking hands and begged her,

"Anna Grigorevna, dearest, don't tell Vladimir Ivanovich!"

"Ha, as if Vladimir Ivanovich won't see it!" Anna Grigorevna answered maliciously.

"Say that you broke it yourself."

"I—break Vladimir Ivanovich's favorite cup! Have you gone mad, Wanda? No, my dear, I won't protect you, you settle it yourself. You will show the fragments to Vladimir Ivanovich yourself."

Wanda burst into tears. The girls began to gather up the fragments.

"Yes, yes, you will show him yourself. He will thank you, my little one," Anna Grigorevna said acidly.

"Don't tell him, for God's sake, Anna Grigorevna," Wanda began to implore her again. "Punish me yourself, but tell Vladimir Ivanovich that the cat broke it."

Sasha, who was carefully collecting the tiny fragments and piling them in the hollow of her hand, again snorted with laughter.

"A Puss in Boots!" she cried, her voice constrained from laughter.

Katya quieted her with a whisper:

"So why are you laughing? If you had broken it, you would be howling too, most likely."

Anna Grigorevna removed Wanda's hands and repeated:

"And you had better not ask; I certainly will tell him. Really, your constant fooling around! No, my pet, you have to be reprimanded, but good. So, is it all picked up?" she asked the girls. "Give it here."

Anna Grigorevna placed the fragments on a plate and carried them into the living room, to the table, the most visible spot; Vladimir Ivanovich would notice it as soon as he came in. Satisfied with her ingenuity, Anna Grigorevna again began running back and forth from the table to the stove and quietly, maliciously kept hissing at Wanda. Wanda dejectedly and hopelessly followed Anna Grigorevna about and begged her to take away the fragments.

"At least wait until after dinner for Vladimir Ivanovich to see it," she said, crying bitterly.

"No, my dear, we'll let him see it right away," Anna Grigorevna answered maliciously.

Bursts of malice at Anna Grigorevna's cruelty welled within Wanda, and she clasped her hands desperately and cried out quietly:

"I beg you! It would be better if you were to beat me!"

The other girls sat quietly and spoke in whispers.

II

Vladimir Ivanovich was returning home and daydreaming sweetly about tossing off a few vodkas, staving off the tapeworm with a bite, and then having a square meal. It was a clear, frosty day. The sun was setting. Now and then the wind, a frequent guest in Lubyansk, started up and tore off clusters of fluffy flakes from the snowdrifts. The streets were empty. Little low wooden houses jutted out here and there from under the snow, glowing pink in the sun; stretched out endlessly were long, half-rickety fences with mean, silver-frosted tree trunks peering out from behind them.

Rubonosov made his way along the narrow wooden sidewalks, stepping sprightly with bent legs and looking around cheerfully, his tiny little eyes shining with a metallic lustre in his red, freckled face. Suddenly he glimpsed his enemy, Anna Fominichna Pikileva, the high school teacher, an old maid of forty with a very wicked tongue. Vladimir Ivanovich was annoyed: must he give way to her and risk falling into the snow? But she was coming straight on, her little snakelike eyes lowered modestly, and her hateful lips pursed in that peculiar way which always irritated Vladimir Ivanovich. In his right hand he held a heavy cane made from circles of birch bark tightly fitted to a steel rod; he advanced resolutely toward the enemy. Finally, they came right up against one another and exchanged burning looks. Vladimir Ivanovich was the first to break the silence.

"Bitch!" he exclaimed solemnly.

Only then did he notice that plodding along behind Anna Fominichna was Mashka, her servant girl, who was carrying her mistress's books. Vladimir Ivanovich was sorry that he could not curse her out more, but there was a witness.

Anna Fominichna whispered in a hissing voice:

"The totally ignorant cavalier!"

Vladimir Ivanovich spread his legs wide and, leaning on his cane spoke, chuckling and showing his decayed teeth:

"So go on by, what are you standing there for?"

"Can't you step aside?" Anna Fominichna asked meekly.

"What do you mean—that I should crawl in the snow for the likes of you? No, sister, you must be joking; my health is precious to me. Pass on by, pass on by; don't block the road."

And he bumped Anna Fominichna ever so slightly as he passed by, but somehow not so carefully, because she fell in the snow and began to scream in a shrill voice, having suddenly lost all her sugary meekness:

"Ooh, he's hurt me! Oh, the scoundrel!"

The servant girl jumped after her; Vladimir Ivanovich encouraged her with a light blow from his cane below the knees, and she was floundering in the snow, helping her lady to get up and yelling and cursing at the top of her voice.

Having cleared the path, Vladimir Ivanovich proceeded

further. His face burned with the proud joy of victory. Masha yelled after him:

"You crook, you mangy cuss! We'll report you to the authorities."

On reaching the intersection, Vladimir Ivanovich turned around, threatened them with his cane, and yelled:

"Curse away, you nitwit, and you'll catch it again."

In answer, Mashka stuck out her tongue, gave him the finger four times in succession, and yelled loudly:

"We dare you, we dare you. You don't scare us!"

Vladimir Ivanovich thought it over and decided that it wasn't worth bothering about. He spat, swore energetically, and set off for home, joyfully noting that his appetite had doubled.

III

The girls, who had been tensely waiting, gave a start. A sharp, authoritative ring sounded: this meant that Vladimir Ivanovich had returned. Anna Grigorevna threw a maliciously joyful glance at Wanda and flew to open the door. Zhenya repeated both her sister's maliciously joyful look and the fidgety rush into the entry hall. Wanda, dying from fear, ran after Anna Grigorevna and quietly implored her not to tell. Anna Grigorevna pushed her away angrily.

Vladimir Ivanovich, freeing himself from his fur coat with the help of his wife and the obliging Zhenya, exclaimed loudly:

"I gave it to her, the goose. She'll remember till doom's day, the nitwit!"

Fear gripped Wanda: she imagined that through some kind of miracle Vladimir Ivanovich had found out about the broken cup. But soon she understood from his broken exclamations that he was talking about something else. A dim hope stirred within her: perhaps it could be put off until after dinner when, after several glasses of vodka, Rubonosov would be in a better mood—and sleepy. She went back hurriedly to the living room and stood in front of the table, trying to screen the fragments of the cup.

Katya helped her by moving the lamp on the table so that from the side, it hid the plate.

Vladimir Ivanovich entered the living room, brandishing a fist and repeated, to Anna Grigorevna's questioning:

"Wait, I'll tell you everything in order; let me wet my whistle."

He stopped in front of the mirror and looked at himself with self-satisfaction—he saw himself as the best-looking man in town. Then he took off his coat, threw it to Wanda, and yelled:

"Wanda, take this into our bedroom!"

Trembling, Wanda caught the coat and dejectedly took it into the couple's bedroom, carefully holding it by the loop of the collar and raising it high, as if it were made of glass. To be even more careful, she tiptoed. Sasha, who laughed so easily, covered her mouth with her hand, and ran out of the room. Wanda's cheeks were covered with a bright flush of shame and vexation.

Rubonosov, in his waistcoat, looked at himself in the mirror once more and began to comb his slick light hair, which was parted in the middle. When he turned away from the mirror, he caught sight of the plate on the table and the fragments in it. He instantly recognized them as the remains of the large cup from which he customarily drank his tea, and he felt himself cruelly offended.

"Who broke my cup?" he yelled in a ferocious voice. "This is an absolute outrage—that's my favorite cup!"

He began to pace about the room angrily.

"Obviously who else but Wanda," Anna Grigorevna began in her malicious, hissing voice.

Zhenya, hastening to be of service, gave an emotional repeat of her story about Wanda breaking the cup. Then she spread her arms wide and began to whirl around, imitating Wanda. Her slightly lowered greenish face with its blunt nose expressed a zealous concern, her malicious lips were unsmiling, and her back was hunched repulsively.

"This constant fooling around!" hissed Anna Grigorevna.

"There's no controlling that child. It's up to you to put her in her place; otherwise all of our dishes will be broken. They certainly aren't making us rich—it's just one trouble and worry after another with them."

"She almost broke the plates, too." Zhenya intervened again. "Malanya was carrying the plates out of the kitchen, and she flew right into her! Malanya just barely caught them, or all the plates would have been shattered to pieces."

Rubonosov gradually became furious; he turned purple and snarled angrily. Wanda was standing behind the living room doors, crying and praying quietly, crossing herself hurriedly. Through the crack in the door she was looking at Vladimir Ivanovich's purple face, which seemed repulsive and terrifying. Rubonosov yelled:

"Wanda, come in here!"

Wanda, trembling all over, entered the drawing room.

"What have you done, you goose?" Vladimir Ivanovich began to yell at her.

Wanda caught sight of the whip in Rubonosov's hand which he used to quiet Nero.

"Come, come a little closer!" Vladimir Ivanovich said spattering saliva, "I want to pet you with this whip."

He began to wave the whip fiercely and whistle shrilly. Wanda was frightened, and started to move backwards toward the doors; but he grabbed her by the shoulder and, twitching nervously, he pulled her into the middle of the room. Wanda fell to her knees, crying loudly. Rubonosov brandished the whip. Wanda screamed desperately when she heard the whip whistle in the air. She evaded the blow with a quick convulsive movement, jumped to her feet, and flew into the entry hall, where she hid behind a cupboard in the narrow, dusty corner. Her hysterical screaming echoed throughout the whole house. Vladimir Ivanovich rushed forward to drag Wanda out, but Anna Grigorevna, frightened by the girl's wild eyes and frenzied screams, stopped her husband:

"That's enough now, Vladimir Ivanovich; let her be," she

said, "You'll only have more trouble with her. Just look at her
eyes—she may start biting you. Once a troublemaker, always a
troublemaker."

Rubonosov stood in front of the cupboard, behind which
Wanda was shaking and struggling.

"Hide from me, will you, you nitwit!" he said slowly, all purple
with indignation, accenting his words fiercely. "All right! But just
wait, I'll get at you some other way."

Wanda became quiet and listened.

"You won't hide from me, you goose!" Vladimir Ivanovich
continued, apparently searching for a worse threat: "I know what
I'll do with you. Just wait until tonight, when you are about to fall
asleep. I'll slip a worm down your throat. Do you hear, you
goose—a worm!" Vladimir Ivanovich gave the word worm a
threatening, roaring emphasis and angrily threw the whip on the
floor. From behind the cupboard the black, wide eyes stayed
fastened on him and the swarthy face, now pale, was motionless.

"I'll fix you!" Rubonosov said. "The worm will crawl right
down your throat, you nitwit! It will crawl right along your
tongue. It will scratch your whole insides raw. It will swallow you
up, my dear!"

Wanda listened keenly, attentively; her frightened eyes glistened unmovingly among the shadows enveloping her in the
dusty, dark corner behind the cupboard. And Vladimir Ivanovich kept repeating his strange, malicious threats and he seemed
to Wanda, from her suffocating corner, like a sorcerer calling
down upon her mysterious evil spells which were irresistible and
horrible.

IV

The story about the worm pleased Rubonosov; he repeated it
several times both at dinner and in the evening after dinner. The
joke also pleased Anna Grigorevna and the girls—they all
laughed at Wanda. Wanda was silent and looked at Vladimir

Ivanovich with frightened eyes. Sometimes she thought that he was joking; after all, what kind of worm could it be? Sometimes she was terrified.

The whole evening she was not herself. She felt both guilty and offended. She would have like to be left alone, to hide in a corner somewhere and cry a little, but that was impossible. Her girl friends were quietly buzzing around her, and she herself had to sit with them over the hateful books and boring notebooks; in the neighboring room the Rubonosovs were talking. Wanda waited impatiently for night to come, so that she could shield herself, if only with a blanket, from these annoying, unnecessary people.

Wanda sat there and pretended that she was studying her lessons. Shutting herself off from her friends with her hands, she tried to imagine her father's house and the dense forest. She squinted her eyes and pictured her distant homeland.

The fire is crackling cheerfully in the stove. Wanda is sitting on the floor and stretching her red hands, stiff from the cold toward the fire; she has just come running home. A winter day, frosty and bright looks in through the window. The setting sun turns the sparkling crystal patterns on the windows red. It is warm and cozy; her own family surrounds her—good-natured laughter, jokes.

Then Rubonosov walked in and asked:

"What, Wanda? Were you meditating? Did you long for the worm, you nitwit? Most likely, during the night it will crawl right into your innards."

The girls were laughing. Wanda looked around confusedly with her wide, black eyes.

"The worm!" she repeated quietly with just her lips, and she pondered this word. The very sound of it seemed strange and somehow coarse. Why, in Russian, "chervyak?" She broke the word into syllables and sounds; the vile hissing at the beginning, then a threatening rumble, then the slippery, repulsive ending. Wanda moved her shoulders with disgust and a shiver ran along her spine. The senseless and ugly syllable "vyak" repeated itself over and over again in her mind; it was repulsive to her, but she could not get rid of it.

V

It was late. The girls got undressed and went to bed in the bedroom where their five beds stood uncomfortably in a single row. Wanda's bed was the second from the end. Dunya Khvastunovskaya slept on her left by the wall, on her right was Sasha, and then Katya; Zhenya was over by the door that led into the Rubonosovs' bedroom.

Wanda looked around the bedroom with melancholy, angry eyes. Gloomy shadows in the corners looked at her hostilely and, it seemed to her, they were watching her.

The walls were covered with an unattractive, dark wallpaper; it had crudely botched violet flowers on it, with the color applied hit or miss. The wallpaper was pasted on sloppily, and the pattern did not join properly. The ceiling, which was papered, was low and gloomy. To Wanda it seemed to be sinking down, taking the air along with it and squeezing her chest. The iron beds also seemed to Wanda to smell of something unpleasant and sad, like a jail or a hospital.

Across from the beds, right before Wanda's eyes, stood the wardrobes for the girls' clothes; they were full of chinks, knocked together out of rotten wood with little doors which did not fit properly. When anyone walked past the cupboards, their doors quivered and squeaked slightly. It annoyed Wanda that the cupboards had the pitiful and puzzled appearance of frightened, decrepit old men.

Vladimir Ivanovich entered the girls' bedroom and yelled loudly:

"Wanda, listen, that worm will crawl down your throat tonight."

The girls began to titter and looked at Wanda and at Vladimir Ivanovich. Wanda was silent. From under the blanket her large black eyes flashed at Vladimir Ivanovich.

Rubonosov left. The girls began to tease Wanda. They knew that it was easy to tease Wanda to the point of tears, and that was why they loved to tease her. Wanda had a harassed, distrustful heart, receptive only to dreams about her distant homeland.

Wanda sadly kept silent, with her sorrowful eyes looking dully at the gloomy ceiling. The girls chattered and exchanged smiles. Vladimir Ivanovich was fed up with all this; he was getting ready to go to sleep. He yelled from his bedroom:

"Hey, nitwit! What are you cackling in there for, you clowns! I'll get the whip after you!"

The girls quieted down.

"All he can think about is the whip!" Wanda thought with annoyance. She recalled the affectionate, kind people at home, and Vladimir Ivanovich in comparison with them seemed uncouth, coarse. But suddenly she felt ashamed to be judging him—for after all she was guilty before him.

Soon, from the neighboring bed came the sleepy puffing of Dunya, who was rapidly falling asleep. Tonight Wanda found it repulsive. In the warm, close air, breathing was difficult and sad. It seemed to her that it was crowded, and that there was little air. A feeling of melancholy and a strange annoyance with something crowded in her breast.

She covered her head with the blanket. Angry thoughts raced through her head—and then died down, being replaced by happy, distant daydreams.

Wanda started to fall asleep. Suddenly she felt something unpleasant on her lips, as if it were crawling. She was shaking from fear. Her sleep literally sprang away from her.

Her eyes were wide open and melancholy. Her heart stopped, then began to pound rapidly and vigorously until it hurt. Wanda quickly raised her hand to her mouth and pulled out a corner of the sheet, slightly wet from saliva, which had accidentally fallen there. That was what had caused the sensation which had so frightened her.

Wanda experienced the joy of having escaped danger. She

noted that her heart was beating hard. She held a hand to her breast and felt her rapid pulse with burning fingers; she smiled at her abating fright.

And in the dusk of night surrounding her, something threatening and unknown stirred dimly and vaguely. Her joy was strained and her smile pale, and once more her heart grew quietly still from that very same dark, hidden foreboding.

Wanda felt melancholy and languid. She turned restlessly from side to side. She was suffocating. The blanket hindered her breathing. There was an unpleasant sensation in her legs: a languid weariness filled with a painful heaviness; her insteps hurt from the tight shoes she had worn during the day. She sensed an uncomfortableness in her whole body. She wanted to sleep; but she could not fall asleep, and her eyes seemed heavy and dry.

The wind gave a howl in the chimney, mournful and thin. One of the girls mumbled something in her sleep. The anguished melancholy of sleeplessness clasped Wanda in a suffocating embrace. It was painfully uncomfortable for her to lie on the coarse folds of the sheet and nightshirt which she had mussed while tossing and turning.

Wanda tried to daydream, to summon the sweet and gentle feelings within herself, but she did not succeed. The girls were sleeping soundly, and at times it seemed to Wanda that they were unalive and terrifying.

Thus she lay one whole, long hour and finally she fell asleep.

VI

Wanda awakened suddenly as if she had been given a push. It was still the dead of night; everyone was sleeping. Wanda shot up and sat on her bed, frightened by something, by some sort of dim dream, some kind of vague sensations. She stared tensely into the gloom of the bedroom, thinking fragmentary, unclear thoughts about something incomprehensible to her. Melancholy gripped her heart. There was an unpleasant dryness in her mouth, making Wanda yawn abruptly. Then she felt as if some foreign object was crawling along her tongue, to the very root, something sticky and repulsive; it crawled into the depths of her mouth and tickled her pharnyx. Unconsciously, Wanda made several swallowing movements. The sensation of something crawling on her tongue ceased.

Suddenly Wanda remembered the worm. Naturally she thought that that very same worm had crawled into her mouth and she had swallowed it alive. Terror and revulsion enveloped her. Wanda's desperate and shrill cries spread throughout the gloomy quiet of the room.

The frightened girls jumped from their beds, uncomprehending, chattering and sobbing and rushing about confusedly in the darkness, colliding with one another. Wanda became quiet. Anna Grigorevna, who recognized Wanda's voice, ran in from her bedroom undressed, lighting a candle on the way. Behind the door one could hear Vladimir Ivanovich turning over heavily in the bed which creaked under him, angrily mumbling and then beginning to search for his clothes.

Anna Grigorevna went up to Wanda.

"Wanda, what is it?" she asked. "Why are you howling! What are you afraid of, you mad thing?"

In the candlelight, the girls also realized that it was Wanda who was yelling, and they crowded around her bed, half awake, snuggling together from the cold and rubbing their sleep-filled eyes. Wanda was sitting on the bed, bent over, cross-legged. Her whole body was shaking, and she looked timidly at Anna Grigorevna. Her wide-open eyes burned and expressed uncontrolled terror. Anna Grigorevna touched her on the shoulder.

"What's the matter with you, Wanda? Speak up!"

All at once Wanda began to cry, loudly, with childish, desperate screams and she began to murmur:

"The worm, the worm!"

Her teeth made a strange and noisy clicking sound. Anna Grigorevna did not immediately remember what worm she was talking about.

"What worm?" she asked with annoyance, turning now to Wanda, then to the other girls.

Wanda began to cry even louder, screaming:

"Oh, my God help me! The worm has crawled inside me!"

She feebly opened her mouth and poked her fingers inside, unconsciously bit them, pulled them out of her mouth and again began to sob. Katya explained:

"She must have dreamed that the worm Vladimir Ivanovich spoke about crawled into her mouth."

Vladimir Ivanovich himself came in and yelled while still on the threshold:

"What's going on here? You clowns, you don't let anyone sleep."

"There you see," answered Anna Grigorevna, "you went on so much about that worm to Wanda that she has even begun to believe it."

"Fool," said Rubonosov, "of course I was joking; there's no worm."

The girls began to laugh, pressing up closer to Wanda and they began to caress and soothe her:

"You only dreamed it, Wanda. Where could a worm come from?"

"What a fool you are! Can't even joke with you!" exclaimed Rubonosov, and he returned to his bedroom.

Dunya brought Wanda some water in a ladle and coaxed her to take a drink. Anna Grigorevna sat next to Wanda on the bed and tried to convince her. Little by little Wanda was calmed, and she fell asleep quickly.

VII

Wanda dreamed of her own home, her father, her mother, her little brothers, the dear forest, and faithful Polkan.

Their little one-storied house, half-covered with snow, sits at the edge of the small town. Blue smoke curls gaily above the steep roof. Not far off is the white forest with its beckoning sadness.

The quiet skies are illuminated by an early pink sunset. Then she dreamed about summer. The winding river is flowing slowly. There are yellow water-lilies not far from the bank. Above the river there are steep clay precipices. Swift birds cry out and soar in the thin air. Her mother is there, affectionate, gay. She has bright blue eyes, a resonant voice, and she is singing a quiet, peaceful song. Her father looks like such a stern man. But Wanda is not afraid of his long, stiff, graying moustache or his thick, frowning brows. Wanda loves to listen to his stories about his homeland—far away and fantastic. Wanda was born and grew up here among these snows in her mother's homeland, and she interprets her father's stories in her own way, as if they were splendid fairy tales.

There is movement in the bedroom; the girls' voices and laughter awakened Wanda. She opened her eyes. Everything she looked at appeared strange and incomprehensible to her. So sharp was the transition from her beloved dreams to these dusty walls, to this coarse wallpaper with its absurd flowers, that for half a minute she continued to lie still, not understanding where she was and what was the matter with her—half-consciously grasping at the fleeting snatches of her interrupted dream.

And then the walls of the room looked at her with the familiar melancholy; her heart ached with the familiar melancholy. Sadly she remembered that once more, for a whole day, she would have to be among strangers who would tease her about the worm and about her name—which they found odd—and other offensive things. This premonition that she would be offended began to stir painfully in her heart.

VIII

The Rubonosovs and the girls were drinking tea. Wanda was still pale from the night's scare. Her head ached, she was languorous and melancholy, and she drank and ate half-heartedly.

She had a bad taste in her mouth, and the tea seemed musty or sour to her.

Vladimir Ivanovich drank from his saucer, and smacked his lips loudly. Wanda found this smacking sound repulsive, but he hurried in order to drink up even more, for soon he had to go to work.

Anna Grigorevna noticed that Wanda was sad, and she asked:

"What's wrong with you, Wanda? Do you have a headache?"

"No, it's nothing, Anna Grigorevna. I'm fine," Wanda answered, rousing herself to smile.

"It's because of her scare that she is so pale," Katya explained.

Sasha, remembering the night's commotion, began to laugh, infecting the other girls with her gaiety.

"Wanda, maybe you really are sick and should stay home?" Anna Grigorevna asked.

But Wanda could tell by her voice that she would be angry if she remained and would take it as a sham. And Wanda hastened to say:

"No, Anna Grigorevna, why do you say that? Of course I am well."

"Do you suppose that the worm really and truly did crawl in?" asked Vladimir Ivanovich and he began to roar with laughter.

Everyone began to laugh, and even Wanda smiled. In the light of day, she had ceased to fear the worm. But Rubonosov became annoyed that Wanda was smiling: the good-for-nothing jokester could grin while he had to drink his tea—without his favorite cup! He decided to frighten Wanda some more, so that she would remember from now on.

"What are you grinning about Wanda?" he said, knitting his whitish eyebrows fiercely, "Do you really think I'm kidding? What a fool! The worm has only quieted down for a while—it's just warming itself, but give it time, and it'll begin to gnaw away again; and then you'll scream your head off."

Wanda turned pale, and suddenly, she distinctly felt in the

upper part of her stomach a light tickling. She clutched at her heart. Anna Grigorevna became uneasy; if the girl were to take ill, they would have a lot of trouble with her: the parents lived more than three hundred versts away. She began to quiet her husband:

"Now that's enough from you, Vladimir Ivanovich. Why do you scare the child? She'll start acting up again during the night. I can't waste time with her every night. You're worn out dealing with them during the day."

IX

While Wanda was walking to school with her friends, the worm still continued to tickle her in the very same place. She felt uncomfortable and terrified.

The wind, which was blowing head-on, seemed relentless. The gloomy fences and the cheerless people made her melancholy, and she could not forget that the worm was inside her—small, thin, barely noticeable—and tickling her, as if it were making its way somewhere, tickling in fits and starts: sometimes it would subside, then it would begin again, just like that relentless wind which was raising gusts of swirling snow in an absurd and fitful way. This howling of the wind on the deserted streets was an agonizing reminder to Wanda of that drowsy quiet in the distant forest where, at that very moment, her father's manly voice was resounding loudly beneath the austere pines. But there, in that forest there is space and God's will, while here in this tedious, alien city there are walls and human impotence.

She remembered how lovely it was to hide herself in her father's fur coat—with the sleigh rushing and the wind screeching rakishly and whipping up snowy clouds and with the sun visible through them, its rays broken up into multicolored sprays; one could hear the cheerful snort of the horses and the drawn out humming of the runners sliding across the snow.

A narrow path of firs stretched from the gate of someone's house out onto the street. Wanda's heart contracted with fear.

"Why did I break that cup yesterday!" she thought bitterly, "and why was I jumping around? What was I so happy about?"

X

Sitting in class, Wanda listened to what her worm was doing. Now and then, it seemed to her that it was rising higher, towards her heart. She tried to calm herself, thinking that all this would pass. But there was such an implacable severity emanating from the bare walls of the classroom that she was terrified.

Her friends told all the classes about the worm, and they teased Wanda mercilessly. During recess, the girls came up to her and asked: "Is it true that you swallowed a worm?"

Wanda heard laughter behind her and quiet exclamations:

"Wanda swallowed a worm." (At school they distorted her name to mean "Wanda-Washroom.")

Then they began to tease her in rhyme:

"Wanda-Washroom broke a cup

Found a worm and ate him up."

Wanda turned pale with rage and quarreled with her friends. Suddenly, at the height of a heated argument with a pesty, mocking girl, Wanda felt a light sucking sensation right under her very heart. Frightened, she fell silent, sat down at her place and, oblivious to everything else, began to concentrate on what was happening inside her.

Under her heart, something was quietly obstinately sucking. First it would abate, and then the sucking would begin again.

The wearisome sucking also continued at home, during dinner and in the evening. Whenever Wanda's thoughts, exhausted by the worm, turned to other matters, the worm became quiet. But then she would immediately remember it, and begin to listen for it. Little by little the irksome sucking would begin again.

Sometimes it seemed to Wanda that if she could forget about the worm, it would be quiet. But she could never forget it; they reminded her.

Wanda became more and more melancholy and terrified, but

she was ashamed to say that the worm was sucking away at her. Nestled timidly within her was the faint hope that all this would pass by itself.

XI

The girls were sitting at their lessons. The yellow lamplight irritated Wanda. She listened to the tedious working of the worm, which was sucking ever more skillfully. Wanda leaned her elbows on the table, put her head in her hands, and looked dully at the opened book. An inexplicable melancholy tormented her. It was difficult for her to breathe in this hostile, close air. Trying to comfort herself, Wanda thought:

"There isn't any worm; this all comes from melancholy. I just have to cheer up."

She tried to think about home. Soon it will be spring and they will take her home.

The cool, mossy forest is somnolent. It is filled with the fresh aroma of pines. The water in the creek has a silvery tinkle, tumbling over the stones. The tall bilberry bush, covered with lackluster blossoms, looms darkly amid the green surroundings.

But this daydream took great effort, and soon Wanda wearied of making herself dream.

Voices came to her from the dining room. Anna Grigorevna was hurrying Malanya: Vladimir Ivanovich had gotten up from his after-dinner nap and was angry because there still was no tea ready.

Wanda abruptly pushed back her chair and went into the dining room. Her swarthy face was so pale that her full cheeks seemed to have fallen away during the past twenty-four hours. Her tired eyes staring straight ahead, she went up to Anna Grigorevna and spoke quietly:

"Anna Grigorevna, it is sucking away at me in the pit of my stomach."

"What's that?" impatiently asked Anna Grigorevna, who had failed to hear.

"In the pit of my stomach. . .it's sucking away. . . the worm."
Wanda said with a falling voice.

"You fool, you!" Anna Grigorevna yelled angrily. "I have
better things to do than waste time with you."

"Oho! The worm!" cried Vladimir Ivanovich triumphantly.

He laughed uproariously, exclaiming violently:

"It's sucking away, you nitwit! I've fixed you! Volodka Rubonosov is no fool!"

Attracted by the laughter, the girls ran into the dining room.
Laughter swirled loosely around Wanda. Her head began to spin.
She sat down on a chair and obediently and hopelessly swallowed
some distasteful medicine which Anna Grigorevna quickly con-
trived for her.

She saw that no one pitied her, and that no one wanted to
understand what was happening to her.

XII

At night Wanda could not get to sleep. The worm had nestled
in under her heart and was sucking incessantly and tormentingly.
Wanda raised herself and leaned on the pillow with her elbows.
The blanket slipped from her shoulders. In the weak light from
the icon lamp, lit for the approaching holiday, Wanda's nightshirt
appeared whitish; her bare arms seemed swarthy and her wide,
black eyes burned with fright in her pale face. It seemed to
Wanda that the pain was becoming unbearable. She began to cry
quietly. But she did not dare awaken Anna Grigorevna. A vague
fear of people's hostility prevented her from calling for help. She
pressed her face to the pillow in order to muffle the sounds of her
crying. But her sobs squeezed her breast. The quiet, but desperate sighing of the sobbing girl resounded through the bedroom.

"What can I do?" exclaimed Wanda quietly and sadly. "And
what was I so happy about, fool that I was! Just because I
memorized a lesson! Oh, God! Is it possible to perish from a
broken cup?"

Wanda got up from the bed. The girls were sleeping; one could hear their measured, deep breathing. Wanda knelt before her icon, which was fastened to the head of her bed. She prayed, crossing herself and quietly whispering words of despair and hope with her trembling, dried-out lips. She got carried away and began to whisper a little more loudly and to sob. Sasha began to toss in bed and mumble something. Wanda was frightened and grew quieter; she settled back on her knees and waited anxiously. Everything became quiet again; no one woke up.

Wanda prayed for a long time, but prayer did not calm her. The silence and half-light responded to her prayer with hostility. It seemed to Wanda that someone quiet was passing nearby, that something was moving and mysteriously fluttering, but it all goes past her with its sorcery and power and has nothing to do with her. Alone, lost in this alien region, she is needed by no one. The meek angel flies by above her toward the happy and meek—and will not press close to her.

XIII

Tedious days and terrible nights passed. Wanda rapidly grew thin. Her black eyes, set off now by the blue spots under them, were dry and troubled. The worm was gnawing at her heart, and at times she cried out indistinctly from the tormenting pain. It was terrible, and difficult to breathe, so difficult that there was a thumping in her breast when Wanda took a deeper breath.

But she could no longer ask for help. It seemed to her that everyone was for the worm and against her.

Wanda imagined her tormentor clearly. Before, it had been thin, grayish, with weak jaws; it barely moved and could not hold on by suction. But by now it has warmed itself and become stronger: it is red now, and corpulent; it chews unceasingly and moves tirelessly, seeking out still other uninjured places in her heart.

Finally Wanda decided to write to her father so he would come and fetch her. She had to write on the sly.

Having found a moment, Wanda went up to Rubonosov's

desk, pulled an envelope from under a marble table weight in the shape of a woman's hand, and hid it in her pocket. Just then, she heard light footsteps. She gave a start as if she had been caught, and jumped awkwardly away from the table. Zhenya walked by. Wanda could not decide whether or not Zhenya had seen her take the envelope. Sitting at her lessons, she kept looking at Zhenya attentively. But Zhenya was immersed in her books.

"Of course she didn't see me," Wanda decided, "otherwise she would have tattled immediately."

Wanda wrote her letter, screening it with her notebooks. She had to tear herself away continually: either Anna Grigorevna was passing by, or her friends were looking at her. This is what she wrote:

Dear Papa and Mama,
    Please take me home. A worm has crawled into me and I am very ill. I broke Vladimir Ivanovich's cup while fooling around and he told me that a worm would crawl inside me and a worm did crawl in me and if you do not fetch me, I will die and you will be sorry for me. Send for me as soon as possible; I will get well at home, but I can't live here. Please take me at least until autumn and I'll study by myself and then I will go into the fourth grade, but if you don't take me, then the worm will eat away my heart and I'll soon die. And if you do take me I will teach Lesha reading and arithmetic. Forgive me for not putting a stamp on; I have no money and I dare not ask Anna Grigorevna. I kiss you dear daddy and mama and little brothers and sisters and Polkan.
                                                                    Your Wanda.
    And I have not been lazy and I have good marks.

Meanwhile, Zhenya went to Anna Grigorevna and began to whisper something to her. Anna Grigorevna listened silently and her malicious eyes glittered. Zhenya returned and with an innocent air, started working at her lesson.

Wanda was addressing the envelope. Suddenly she felt uneasy and apprehensive. She raised her head; all of her friends were looking at her with dull, strange curiosity. From their expressions it was obvious that there was someone else in the room. Wanda felt cold and terrified. With an agonizing shiver, she turned around, forgetting even to conceal the envelope.

Behind her stood Anna Grigorevna and she was looking at her notebooks under which the letter was visible. Her eyes glittered wickedly, and her canine teeth appeared yellow in her mouth under her lip which was quivering in rage.

XIV

Wanda was sitting by the window and looking sadly at the street. The street was dead, the houses were standing on a shroud of snow. Wherever the rays of the sunset fell on the snow, it sparkled magnificently and rigidly like the silver brocade on a smartly decked-out coffin.

Wanda was sick and was not allowed to go to school. Her emaciated cheeks glowed with a magnificent, never-changing flush. Anxiety and terror wearied her, timid impotence chained her will. She had grown used to the tormenting work of the worm and it was all the same to her whether it was silent or gnawing at her heart. But it seemed to her that someone was standing behind her and that she dare not look around. She looked at the street with frightened eyes. But the street lay dead in its magnificent silk brocade.

And it seemed to her that there was a faint smell of incense in the room.

XV

It was a clear, sunny day. But the ailing Wanda was lying in bed. They had moved her into another room, where her bed stood alone. It smelled of medicines. Wanda lay, terribly emaciated, her feeble hands on top of the covers. She indifferently surveyed the new walls, already hateful to her. A tormenting cough was rapidly overstraining the dying child's breast. The stationary spots of a consumptive flush flamed brightly on her sunken cheeks; their swarthy color had taken on a waxy hue. A cruel smile distorted her mouth; because of the terrible thinness of her face it no longer closed tightly. She murmured disjointed, incoherent words in a hoarse voice.

Wanda no longer feared these strangers; it terrified them to hear her malicious words.

Wanda knew that she was dying.

The Hoop

I

One morning, a woman and her child of about four years were walking on a deserted street on the outskirts of the city. The woman was well-dressed and young; her child was lively and red-cheeked. Happy and smiling, the woman kept a careful watch on her son. The boy was rolling a hoop, a large, new, bright-yellow one. With movements that were still awkward, the boy urged it on, laughing, rejoicing, stamping his chubby little legs, bare to the knee, and waving his stick about. He didn't really have to raise his stick so high above his head, but why not!

What joy! There had not been this hoop before, and now it runs along so briskly! And everything is such fun!

And none of this really had existed before; for the boy—all of this is new: the streets in the morning and the cheerful sun and the distant city noises. Everything is new to the boy—pure and joyous.

Indeed, everything is pure: children themselves do not see the filthy side of things until adults show them.

II

A poorly dressed old man with coarse hands stopped at the intersection; he pressed himself against the fence to let the woman and the boy pass. The old man looked at the boy with dim eyes and grinned dully. Vague, slow thoughts crept into his bald head.

"A young gentleman!" he thought, "and he's such a small

fellow. And look how merry! A child, but a gentleman's child—imagine!"

There was something he did not understand; something seemed strange to him.

"Here's a child, but aren't children to be pulled about by the hair? Play is mischief isn't it? Children, as everyone knows, are mischief-makers.

And his mother does nothing: she doesn't quiet him or yell, or threaten him. Well-dressed and all shiny. What's she need more? Sure, they live high on the hog."

But when he, the old man, was a little boy, it was a dog's life. It wasn't so sweet even now, but at least he wasn't beaten, and he had plenty to eat. But back then, just hunger, cold, and brawls. There was no such mischief as a hoop or other high-class toys. And so his whole life had passed—in poverty, worry, bitterness. And there was nothing to remember—not one single joy.

He smiled at the boy with his toothless mouth, and envied him. He was thinking.

"What a stupid thing he's having fun with."

But his envy tormented him.

He walked on to work—to the factory where he had worked since childhood, where he had grown old. And all day he thought about the boy.

His thoughts were fixed; he simply kept recalling the boy—laughing, running, stamping his feet, rolling his hoop. And his little legs were chubby and his knees were bare. . . .

All day in the noise of the factory wheels, he remembered the boy with the hoop. And that night he dreamed of the boy.

III

The next morning daydreams again overpowered the old man.

The machines are pounding, the work is monotonous, there is no need to think. His hands go about their accustomed task; the toothless mouth grins at the amusing daydream. The air under the high ceiling grows misty from the dust, up above under the high ceiling where the endless belts slide from wheel to wheel with a rapid whine. The far corners are wrapped in a noisy haze. People are scurrying about like ghosts; the human voice is inaudible under the reverberating song of the machines.

And the old man imagines that he is small and that his mother is a lady and he has a hoop and a stick and he is playing—rolling the hoop with the stick. He is dressed in white, his little legs are chubby, his little knees are bare. . . .

Day after day there is the very same labor, and the very same daydream.

IV

Once toward evening, when the old man was returning home, he saw in the courtyard the hoop from an old barrel, a black, rough rim. The old man began to shake with joy, and tears appeared in his dim eyes. A quick, almost unconscious longing flashed in his soul.

The old man looked around cautiously, bent down, and with trembling hands, grabbed the hoop and carried it home, smiling bashfully.

No one noticed, nor asked. And who would care about such a thing? A little old man in rags carrying an old, broken thing no one needed; who would look at him!

But he carried it stealthily, afraid of ridicule. Why he took it and why he carried it, he himself did not know. It was similar to the one the boy had, so he had taken it. So what, he could let it just lie around.

Looking at it and touching it made his daydreams more alive, the factory whistles and noises seemed dimmer and the noisy haze even hazier. . . .

For several days the hoop lay under the old man's bed, in his wretched, cramped corner. Sometimes the old man pulled the hoop out and looked at it; this filthy gray hoop comforted him, and his constant daydream about the happy boy became more vivid.

V

One clear, warm morning, when the birds were twittering in the stunted city trees more cheerfully than the day before, the old man got up earlier than usual, took his hoop, and walked out of the city a little way.

Coughing slightly, he made his way among the old trees and thorny bushes in the woods. The silence of the gloomy trees, covered with dry, dark, cracked bark, was incomprehensible to him. And the odors were strange and the flies astonished him and a fantastic fern grew there. There was no dust or noise and a gentle, marvelous haze lay behind the trees. The old feet slid along the flooring of needles and stumbled over ancient roots.

The old man broke off a dead branch and hung his hoop on it.

A little meadow lay before him—radiant, quiet. Multicolored, innumerable little dewdrops sparkled on the green blades of recently mown grass.

And suddenly the old man tossed the hoop from his stick, he hit the hoop with the stick—the hoop began to roll silently about the little meadow. The old man began to laugh. He beamed, then ran after the hoop, just like the little boy. He kicked up his heels and drove the hoop with the stick and he raised the hand with the stick just as high over his head as the boy had.

It seemed to him that he was small, affectionate, and cheerful. It seemed to him that his mother was walking behind him, looking at him and smiling. Like a child, experiencing it for the first time, he felt refreshed in the gloomy forest on the cheerful grass, on the quiet mosses.

The goatlike, dusty-gray beard on his slack face trembled, and rattling sounds of laughter and coughing flew from his toothless mouth.

VI

And the old man came to love walking to the woods in the morning and playing with his hoop in that little glade.

Sometimes he thought he might be seen and ridiculed, and this thought would make him suddenly feel unbearably ashamed. And his shame resembled terror: he grew so weak that his legs gave way under him. The old man would look around, timid and shamefaced.

But no, no one was to be seen, no sound heard. . . .

And, having played as much as he wanted to, he would walk back peacefully to the city, smiling gently and joyfully.

VII

And so no one ever did see him. And nothing more happened. The old man played quietly for several days, and on one very dewy morning, he caught cold. He took to bed and soon died. When he died in the factory hospital among indifferent strangers, he was smiling clearly.

And his memories comforted him, for he too had been a boy, laughing and running across the fresh grass, under the gloomy trees—and his beloved mama was watching after him.

Hide-and-Seek

I

Lelechka's nursery was bright, pretty, and cheerful. Lelechka's ringing voice delighted her mother. Lelechka is a charming child. No one has another child like her, and never did, or ever could. Serafima Aleksandrovna, Lelechka's mother, was sure of that. Lelechka's eyes are dark and large, her cheeks rosy, her eyes made for kisses and for laughter. But this is not Lelechka's greatest or sweetest charm for Serafima Aleksandrovna.

Lelechka is her mother's only child. That is why Lelechka's every movement charms her mother. What bliss it is to hold Lelechka in her lap, caress her, and feel the little girl under her hands, lively and gay as a little bird.

To tell the truth, it is only in the nursery that Serafima Aleksandrovna feels happy. With her husband she feels cold.

Perhaps this is because he himself loves the cold—cold water, cold air. He is always fresh and cold, with a cold smile—and wherever he passes, cold currents seem to move in the air.

The Nesletevs, Sergey Modestovich and Serafima Aleksandrovna, had not married from love, nor from calculation either, but because it was the accepted thing. He was a young man of thirty-five and she a young woman of twenty-six, both from the same circle and well brought up, so they came together: it was appropriate that he take a wife, and it was time for her to marry.

It even seemed to Serafima Aleksandrovna that she was in love with her fiancé, and this made her very happy. He was refined and clever, always kept a significant expression in his intelligent, gray eyes, and he carried out the duties of one betrothed with irreproachable tenderness.

Sergey Modestovich did not feel himself to be in love and he was not particularly happy, but he was comfortable—as was everything in his well-regulated, temperate life.

His bride was pretty, but not too much so: she was a tall, dark-eyed, dark-haired woman, somewhat shy in manner, but she had great tact. He was not after her dowry, but he was pleased to know that his wife had something. He had connections, and his wife had good, influential relatives. This could prove useful on the right occasion. Nesletev, always correct and tactful, was advancing in his work neither so rapidly that he was envied, nor so slowly that he envied others, but moderately and opportunely.

Never once, from the time they were married did Sergey Modestovich's outward and visible behavior give his wife occasion to accuse him. Later, when Serafima Aleksandrovna was already pregnant, Sergey Modestovich began to indulge in easy and casual liaisons on the side. Serafima Aleksandrovna found out about it and to her own surprise, was not particularly distressed; she awaited the baby with an anxious feeling which absorbed her.

A daughter was born: Serafima Aleksandrovna devoted herself to attending to her. In the beginning, she would report to her husband enthusiastically all the details of Lela's life which so delighted her. But she soon noticed that Sergey Modestovich listened to her without any real interest but solely from his habit of social politeness. Serafima Aleksandrovna grew more and more distant from him. She loved her little daughter with the ungratified passion with which other women, whose lives have gone wrong, betray their husbands with chance young men.

"Mama, let's play hide-and-seek," cried Lelechka, pronouncing the k as t, so that instead of "seek," she said "seet."

This sweet clumsiness in her speech touched Serafima Aleksandrovna and made her smile tenderly. Lelechka ran off, her chubby little feet stamping over the rugs, and hid behind the curtains by her little bed.

"Peek-a-boo, Mommy!" she cried out in her laughing, tender voice, peeking out with one dark, mischievous little eye.

"Where's my little girl?" her mama asked, pretending that she was searching for Lelechka and could not see her.

But Lelechka burst into ringing laughter in her hiding place. Then she edged out a bit more and her mother acted as if she had just then caught sight of her and she clasped her little shoulders and exclaimed joyfully:

"Here she is, my Lelechka!"

Lelechka laughed long and loud, pressing her head against her mother's knees and wriggling in her mother's white arms. Her mother's dark eyes burned excitedly and passionately.

"Now, mama, you hide," said Lelechka, having tired of laughing.

Her mother went to hide; Lelechka turned away, as if not looking, but she stealthily observed where her mama was going. Her mother hid behind the wardrobe and cried out:

"Peek-a-boo, little daughter!"

Lelechka ran around the room, peeking in all the corners, pretending, just as her mother had done, that she was searching—though she knew full well where her mama was standing.

"Where is my mama?" asked Lelechka. "Not here and not here,"—she was saying, running to another corner.

Her mother was standing, holding her breath, her head leaning against the wall, her coiffure crushed. A blissfully excited smile played about her ruddy lips.

The nurse, Fedosya, a rather stupid looking, but kind, pretty woman, grinned as she looked at her mistress with her usual expression of agreeing not to quibble about the nobility's whims, and she thought to herself:

"The mother's just like a little kid herself—just look at how flushed she is."

Lelechka was getting close to her mother's corner—and her mother was becoming more and more excited, entering into the spirit of the game; her mother's heart was beating intensely and rapidly and she pressed herself more closely to the wall, mussing her hair. Lelechka peeked into her mother's corner and squealed with joy:

"I sound you!" she cried out loudly and joyfully, once more delighting her mother by mispronouncing the f.

She pulled her mother by the hand to the middle of the room—both of them were happy and laughing—and once more she dropped her head onto her mother's lap and prattled, end-lessly prattled her sweet little words, pronouncing them so splen-didly and awkwardly.

At that moment, Sergey Modestovich was approaching the nursery. He had heard the laughter, the joyful exclamations and noisy row through the partly closed doors. Smiling coldly, but politely, he entered the nursery—fresh, erect, impeccably dressed and emitting an aura of cleanliness, freshness, and cold-ness. He entered in the midst of the lively game and confused everyone with his serene coldness. Even Fedosya was ashamed and didn't know whether for her mistress or for herself. Serafima Aleksandrovna was instantly calm and to all appearances, cold—and her mood was conveyed to her little daughter, who ceased laughing and looked at her father silently and attentively.

Sergey Modestovich cast a fleeting glance about the room. Everything there pleased him: the furnishings were pretty— Serafima Aleksandrovna had seen to it that from the tenderest age, her little daughter was surrounded only by beautiful things. Serafima Aleksandrovna was smartly and flatteringly dressed— she always did the same for Lelechka, and with the same care. There was only one thing Sergey Modestovich would not ap-prove of—that his wife was nearly always in the nursery.

"I wanted to say . . . I just knew that I would find you here," he said with a mocking and condescending smile.

They walked out of the nursery together. Showing Serafima

Aleksandrovna to the door of his study, Sergey Modestovich said, indifferently, as if in passing and without giving any significance to his words:

"Don't you find that it would be good for the little girl to manage without your company sometimes? You understand, in order for the child to feel its own separate personality," he explained to Serafima Aleksandrovna's astonished look.

"She's still so little," said Serafima Aleksandrovna.

"However, this is only my humble opinion. I don't insist—that's your realm there."

"I'll think it over," answered his wife, smiling as coldly and politely as he.

And they began to talk about other things.

II

That evening, in the kitchen, the nurse Fedosya was telling the taciturn housemaid Darya and the argumentative old cook Agafya, how much the child loved to play hide-and-seek with the mistress—hiding her little face and crying peek-a-boo!

"And the mistress herself is like a little kid," Fedosya said, grinning.

Agafya listened, shaking her head disapprovingly, and her face became severe and reproachful.

"As far as the mistress is concerned, it doesn't make any difference," she said, "but for the young lady to be hiding all the time is bad."

"What do you mean?" Fedosya asked with curiosity.

Her kind, rosy face, with its expression of curiosity, resembled the face of a crudely painted wooden doll.

"It's bad," Agafya repeated with conviction, "Really bad!"

"Well?" Fedosya asked again, the expression of curiosity on her face growing still more comical.

"She'll hide and hide and hide herself away for good," said Agafya in a mysterious whisper, looking at the door apprehensively.

"What are you saying!" exclaimed Fedosya with fright.

"I'm telling the truth, just you remember my words," Agafya said confidently and just as mysteriously, "this is the truest sign."

But the old woman had invented this sign herself, all of a sudden, and now, she was obviously very proud of it.

III

Lelechka was sleeping, and Serafima Aleksandrovna was sitting in her own room joyfully and tenderly daydreaming about Lelechka. In her dreams, Lelechka was a dear baby girl, then a dear young girl, then again a charming baby girl, but always, endlessly, she remained her mother's Lelechka.

Serafima Aleksandrovna did not notice that Fedosya had come and was standing before her. Fedosya's face was worried and frightened.

"Mistress, oh mistress," she called softly in a quivering, agitated voice.

Serafima Aleksandrovna awakened. Fedosya's face made her uneasy.

"What do you want, Fedosya," she asked anxiously. "Is something wrong with Lelechka?"

She quickly got up from the chair:

"No, mistress," answered Fedosya, waving her arms so her mistress would calm herself and sit down. "Lelechka's asleep, God be with her. It's just that I . . . you know, I tell you, it's . . . Lelechka's hiding all the time—it's just no good."

Fedosya looked at her mistress with unmoving eyes, round with fear.

"Why isn't it good?"—Serafima Aleksandrovna asked with vexation, involuntarily submitting to a vague uneasiness.

"Because it isn't, it's not done," said Fedosya, and her face expressed steadfast certitude.

"Please talk sense," Serafima Aleksandrovna ordered dryly, "I don't understand a thing."

—"Well, mistress, there's a kind of sign," explained Fedosya, suddenly ashamed.

"Nonsense," said Serafima Aleksandrovna.

She did not want to hear any more about what the sign was, or what it presaged. But it began to seem to her, if not terrifying, somehow terrible—and insulting, that some obviously absurd invention could destroy her sweet dreams and disturb her so agonizingly.

"Everybody knows that gentlefolk don't believe in signs, but this one's a bad sign," said Fedosya in a doleful voice, "the little girl hides, she hides . . . ."

Suddenly she began to cry, her voice choked with sobs.

"She hides and hides—and the sweet little angel will hide herself away in a damp little grave," she kept saying, wiping her tears with her apron and blowing her nose.

"Who told you that?" asked Serafima Aleksandrovna in a stern and weak voice.

"Agafya says so, mistress," answered Fedosya. "And she knows."

"She knows!" said Serafima Aleksandrovna vexedly, visibly wanting somehow to defend herself from this sudden uneasiness. "What nonsense! Please, in the future don't speak to me of such rubbish. Go."

Fedosya, with an offended and dejected face, went out.

"What rubbish! As though Lelechka could die," thought Serafima Aleksandrovna, trying to think rationally so as to conquer the sensation of coldness and fear which overcame her at the thought that Lelechka could die.

Serafima Aleksandrovna thought that these women were ignorant and that this was why they believed in signs. She, however, understood clearly that there could be no connection between this children's game, which any child could love, and that child's life span. She made a particular effort that evening to keep busy with something else—but her thoughts involuntarily kept returning to the fact that Lelechka liked to hide.

When Lelechka was still very small and had just recently
learned to recognize her mother and her nurse, she would sometimes, while looking at her mother, suddenly make a mischievous
face, and then burst out laughing and hide behind the shoulder
of the nurse, in whose arms she was lying. Then she would peek
out and give a sly look.

Just recently, during those few moments when Serafima Aleksandrovna had to leave the nursery, Fedosya had taught Lelechka how to hide again; and when her mother saw how charming Lelechka was when she hid, she herself began to play hide-
and-seek with her little daughter.

IV

The next morning Serafima Aleksandrovna was absorbed in
her joyful attentions to Lelechka, and she forgot all about Fedosya's words of the previous evening.

But when she had left the nursery to order dinner and then
returned to find Lelechka hiding under the table and crying out
"peek-a-boo!" Serafima Aleksandrovna suddenly felt terrified.
Although she reproached herself at once for this unfounded,
superstitious terror, still she could not bring herself to play hide-
and-seek with Lelechka, and she tried to divert Lelechka's attention to something else.

Lelechka is an affectionate, obedient, little girl. She willingly
does what her mother wants. But because she was used to hiding
from her mother and crying out "peek-a-boo!" from some hiding
place, today she kept returning to it.

Serafima Aleksandrovna tried earnestly to occupy Lelechka.
But it was no easy task! Especially when disturbing, threatening
thoughts were interfering constantly.

"Why does Lelechka keep remembering her 'peek-a-boo?' Why
doesn't she get bored doing the same thing over and over—closing her eyes and hiding her face? Perhaps," thought Serafima

Aleksandrovna, "Lelechka does not have that strong attraction to the world that other children have who look at things persistently. But if this is so, then isn't that a sign of an organic weakness? Isn't it the germ of an unconscious unwillingness to live?"

Forebodings tormented Serafima Aleksandrovna. She was ashamed in front of Fedosya and herself to give up playing hide-and-seek with Lelechka. But the game became agonizing for her, particularly agonizing because she still wanted to play it. And she was drawn all the more to hiding from Lelechka or seeking out the hiding Lelechka. Sometimes, even Serafima Aleksandrovna herself would start the game—with a heavy heart, suffering as if from some kind of evil deed that you know you shouldn't do but that you go ahead and do anyway.

It was a bad day for Serafima Aleksandrovna.

V

Lelechka was getting ready to go to sleep. Her little eyes could barely stay open from weariness as she climbed onto her little bed, enclosed by net guards. Her mother covered her with a blue blanket. Lelechka freed her soft, tiny white hands from under the blanket and reached out to embrace her mother. Her mother bent down. Lelechka, with a tender expression on her sleepy face, kissed her mother and lowered her head onto the pillows. Her arms were hidden under the blanket and Lelechka whispered:

"Peek-a-boo little arms."

Her mother's heart stopped beating. Lelechka was lying there so small, frail and quiet. Lelechka smiled weakly, closed her eyes and said quietly:

"Peek-a-boo little eyes."

And then even more quietly:

"Peek-a-boo Lelechka."

With these words she fell asleep, her cheek pressed to the pillow; covered by the blanket, she was so small and frail. Her mother looked at her with grieving eyes.

Serafima Aleksandrovna stood for a long time over Lelechka's little bed looking at Lelechka with tenderness and fear.

"I am her mother. Is it not possible for me to protect her?" she thought, imagining various misfortunes which could threaten Lelechka.

She prayed for a long time that night—but prayer did not relieve her grief.

VI

Several days passed. Lelechka caught a cold. At night she developed a fever. When Serafima Aleksandrovna, awakened by Fedosya, went to Lelechka and found her feverish, restless, and suffering, the first thing she thought of was that ominous "sign"—and in that first moment, hopeless despair seized her.

They called the doctor and did everything that one does in such cases, but the inevitable happened. Serafima Aleksandrovna tried to console herself with the hope that Lelechka would recover and smile again and play—yet that seemed to her such an unrealizable happiness! And Lelechka was becoming weaker with each passing hour.

Everyone pretended to be calm so as not to frighten Serafima Aleksandrovna—but their insincere faces made her grieve.

And her grief became dire when she heard Fedosya's sobbing and lamentations:

"She's hid, Lelechka's hid."

But Serafima Aleksandrovna's thoughts were confused, and she did not really grasp what was going on.

Lelechka was burning all over, and she kept dropping off by the minute and was delirious. Whenever she regained consciousness, she bore her pain and lassitude with tender meekness, and she would smile wanly at her mama so her mama would not think that she was in much pain. Three days passed as agonizing as a nightmare. Lelechka had become extremely weak. But she did not understand that she was dying.

She looked at her mother with her fading eyes and prattled in a barely audible, hoarse voice:

"Peek-a-boo, mama! Make peek-a-boo, mama!"

Serafima Aleksandrovna hid her face behind the little curtains of Lelechka's bed. Such grief!

"Mama!" called Lelechka in a barely audible voice.

Her mother bent over Lelechka—and Lelechka, with dimming eyes, saw her mama's pale, despairing face for the last time.

"A white mama!" Lelechka whispered.

Her mama's pale face faded and everything became dark for Lelechka. She caught feebly at the edge of the blanket with her hands and whispered:

"Peek-a-boo."

Something wheezed in her throat; Lelechka opened and closed her rapidly paling lips and died.

Serafima Aleksandrovna, numb with despair, left Lelechka and walked out of the room. She met her husband.

"Lelechka is dead," she said quietly, in an almost soundless voice.

Sergey Modestovich looked cautiously at her pale face. He was struck by the strange torpor in the features of this formerly animated, beautiful face.

VII

Lelechka was dressed, placed in a little coffin and carried into the hall. Serafima Aleksandrovna stood by the coffin, looking dully at her little dead daughter. Sergey Modestovich went up to his wife, and with cold, empty words of consolation tried to draw her away from the coffin. Serafima Aleksandrovna smiled.

"Go away," she said quietly. "Lelechka is playing. She'll get up in a minute."

"Sima, my dear, don't upset yourself," Sergey Modestovich said in a whisper. "You have to resign yourself to fate."

"She'll get up," Serafima Aleksandrovna repeated stubbornly, resting her eyes on her little dead daughter.

Sergey Modestovich looked around cautiously: he had a fear of impropriety and of the ridiculous. "Sima, don't upset yourself," he said again. "That would be a miracle, but miracles don't happen in the nineteenth century." Having said these words, Sergey Modestovich dimly felt their disparity with what had happened. He felt awkward and angry. He took his wife by the arm and cautiously led her away from the coffin. Serafima Aleksandrovna did not resist.

Her face seemed calm and her eyes were dry. She went into the nursery and began to walk around, glancing in those places where Lelechka used to hide. She went all around the room, stooping in order to glance under the table or under the little bed and she kept repeating in a cheerful voice:

"Where's my little daughter? Where's my Lelechka?"

Having circled the room, she began her search anew. Fedosya was sitting motionless in the corner, her face doleful. She cast a frightened look at her mistress, then she suddenly began to sob and cried out with all her might:

"She's hid, Lelechka, my angel's hid."

Serafima Aleksandrovna shuddered and stopped; she looked at Fedosya in bewilderment, began to cry, and walked quietly out of the nursery.

VIII

Sergey Modestovich hurried the funeral. He realized that Serafima Aleksandrovna was terribly shaken by the sudden sorrow and, fearing for her sanity, he thought that Lelechka should be buried as quickly as possible so her mother could be distracted and consoled.

Serafima Aleksandrovna dressed that morning especially carefully—for Lelechka. When she came into the hall, there were many people between her and Lelechka; the priest and the deacon were pacing about, blue smoke floated in the air, and it smelled of incense. With a dull heaviness in her head, Serafima Aleksandrovna went up to Lelechka. Lelechka lay quiet and pale and was smiling pitifully. Serafima Aleksandrovna placed her cheek on the edge of Lelechka's coffin and whispered:

"Peek-a-boo, little daughter!"

Her little daughter did not answer. Some kind of movement, bustle was going on around Serafima Aleksandrovna—strange, unwanted faces bent over her, someone supported her—and they began to take Lelechka away somewhere.

Serafima Aleksandrovna straightened up, gasped in bewilderment, smiled, and said loudly:

"Lelechka!"

They were taking Lelechka away—the mother threw herself after the coffin with a despairing wail—they restrained her. She rushed to get behind the door through which they were carrying Lelechka, sat down there on the floor and, looking through the crack, she shouted:

"Lelechka, peek-a-boo!"

Then she leaned her head out from behind the door and began to laugh.

Lelechka was hurriedly carried away from her mother, and the procession began to look like a stampede.

Beauty

In the austere silence of the waning day, Elena was sitting
alone, erect and unmoving, her pale, slender hands placed in her
lap. Her head unbowed, she was crying; large, slow tears rolled
down her face and her dark eyes glimmered.

She had just that day buried her mother, whom she loved
tenderly, and because noisy grief and people's coarse concern
were repulsive to her, she had restrained herself from crying at
the burial, both beforehand and then later, while accepting
condolences. Finally she had been left alone in her own white
room, where everything was chastely pure and austere—and sad
thoughts had wrenched the quiet tears from her eyes.

Elena's dress, austere and black, lay upon her mournfully—as
if, enshrouding Elena on her day of sorrow, the insensitive
clothing could not help reflecting her darkened soul. Elena
recalled her late mother, and she knew that her former life—serene, bright, and austere—had died forever. Before something
different should begin, Elena, with her cold tears and still sadness, was memorializing the past.

Her mother had died while still young. She had been as beautiful as some goddess of antiquity. All of her movements were slow
and stately. Her face had seemed haunted by melancholy dreams
of something eternally lost or of something desired and unattain-
able. And a languid pallor, auguress of death, had long marked
her features. A great weariness seemed to be inclining that beautiful body toward tranquillity. The white hair amidst the black
became ever more noticeable on her head—and it was strange

for Elena to think that her mother would soon be an old woman. . . .

Elena got up, walked to the window and slowly pulled back the heavy curtain to disperse the twilight which she did not like. But the gray, dim, half-light from outside was a further torment to her eyes—and Elena sat down again and waited patiently for the black of night and shed cold, slow tears.

And finally night came; a lamp was brought into the room and once more Elena went up to the window. A thick darkness was cloaking the street. The wretched and coarse objects of tedious convention were hidden in the black cover of night—and there was something triumphant in this melancholy blackness. Opposite the window where Elena was standing, on the other side of the street, the blacksmith's small brick-red house was barely visible in the light of occasional street lamps. The lamps stood far off making it seem just a black shape.

Suddenly a huge red spark slowly drifted from the open forge to the gates, and the gloom surrounding it seemed to thicken. It was the blacksmith carrying a piece of glowing iron along the street. A sudden joy flamed up in Elena's soul and made her laugh quietly—her ringing and joyful laughter spread throughout the expanse of the silent room.

And when the blacksmith had passed and the red spark had vanished in the black gloom, Elena marveled at her sudden joy and she marveled that it played on, tenderly and timidly, in her soul. Why did it arise, where did it come from, this joy that wrenches laughter from the breast and lights fires in eyes which have just been weeping? Wasn't it beauty that brought her joy and agitation? And wasn't every appearance of beauty joyful?

It was a momentary thing, born of a base substance and it had spread through the gloom and faded away, which is the way it must be with beauty: it appears and it passes, gladdening but not satiating the eye with its bright and transient brilliance.

Elena went out into the unlighted hall where it smelled faintly of jasmine and vanilla and opened the piano; festive and simple melodies poured forth from beneath her fingers, and her hands moved slowly across the white and black keys.

II

Elena loved being alone, among the beautiful things in her rooms, where the color white dominated the decor; where light and delicate fragrances drifted in the air; where it was so easy and joyful to dream about beauty. Everything there was redolent with slightly different aromas: Elena's clothes smelled of roses and violets, the curtains of white acacia; flowering hyacinths spread their sweet and languorous odors. There were many books— Elena read a great deal, but only selected and austere works.

It was painful for Elena to be with people—people speak untruths, they flatter, fuss, express their feelings in exaggerated and unpleasant ways. There is much that is absurd and ridiculous in people: they submit to fashion, use foreign words for some reason, have vain desires. Elena was reserved with people and was unable to like a single person whom she met. The only one worthy of her love was her mother—because she was serene, beautiful, and true. Elena wished that all people might someday become that way; that they would understand that beauty was the only aim in life; and that they would build themselves a dignified and wise life. . . .

The lamps were burning; their bright light was unmoving, white. It smelled of roses and almonds. Elena was alone.

She locked the door, lit the candles in front of the mirror and slowly bared her beautiful body.

All white and calm, she stood before the mirror and gazed at her reflection. The reflected lights from the lamps and the candles ran over her skin and made Elena happy. She stood there tender as a barely opened lily with its soft, little leaves still flattened, and a chaste scarlet hue was spreading over her virginal body. The sweet and bitter almond fragrance wafting in the air seemed to come from her naked body. A sweet excitement tormented her, and not a single impure thought disturbed her virginal imagination. And she dreamt of tender, innocent kisses, quiet as the touch of a midday wind, and joyous as blissful dreams.

The naked beauty of her tender body was a joy for Elena. Elena was laughing, and her quiet laugh echoed in the solemn quietude of her imperturbable room.

Elena lay breast down on the rug and inhaled the faint odor of mignonette. Down there, where it was strange to be looking at the lower halves of objects, she became still happier and more joyful. She laughed, like a little girl, rolling about on the soft carpet.

III

Each evening, for several days in succession, Elena admired her beauty in the mirror—and it never wearied her. Everything in her chamber was white—and amid this whiteness, the scarlet and yellow tones of her body shimmered, recalling the most delicate shades of mother-of-pearl and pearls.

Elena would put her arms above her head and, raising herself a little, she would stretch and bend and sway on her tensed legs. The delicate flexibility of her body delighted her. She took pleasure in seeing how the powerful muscles of her beautiful legs tensed resiliently beneath the delicate skin.

She moved about the room naked, and whether she stood or lay down, all of her positions, and all of her languorous movements were beautiful. And she rejoiced in her beauty and spent long hours unclothed—sometimes lost in reverie and admiration of herself, sometimes reading through the pages of marvelous and austere poets. . . .

An aromatic liquid gleamed whitely in an engraved silver amphora: Elena had mixed fragrances and milk in the amphora. Elena slowly raised the chalice and inclined it over her high breast. The white odorous drops fell quietly onto her scarlet skin, which shuddered from their touch. There was the sweet odor of lilies-of-the-valley and apples. The fragrance enveloped Elena in a light and delicate cloud. . . .

Elena let down her long, black hair and strewed it with red poppies. Then a garland of white flowers encircled her slender figure and caressed her skin. And these fragrant flowers were beautiful on the naked beauty of her fragrant body.

Later she took off the flowers and again gathered her hair into a high knot, draped her body with a sheer garment and secured it on her left shoulder with a golden clasp.

She had made this garment herself out of sheer linen, so no one had ever seen it.

Elena lay down upon a low couch, and dulcet daydreams drifted through her mind—dreams of sinless caresses, of innocent kisses, and of unconstrained dances upon meadows sprinkled with a delightful dew, beneath clear skies where a gentle and benevolent luminary shines.

She looked at her bare legs—the undulating lines of her shins and thighs ran softly out from under the folds of her short dress. The delicate yellowish and scarlet tones of her skin next to the monotonous, yellowish whiteness of the linen delighted her eyes. The protruding edges of the little bones of her knees and feet, and the little hollows next to them—Elena examined everything lovingly and joyfully and she explored everything with her hands—and this brought her new delight.

IV

Once, in the evening, Elena forgot to lock the door before undressing. She was standing nude in front of the mirror, her arms raised above her head.

Suddenly the door opened slightly. A head appeared in the narrow opening—it was the maid peeking in, Makrina—a pretty girl with an obligingly cunning expression on her ruddy face.

Elena glimpsed her in the mirror. It was so unexpected—Elena could not think what to do or say and remained standing, without moving. Makrina immediately vanished just as noiselessly as she had appeared. One could have thought that she really had not come to the door, that it was only a dream.

Elena felt vexed and ashamed. Although she had just managed to catch a glimpse of Makrina, it seemed to her that she had seen a dirty smile flit across Makrina's face. Elena walked hurriedly to the door and locked it. Then she lay down on the soft low couch and her thoughts were sad and confused. . . .

Vexatious suspicions awoke inside her. . . .

What would Makrina say about her? By now of course she is in the servants' room telling the cook all about it in a whisper and with a vile laugh. A wave of shameful terror ran over Elena. She thought of the cook Malanya, a ruddy, jolly young wench who had a sly laugh. . . .

Just what is Makrina saying now? It seemed to Elena that someone was whispering Makrina's words in her ear:

"And I see it through the crack in the door. There's the mistress standing in front of the mirror, naked as the day she was born, everything sticking out."

"What are you saying!" Malanya exclaims.

"I swear to God!" Makrina is saying, "All naked, and striking poses—and turning this way and that. . . ."

Makrina prances about, pretending to be her mistress and they both guffaw. The cynical, coarse words resounded with merciless and vile clarity; Elena's face was covered by a burning flush of shame and offense from the words and coarse laughter of the maid and cook.

She felt shame in her whole body—it spread like a flame, like an illness consuming her body. For a long time Elena lay still, in a kind of strange and dull perplexity—then she began to dress slowly, knitting her brows as if trying to resolve some kind of difficult question, and examining herself carefully in the mirror.

V

In the days that followed, Makrina behaved as if she had not even been passing by—and this pretense of hers irritated Elena. And everything about Makrina, which had always been there, but which Elena had never noticed, now became disgusting to her. It was unpleasant to dress and undress in Makrina's presence, to accept her services, or to listen to her flattering words, which in the past had always been lost in the babbling sounds of the streams of water splashing over Elena's body, but which now were striking her ear.

And the very first time that Makrina began to speak as she used to, Elena listened attentively to her words, and gave free reign to the irritation.

In the morning, when Elena went to bathe, Makrina, supporting her by the elbow, said with a flattering smile:

"Who wouldn't fall in love with such a darling as you! You'd have to be blind not to notice you. Such little hands and feet!"

Elena blushed.

"Please stop," she said sharply.

Makrina gave her a look of surprise and lowered her eyes, and then—or did it just seem that way to Elena?—she grinned slightly. And this grin irritated Elena still more, but she had control of herself now and remained silent. . . .

Obstinately, and without her former pleasure, Elena continued each day to bare her beautiful body and look at herself in the mirror. But her thoughts were now somehow malicious and apprehensive. She did it even more often than before, not only in the evening by lamplight, but during the day as well, with the curtains pulled. She no longer neglected to lower the door curtain so that there would be no spying and eavesdropping on her from the outside, and in this way, shame began to make all of her movements awkward.

But now Elena's body no longer seemed as beautiful to her as before. She found imperfections in this body, and she sought them out diligently. There appeared to be something repulsive in it—some evil which was corroding and tainting the beauty, as if it were a kind of film, a cobweb or slime—something disgusting but impossible to shake off.

It often seemed to Elena that an alien and terrifying gaze was resting oppressively upon her naked body. Although no one was looking at her, it seemed to her that the whole room was looking at her and because of this it was embarrassing and terrifying.

If it was during the day, it seemed to Elena that the light knew no shame and that its sharp rays were peeping through the cracks from behind the curtains and that it was laughing. In the evening the shadows without eyes looked at her from the corners and moved unsteadily and their movements produced by the quivering candlelight seemed to Elena like soundless laughter.

It was terrifying to think of this soundless laughter; Elena was unable to convince herself that these were ordinary, lifeless, and insignificant shadows. Their flickering hinted at some alien, unsightly, taunting life.

Now and then, she would suddenly imagine someone's flabby, fat face with rotten teeth—and the face would be looking at her lewdly, with small, repulsive eyes.

And at times, Elena saw in her own face, reflected in the mirror, something impure and nasty, and she could not understand what it was.

She thought about this for a long time and did not feel convinced that something foul had been born in the secret recesses of her grieving soul; at the same time, in her body, all bared and white, a searing wave of shuddering and passionate agitation was rising ever higher.

Terror and disgust tormented her.

And Elena understood that she could not live with all this darkness on her soul. She thought:

"Is it possible to live when coarse and dirty thoughts exist? Even if they are not mine and did not originate in me—didn't these thoughts indeed become mine as soon as I acknowledged them? And isn't everything in the world mine and isn't everything connected by unbreakable bonds?"

VI

Resnitsyn was sitting in Elena's drawing room; he was a young man, fashionably dressed, somewhat indolent, but totally in love with himself and convinced of his own worth. His attentions today had no more success with Elena than they ever had. But whereas she had used to hear him out with that general and impersonal graciousness which is customary for people of so called "good society," now she was cold and silent.

Resnitsyn felt utterly deflated and was therefore angry and played nervously with his monocle. He would not have been averse to calling Elena his fiancée, and her coldness appeared to him as rudeness. But the superficial flitting from subject to subject in his conversation wearied Elena more than ever before. She herself always spoke concisely and precisely, and verboseness in anyone was distressing to her. But people are almost all like that—undisciplined and disorderly.

Elena was looking at Resnitsyn calmly and attentively, as if finding in him a kind of sad correspondence to her own bitter thoughts. Suddenly surprising him, she asked:

"Do you like people?"

Resnitsyn smiled ironically, in an off-hand manner, and with an air of intellectual superiority, he said:

"I myself am a person."

"Well, do you like yourself then?" Elena asked again.

He shrugged his narrow shoulders, smiled sarcastically, and said in an affectedly polite tone of voice:

"People do not please you? In what way, may I ask?"

It was obvious that Elena's raising the possibility of not liking people had offended him on their behalf.

"Is it really possible to like people?" asked Elena.

"Well why on earth not?" he repeated dumbfoundedly.

"They don't like themselves," Elena said coldly, "and why should they? They don't understand the one thing that's worthy of love—they don't understand beauty. They have banal ideas about beauty, so banal that I am ashamed to have been born on this earth. I don't want to live here."

"But still, you do live here!" Resnitsyn said.

"Just where am I to live!" Elena uttered coldly.

"Just where are people better?" asked Resnitsyn.

"Yes, they are the same everywhere," Elena answered and a light, contemptuous smile flashed across her lips.

Resnitsyn did not understand. This conversation inhibited him, seemed improper and strange to him. He made haste to say good-bye and leave.

VII

Evening was approaching. Elena was alone.

In the quiet air of her chamber, the vanilla odor of heliotrope refused to blend with the honeyed fragrance of bird cherries or with the sweet aroma of roses, and it overpowered them.

"How can I construct a life according to the ideals of goodness and beauty! With these people and with this body!" Elena was thinking bitterly. "It is impossible! How can I shut myself off from human banality, how can I shield myself from people! We all live together, and it's as if one soul were languishing in all of multifaceted humanity. The whole world is within me. But it is terrifying that it's the way it is—and the moment you understand it, you see that it should not exist, because it wallows in vice and evil. It ought to be condemned to execution—and yourself along with it."

Elena's melancholy eyes settled on a gleaming object, a pretty plaything that had been left on the table.

"How simple it is!" she thought.

"Why just this knife is enough."

Lying on the desk was a slender, gilded dagger, like those sometimes used to cut the pages of books; it had a double-edged blade and its handle was decorated with intricate carvings. Elena took it in her hands and admired it for a long time. She had bought it recently, not because she needed it, but because her eye had been drawn to the strange, elaborate pattern of the carving on the handle.

"A fine instrument of death," she thought and smiled. Her smile was calm and joyful, and her thoughts passed through her mind clear and cold.

She stood up—and the dagger gleamed against the folds of her greenish-yellow dress as she lowered her bared hand. She went off to her own bedchamber and lay the knife on the pillows, cutting edge to the head of the bed. Then she put on a white dress which smelled sweetly and heavily of roses, and took the knife again and lay down with it on the bed, on top of a white blanket. Her white shoes rested against the foot of the bed. She lay for several moments without moving, with her eyes closed, listening to the quiet voice of her thoughts. Everything in her was clear and calm, and only her dark contempt for the world and for this life here tormented her.

And now, it was as if someone had told her, with authority, that her hour had come.

Slowly and powerfully she plunged the dagger into her breast, up to the very hilt and right against her evenly beating heart,— and she died quietly. Her pale hand grew limp and fell upon her breast, beside the handle of the dagger.

The
Beloved Page

I

In a certain blest and flourishing country, along the high banks of a beautiful river which flowed from eternally snowcapped southern mountains to the great north sea, there lay the vast lands of a powerful lord. Atop the very highest cliff, and towering inaccessibly above all the surrounding arteries, proudly stood the count's splendid castle.

The count was already in his declining years, and already he had buried six young and beautiful, though barren wives. The ancient line would have come to an end with his death, had not fate chosen to restore, albeit in a strange manner, the splendor and longevity of a house renowned far and wide.

The count was wealthy. Campaigns against the lands of the disloyal and numerous raids upon nearby foreign enemies in which, during the years of his youth and mature manhood, he had loved to take part, had enriched him with many elegant and expensive things—with tapestries, weapons, and all manner of goods and raiment—so that the count's castle was adorned in wondrous splendor.

From his eastern campaigns, the count had acquired a weakness for luxury and beauty, for sweet wines, for aromatic incense and spice-laden oils. The count loved to caress beautiful women and he loved his eye to be caressed by the beauty of embellished walls and arches, of delicately engraved vessels at feasts and of luxuriant clothes on handsome men and beautiful women. Only those youths of handsome face and well-formed figure, whose agreeable appearance bespoke an affectionate nature, were awarded the great honor of being numbered among the pages of the wise and happy old count.

The count had many manly sword bearers, handsome pages, and diligent attendants, and all of them loved their master and served him devotedly and faithfully as befits good servants, with body and soul and with all the strength of their might. The faithful vassals, and their wives, and their children, punctually brought their established rents and tributes to the gracious count. Every morning, three fat chaplains diligently prayed for the count's sins—for even the deeds of noble lords are in part subordinate to the laws of God and man.

II

Now at that time in the neighboring territory there flourished many young and beautiful maidens of noble birth; and so it was that the old count, having decided once again to enter into marriage, as much for the prolongation of his line as for his own pleasure, soon chose for himself, from among this charming arbour, a wife after his own heart, one who was worthy of his great valour and illustrious name. She was the gentle and modest Edwiga, daughter of one of the neighboring barons, a maiden shining with beauty and intelligence, and trained not only in all the sorts of needlework befitting a woman of the nobility, but even in reading and writing.

Edwiga had a happy disposition, she loved innocent fun and jests at table; and when the old count brought her home as his wife, an even more luxurious and gay life began in his ancient castle. The old count loved the gentle Edwiga more fervently than he had his former wives, and so took great care to provide her much pleasure and joy. But since the count's physical prowess was already on the wane, the countess Edwiga soon began to harbor a secret boredom, and cunning designs entered her heart. Of course the whole world knows that women are fickle and perfidious, and that a woman's fidelity demands careful supervision.

More and more frequently and for ever longer spells, Edwiga's wandering glances would wander over faces of the pageboys, as if the gentle Edwiga were searching for someone to console her. And finally, the beautiful lady's desires came to rest on one of the pages, to which it ought to be said that even the count, a connoisseur of beauty, would have approved of the countess's choice, had he only known and could he have permitted her betrayal.

Adelstan, the dark-eyed, dark-complexioned, slender and agile page, eclipsed in his beauty all the youths about him, just as the brightly shining moon eclipses the light of the stars round about it. Upon his upper lip had already appeared that downy fuzz which so delights the heart of a youth who is on the brink of feeling his manhood. His dark eyes sparkled from beneath long lashes, like brightly burning torches in a dark night—and in the shadows of those long lashes, his dark cheeks glowed, glowed so that not one of the beauties round about could look at them without dreaming of covering them with kisses. And since many of them had already kissed him, claiming—the cunning creatures—that he was still a child, he had become used to kind treatment and the assurance of his own superiority over other youths. And thus he held himself so erect and proud, and carried his head so high, that one would have thought he was a prince rather than the son of just a poor and unknown knight. In addition, Adelstan could play the lute, and had a pleasing and powerful voice; he knew many romantic songs in which beautiful women were exalted, and various other songs as well.

Adelstan always looked at the countess respectfully and tenderly, but sometimes he would smile so boldly that the countess blushed and stood stock still, while a promise of joyous paradise was revealed to her in the beautiful page's smile.

Once when the count was going off for several days, the countess expressed the wish that Adelstan remain with her in the castle.

"I wish it," she said to the count, "because he is the most modest of the pages, and he has the same eyes as you. Looking at him, I'll think of you, and I'll not be so bored while you're away."

The count granted his wife's wish. He loved Adelstan himself, and he knew that Adelstan was a youth faithful—in everything and to the end.

III

Atop the highest tower of the castle, watching the departing count and waving her white handkerchief as a sign of farewell, the beautiful Edwiga said quietly to Adelstan: "Beloved page, this night is ours. I want you to come to me when the night's darkness falls upon the earth and spreads its sweet shroud over those who are resting from their labor as well as those who are awaiting comforting kisses."

And Adelstan answered Edwiga:

"Gracious Lady, sweet as your kisses are, you still belong to our master, and if our betrayal should be discovered, then the mighty count would shorten the list of our transgressions, both yours and mine, together with the number of our days and the length of our bodies."

"The count will learn nothing," said the merry Edwiga, "and we shall have several sweet nights together."

"Gracious mistress," said Adelstan, "I have sworn to serve my beloved master faithfully, and I am afraid that I will destroy my soul in betrayal and so it would be better for you not to tempt me."

"We'll have time to atone for our sins by prayer," said Edwiga, "but perhaps you love another, more beautiful than I?"

"Gracious Lady," answered Adelstan, "I love only you and my master, and of course not in all the world, neither amid the nobility nor among the simple people, are there women or maidens more charming than you; only Venus herself, born of the sea's foam might be compared in beauty, but she could not surpass you."

Edwiga began to laugh cunningly and asked:

"Beloved page, have you tasted love's joys? Have you mounted the couch of either woman or maiden?"

Adelstan dropped his eyes from modesty and answered Edwiga thus:

"No, gracious mistress, I have not mounted the couch of either woman or maiden."

And to this, Edwiga said:

"Beloved page, how then do you refuse what you know not of? Come to me, and you shall see that a game so tender cannot burden the conscience. I shall bare my body before you. I shall lay you on my couch, and shall teach you all of love's pleasant amusements."

And Adelstan did not know what to answer. The dim fire of desire began to burn in his shining eyes, and shame's crimson coloring covered his dark cheeks, which made him all the more desirable to the youthful Edwiga.

But in vain that night did the beautiful Edwiga wait for Adelstan. Opening the doors to her bed-chamber and dismissing her servant girls, she lay there burning with desire and her eager eyes kept stabbing at the darkness of the night. Each light rustling of fabric, each passing sound that broke the silence of the night for some uncertain reason—for the night is full of things we cannot fathom—each sound seemed to the gentle Edwiga to be the rustle of Adelstan's stealthy footsteps.

And many times Edwiga hurried to the door to give an affectionate greeting and to encourage the timid and tardy youth—and each time, in vain.

IV

The next day, exhausted by a sleepless night, burning with unfulfilled desires, Edwiga summoned Adelstan to her chambers. She showered him with cruel reproaches, slapped his cheeks, scratched, and pinched him.

Adelstan submissively endured her frenzy, though he shed many tears, and then he said to her:

"Gracious mistress, I must remain faithful to my master, it was you who planned this vile and obscene affair. If we act according to your loathsome desire, we both shall perish from a cruel death at the hands of the executioner, and the accursed demons will drag our souls straight to hell, to the undying fire, to the eternally boiling pitch."

"Beloved page," said the countess, "do you think no one would pray for us? And did the count leave you with me so that you could show disobedience to your mistress? You stupid child, you yourself had no pleasure, and the excruciating torment of last night exhausted me, and I am still tired as I inflict upon you the blows which you have deserved. I can no longer stand such torment and travail—come to me tonight and if you do not come, then tomorrow I will subject you to cruel tortures."

Adelstan answered nothing.

But that night, Edwiga awaited him in vain.

V

The next morning, she walked about the castle feeling tired and malicious, and nothing in the luxurious castle cheered her eye. Suddenly she heard, somewhere nearby, the sounds of a lute, a tender voice and laughter. Her glance flashing with anger, she went quickly to the source of the sounds. Their gaiety was so incompatible with her anguish that it brought new and the bitterest of torments to her heart.

The pages had gathered in the courtyard; Adelstan was singing gay, amusing songs to them, as if he had already forgotten the entreaties and threats of his mistress. The pages were listening to him, laughing and praising the songs and the singer.

The countess's passion flared up still stronger. Everything

irritated her: the captivating sounds of his voice, his tender beauty, and his shapely, bare legs. The pages were not expecting their mistress to visit them and they had not had time to put on their leggings—entranced as they were by the singing of the charming page Adelstan. Edwiga drove the external signs of anger away from her face—well-bred ladies and gentlemen excel in the art of hiding their feelings and obscuring the mirror of their souls with deceptive expressions of good will—and she went up to the pages and said:

"I weep and lament at being parted from my beloved lord. I am lonely—and what have I to console me while my lord is far away? Your laughter I find unpleasant, your tears would be more to my liking."

The cheerful, blue-eyed Heinrich, youngest of the pages, and therefore the boldest in addressing the noble lady, answered Edwiga:

"Gracious mistress, our master will soon return, there is no reason for you or for us to weep; rather should you listen along with us to how well and clearly Adelstan sings and be comforted."

"No," Edwiga answered, "I find your songs dull. And do you think that with these songs of yours alone you fulfill your obligation to serve the count and me? Is laughter and merrymaking at feasts the limit of your loyalty?"

"Gracious mistress," said the blue-eyed Heinrich, "our faithfulness to our master and to you is to the last drop of blood and to our last breath."

Edwiga began to laugh and said:

"Then console me now with the shedding of your blood."

And with her sharp dagger Edwiga pricked Adelstan's bare legs above the knees several times,—and after each prick, she licked off the sweet drops of Adelstan's blood from the sharp and gleaming blade with her cunning tongue. And the countess Edwiga took pleasure in looking at Adelstan's bloodied legs.

But that night too, Adelstan did not come to Edwiga—and in the morning the old count returned home.

VI

Edwiga was languishing from passion; and the page's faithfulness came to amaze her even more when she saw how Adelstan
now cast her burning glances full of desire. She noticed that
serving at table, he would try to touch her tender hand or
perchance her dress. These touches of Adelstan's made her
happy, but also bitter, for they inflamed her desires even more
strongly.

The weeks and months passed, and the countess remained
childless. She was always sorrowful now and listless, and it
seemed as if she were already wasting away.

"Holy Virgin Mary," she prayed, "what a life I have! An old
husband caresses me, but his caresses are hateful to me; and he
whom I do love, dares not partake of his lady's joy."

The count himself had by now taken note of her languor and
already jealousy had entered his heart. He observed passionate
glances being exchanged between the countess and the page
before his very eyes, like two daggers crossing in equal and
prolonged combat.

The old count feared alike that Edwiga would sin with the page
and that Adelstan would forget his debt of loyalty.

VII

Not far from the count's castle, in a secluded and wild spot
situated in a ravine amidst the dense forest, stood a dismal
cottage, the dwelling place of an aged wizard.

Now the priests felt malice toward the wizard and threatened
to burn him alive—for it is an impious business to work magic
and practice witchcraft. More than once they had sent men-at-
arms and the town guard to bring him into court, but each time the
wizard had averted the danger by means of black magic: dimming
the searchers' eyesight, making them lose their way, inflicting
storms and the unbearable terrors of the forest upon them. And
as it was, the mighty count himself had no desire to see the wizard
burned just yet, for there was none other nearby and who could

tell when some sorcery might come in handy. But the wizard, knowing that sooner or later his life would nonetheless be cut short by the fire, zealously hoarded his money; and from time to time he would pass it on to his daughter, who was married to a brewer and lived in a nearby town, having nothing to do with witchcraft and at peace with the church, to which she gave generous donations each year.

One night, the countess put on poor, coarse clothes, covered her face with a cloak, and set off to see the wizard barefoot—all this so that by her humility she might merit the favor of the mysterious power, but also the better to conceal her high station. Nonetheless a heavy bag of gold pieces was hanging at her belt.

A stormy and cold wind was blowing directly into the trembling Edwiga's face, and it tore fiercely at her clothes and hampered her steps. Torrents of rain came crashing down from the darkened sky. Now and then, huge trees fell with a crackle and a crash across the road, shattered by the frenzy of the ferocious storm.

Completely soaked, shivering from fear and the cold, her legs scratched and dirtied by the wet clay, the young, beautiful Edwiga reached the wizard's gloomy den. The walls of the hut, sooty from the smoke of magical practices, were unfriendly; and the green eyes of an immense cat glittered, inspiring a terrible fear in Edwiga.

The tall, gaunt, gray-bearded old man gave Edwiga a piercing look and asked:

"Gracious Lady, why have you come on such a terrible night—and terrible not for you alone—to this god-forsaken place, abandoning your proud castle and warm bed, and not fearing the furor of the raging storm?"

"I am not a lady," said Edwiga, "I am a simple woman. I've brought you my heavy grief so that you, with your accursed charms, might turn it into joy, for which I'll pay you just as much as I can."

"Gracious Lady," answered the wizard, "the night is dark, the storm howls, but long have the imprints of your charming feet been radiating before me, and I heard the rustle of your steps even from the very gates of the old castle. For although this hut is poorly appointed, great charms dwell here and invincible spells; and zealous servants unseen by those unconsecrated to the mysteries, keep ceaseless watch over all the paths that lead here. Tell me, gracious Lady, what you wish from me?"

The cunning Edwiga began to laugh, and said:

"I see that it is useless to try to hide myself from you, but perhaps you can also guess my wishes, so that I need not tell you what they are."

A terrible smile, like that of a dead man, distorted the wizard's shriveled blue lips, and he said:

"Gracious Lady, to want is not enough; my science does not like mute spells. If you want, say what you want; if not, then go in peace. I can only give you what you ask of me with words; otherwise I give you much too much. Countless and dark are human desires, and man himself cannot know them all. My servants, though, see deep, into the most secret recesses of the soul, and should you fail to guard yourself from their zeal by limiting your words, they'll strangle you in excess of fulfillment."

Then, trembling from shame and fear, Edwiga told him of her grief and her desires, gave him her gold, and falling at his feet and with loud sobbing, she entreated him for help.

The wizard heard her out until the end, weighed her heavy and valuable gift in his hand, and said:

"Powerful spirits are enclosed in this bag, and if you had known how to command them, you would not have come to me. But, rise—everything shall be as you wish—have patience, I will do it. Go in peace."

VIII

A little later that very night, the count too came knocking at the door of the wizard's hut. The wizard greeted him with a low bow. The count said to him:

"I am growing old, I still have no heir; and although my young wife has been with me for more than a year now, yet still she walks about barren. And another grief have I—my beloved wife gazes with lust upon my dear page, and he upon her also. As yet there has been no sin between them, but I fear that there will be."

The wizard heard him out and said:

"Gracious lord, everything shall be as you wish, if you will act according to my words. She is your spouse, but no less is he your servant. And should not he serve you with all his soul, with all his body, and with all the strength of his might?"

And then the wizard spoke with the old count for a long time and gave him extraordinary instructions,—and the count was cheerful when he left the hut and in a gay mood when he returned home on his faithful horse.

IX

At daybreak the count summoned Edwiga and Adelstan to his presence and ordered the page to bolt the doors securely. Adelstan, after fulfilling his master's command, stood before him and said boldly:

"Gracious count, if you wish, judge me, I have been faithful to you."

Edwiga was trembling and pale and remained silent.

The old count said to them:

"Don't be afraid. You both will serve me and my family according to your abilities. Last night, as the storm howled, striking terror even among the brave, I heard wise and prophetic words; and you shall perform a wise and glorious deed, in fulfillment of those prophecies. . . ."

In beauty—like the goddess born of the sea's foam, though crimson-faced from shame, Edwiga stood before her lord. The count looked at her in silence and his heart shuddered with the joy of possession. Adelstan, for his part, was unable to lift his eyes to the countess, but neither could he turn his gaze away. . . .

Somber and ashamed, Edwiga and Adelstan departed from the

count, but the joy of love nonetheless triumphed in their hearts.

At first they were both happy. But soon both Edwiga and Adelstan wearied of caresses at the behest of another, for any kind of compulsion is hateful to love—and they were exhausted to the point of mutual hatred. And both of them began to think of how they might free themselves of the sweet but burdensome bonds of a love commanded by their lord.

"I'll kill the countess!" thought Adelstan.

"I'll kill the page!" thought Edwiga.

And once, when she was dressing, and he had come at her call and had knelt at her feet to put on her slippers, she thrust a slender and sharp-pointed dagger into his heart. Adelstan fell, gave out a rasping sign, and then died.

They removed his body and following the count's orders, hung it naked in the castle's moat, and next to it they hung a dog, so the vassals would think that the page Adelstan had been sentenced to death for some insolent act.

The countess was with child. And soon she gave birth to a son, the heir to the count's renowned and mighty line.

The
Youth Linus

Having successfully carried out the orders to subdue a rebellious village where the unruly inhabitants had refused to offer
sacrifices and to make holy obeisance before the image of the
divine emperor, a detachment of Roman cavalry was returning to
camp. Much blood had been shed, many of the disrespectful had
been destroyed—and the exhausted soldiers awaited with impatience the coming of that gratifying hour when they would be
back in their tents, when nothing would hinder them from taking
their pleasure of the beautiful bodies they had captured in the
rebellious village, the wives and daughters of impious fanatics.

These women and girls had already tasted the sweet but fatigu-
ing violence of hurried caresses at the very outskirts of the
destroyed and burnt-out village, alongside the mutilated corpses
of their fathers and husbands, alongside the tortured bodies of
their mothers, bloodied by the blows of clubs and whips. And the
more the soldiers desired them, these women and girls, the more
they themselves resisted, and the more forced were their embraces. Now they lay tightly bound in the heavy wagons which
were being carted off by powerful horses along the highroad that
led directly to the camp.

The horsemen themselves had chosen a roundabout route, for
a report had come to the oldest centurion that several of the
rebels had managed to escape and were fleeing in that direction.
And although their swords were all nicked and covered with
blood, and their lances had been dulled from the fervent labor of
warriors devoted to the glory and dignity of the emperor—still, a

Roman warrior's sword can never have enough of fallen foes, and it thirsts eternally for yet fresher, hotter, human blood.

It was a sultry day, and the hottest hour of the day, just past noon. The heavens, cloudless and blazing, glared down mercilessly. Fiery and hazy, the celestial Dragon, trembling in worldwide, insane fury spewed out streams of burning wrath from its flaming jaws onto the silent and sad plain. The withered grass lay pressed against the earth, which waited and thirsted for moisture in vain; and the grass shared its grief, and languished, and drooped, and strangled from the dust.

From under the horses' hooves the gray dust rose smokily and hung there, swaying in the motionless air like a barely moving cloud. And the dust settled upon the weary riders' mail which gave off a dull, crimson glimmer. And through the cloud of gray unmoving dust, the whole area seemed to the gaze of the exhausted warriors to be sinister, gloomy, and grievous.

Consumed by the fierce Dragon, the earth lay submissive and impotent beneath the heavy hooves, shod in iron. And beneath those heavy and iron-shod hooves, the desolate dusty road shuddered and droned.

Only rarely did they come across poor villages with pitiful hovels, but the oldest centurion, wearied in the heavy sultriness, forgot about his intention of pillaging along the way; and rocking in his saddle rhythmically, he thought sullenly of how that sultry heat would have to end sometime, and the long journey as well; and then they would lead his warhorse off and take his helmet and shield; and beneath the broad canvas of his field tent there would be coolness and the soft light of the night lamps, and once more the naked slave girl would begin to weep and she would weep in a reedy voice, complaining and lamenting in a foreign and comical tongue, and she would weep, but she would kiss him. And he would caress her, caress her to death in order that she not weep and not lament and not complain and not speak in her reedy voice of the slain, of her dear ones, of mighty Caesar's fallen foes.

A young warrior said to the centurion:

"Look over there, on the right, near the road, I see a crowd. Marcellus, give us the order and we'll tear after these people and scatter them, and with the rapid motion of our steeds, we'll rouse this wind, so lulled by heavy heat, and it will blow away the dusty languor, yours and ours."

The centurion looked attentively in the direction where the young warrior was pointing. The old centurion's eyes were sharp.

"No, Lucilius," he said, smiling, "that's a crowd of children playing by the road. It's not worth dispersing them. Let the urchins look at our mighty steeds and valiant men, and from their youth they'll have engraved within their hearts due awe before the grandeur of Roman arms and the glory of our invincible and divine Caesar."

Young Lucilius dared not argue with the centurion. But his face grew dark. He was displeased as he rode away to his place, and he said quietly to his friend who was a youth the same as he:

"These children may be the spawn of that rebellious scum, and I would gladly cut them to bits. Our centurion's become too sensitive in his old age, and he's lost that stern resolve intrinsic to a valiant warrior."

But Lucilius's friend answered him with noticeable dissatisfaction:

"Why should we battle with children? What glory is there in that? We have enough battles with those who can defend themselves."

Then, flushing from vexation, the young and quick-tempered Lucilius fell silent.

The warriors were drawing close to the playing children. The children stopped by the road and looked at the warriors, marveling at their powerful steeds, their shining armor and their manly, tanned faces. They stood there awe-struck, whispering and gaping with wide-open eyes.

Only one of the children, the handsome youth Linus, was looking at the warriors sullenly, and his dark eyes glittered with the fire of sacred wrath. And when the detachment of horsemen drew even with the children, the youth Linus called out loudly and wrathfully:

"Murderers!"

And he raised his arms and stretched them menacingly toward the centurion. The old centurion looked at him sullenly; he had not heard what the child was shouting, and he rode on by.

The frightened children surrounded Linus and stopped him from shouting, and they whispered:

"Let's run, let's hurry up and run or they'll kill all of us."

And the little girls had already begun to cry. But the handsome youth Linus stepped forward fearlessly and shouted loudly:

"Butchers! Torturers of the innocent!"

And once again, Linus's small, powerless arm was raised menacingly in a fist. His dark eyes glittering angrily, trembling all over and choking with wrath, Linus kept shouting louder and louder:

"Butchers! Butchers! How will you wash the blood of your victims off your hands?"

The little girls raised a howl, drowning out the shouts of the youth Linus, and the boys grabbed him by the arms and led him away from the road. But Linus tore himself away from their hands; he was burning with a sacred wrath and he kept shouting out curses at the warriors of the mighty emperor.

The horsemen came to a stop. The youngest among them exclaimed loudly:

"These are the spawn of rebels. Their hearts are infected with a mutinous spirit. We'll have to destroy them all. There's no place on this earth for those who dare to insult a Roman warrior."

And the old warriors too said to the centurion:

"The impudence of these scoundrels deserves cruel punishment. Marcellus, order us to go after them and to slaughter them all. We have to destroy the seditious brood before they grow up and have the power to revolt and cause great harm to divine Caesar and all-powerful Rome."

And the centurion said:

"Go after them, kill those who shouted, and as for the rest, punish them so they'll remember until the end of their days, what it means to insult a Roman warrior."

And all the warriors turned from the dusty road and galloped after the fleeing children.

Seeing the pursuit, the youth Linus shouted to his companions:

"Leave me. You won't save me, and if you run, you'll all perish under the swords of this profane and ruthless army. I'll go straight up to them and let them kill me alone—I don't want to live in this despicable world, where such brutal things take place."

Linus stopped, and his comrades, weak from running and from fear, were unable to entice him any further. They stood there, weeping loudly, and the horsemen quickly surrounded them in a tight circle.

The unsheathed swords glittered in the sun, and the Dragon's rippling smiles, ruthless and evil, ran over the steel blades. The children began to tremble, and clutching one another with loud sobbing, they huddled close together.

The Dragon, pressing for murder, was inflaming the soldiers' hot blood, clouding the warriors' swollen eyes with the crimson smoke of fury, and from on high it was already rejoicing in this evil, earthly deed. It lay ready to lap up the innocent childrens' blood with the merciless rays of its serpentine eyes, and to drown the defenseless bodies, hacked to pieces by cruel, broad swords, with the festering sultry heat of malice. But the youth Linus stepped boldly out of the crowd and walked up to the centurion. And he said loudly:

"Old man, it was I who called you and your warriors murderers and butchers, it was I who cursed you and all who are with you, it was I who summoned the wrath of the righteous deity on your profane heads. Look, these children are crying and trembling from terror. They are afraid that by your godless order, your accursed warriors will kill us all; and they will kill us and our fathers and mothers. Kill me alone—for these others submit to you and to the one who sent you. Kill only me if you're still not sated with murdering. I do not fear you, I hate your ferocity, I despise your sword and your unjust power, I have no wish to live on an earth which the horses of your frenzied army trample. My arms are still weak and I'm still too small to get at your throat to strangle you—so kill me, quickly kill me!"

The centurion listened to him with great amazement. And he said:

"No, you little snake, it won't be your way,—you'll not die alone."

And he commanded his warriors:

"Kill them all. We cannot let this serpent brood remain alive, because the words of an insolent boy are now embedded in their rebellious souls. Kill them all without mercy, the big and the small, even those who've only barely learned to babble."

The warriors threw themselves at the children and hacked them with their merciless swords. The gloomy valley and the dusty road shuddered from the childrens' wails, and the hazy distances began moaning with an answering moan—like a tenderly piping echo they moaned and then fell silent. And flaring their hot nostrils, the horses were sniffing the smoky blood, and they were slowly and heavily trampling the childrens' bodies with their iron-shod hooves.

Afterwards, the warriors returned to the road laughing joyfully and cruelly. They were hurrying to their camp. They were chatting cheerfully and rejoicing.

But it went on, the dusty, hard road went on in the valley that grieved beneath the angry flaming eyes of the Dragon. The crimson Dragon began to go down, but there was no coolness around, and bewitched by the quiet and the terror, the wind slept.

The sultry Dragon's crimson countenance, while descending, looked into the old centurion's sharp-sighted eyes, and the celestial Snake smiled a quiet and terrible smile. And because it was quiet and sultry and crimson, and because the horses' rhyth-mically-ringing, even gait was heavy, the old centurion grew melancholy and terrified.

And the steeds' heavy tread was so measured and so resound-ing; and the unmoving, hopeless dust was so fine and so gray; and it seemed that there would be no end to the lassitude and terror of the deserted route. And to each step of the tired steed, the deserted distance responded with a resonant, echoing hum.

And resonant moans arose in the deserted distance.

The earth hummed beneath the hooves.

Someone was running. Gaining on them.

A somber voice, like the voice of the youth whom the warriors had killed, was shouting something.

The centurion glanced back at his warriors. Their dust-covered faces were distorted not only by fatigue. A vague terror appeared on the coarse features of the soldiers' sunburned faces.

The young Lucilius's dry lips trembled, he whispered uneasily:

"We should hurry to get to camp."

The old centurion stared hard at Lucilius's tired face and quietly asked the young warrior:

"What's the matter with you Lucilius?"

And Lucilius answered him just as quietly:

"I am terrified."

And, ashamed of his terror and his weakness, he said more loudly:

"It's awfully hot."

And again, not having conquered his terror, he quietly whis-pered:

"That damned boy is chasing us. The witches of the night have him under a spell with their evil charms; and we were unable to slay him so that he'd never arise."

The centurion carefully surveyed the environs. No one was visible—neither close by nor far off. And the centurion said to the young Lucilius:

"Did you lose your amulet given you by the old heathen priest of the foreign god? They say that whoever has such an amulet, the charms of the midnight and midday witches are powerless against him."

Lucilius answered, shaking with terror.

"I have the amulet on, but it is burning my chest. The subterranean gods have already drawn close to us and I hear their somber murmur."

The valley was moaning with a heavy rumble. The old centurion, thinking he could conquer his terror with a pious speech, said to Lucilius:

"The subterranean gods are thanking us—we did considerable work for them today. The voice of the subterranean gods is somber and indistinct, and it is terrifying in the sultry silence of the desert, but surely the honor of a valiant warrior lies in overcoming fear!"

But the young Lucilius said once more:

"I'm terrified. I hear the voice of the youth and he is overtaking us."

Then in the valley's sultry silence, a ringingly piping voice proclaimed:

"Curses, curses on you murderers!"

The warriors shuddered and quickly spurred their horses. The mysterious voice, like the voice of the youth Linus, sounded so close, so clear:

"Murderers! Murderers of innocent people! There's no pardon, no mercy for you."

And the horses flew off, urged on by the warriors. But wrath inflamed the old centurion's heart. And he shouted, holding back his frightened horse, and turning to his riders:

"Aren't we the warriors of the mighty, divine emperor? From whom do we flee? A damned kid, that we didn't finish off, or who was brought back to life by the evil charms of malevolent witches, gathering blood for their nocturnal sorcery; and this kid continues to heap abuses on the invincible army. But Roman arms must prevail not only over the forces of our enemies, but over the evil spirits as well."

The warriors were ashamed. They halted their horses. They listened. Someone was gaining on them, proclaiming and wailing; and in the hazy quiet of the valley's darkening gloom, a child's shout could be heard distinctly:

"Murderers!"

The horsemen turned their horses in the direction of the shouts. And they caught sight of the youth Linus, running towards them in blood-stained, torn clothes. Blood was running down his face and down his arms which were raised at the warriors in a threatening gesture, as if the youth wanted to seize each of them and hurl them down at his blood-covered, dust-covered feet.

The warriors' hearts were filled with wild malice. Unsheathing their swords and rousing their horses to fury with rapid jabs from their sharpened stirrups, they rushed headlong at the youth and hacked him with their swords, and trampled him and sated their fury above his remains; and then they jumped from their horses, and tore the youth's body to pieces, and scattered it about the road and environs.

The warriors wiped their swords with the wayside grass, mounted their horses and rushed on, hurrying to their camp. But again a heavy moan filled the valley which appeared gloomy in the rays of the descending Dragon—and again the sobbing, piping voice brought forth those same merciless words. And again the ringing wail was repeated in the warriors' ears:

"Murderers!"

Then the warriors, wearied by horror and malice, turned their horses round once more—and once more the youth Linus ran toward them in his blood-stained clothes and stretched his blood-covered, threatening arms at them. And again the warriors cut him down, trampled him and hacked his body with their swords, and scattered it and rushed off.

But again and again the youth Linus overtook the warriors.

And the warriors had forgotten now where their camp lay, and in the fury of the endless murdering, midst the wails of the unremitting reproach, they rushed about the valley, and circled the place where the youth Linus and the other children had been killed.

For the whole remainder of the day, the Dragon, flaming in crimson and dying a smoky death, gazed with a furious, merciless eye at the horror and madness of the eternal killing and unending reproach.

And evening burned away and it was night and the stars were twinkling—chaste, innocent, distant.

But in the valley, where the evil deed had taken place, the warriors rushed about, and the youth Linus wearied them with his unending wail. And the warriors rushed about and they killed him again and again but could not kill him forever.

Before sunrise, driven by horror and followed by the eternal moans of the youth Linus, they came rushing to the seashore. And the waves foamed under the horses' maddened stampede.

Thus perished all of the horsemen, and with them, the centurion, Marcellus.

But there, on the distant field, by the road, where the horsemen had killed the youth Linus and the other children, lay their bodies, blood-stained and unburied. At night, cowardly and careful wolves came up to the prostrate bodies, and sated themselves on the innocent sweet bodies of the children.

Death by Advertisement

Rezanov felt so weak and tired and wasted away. His thoughts turned more and more often to eternal tranquility. It seemed that there could be no sweeter rest than on a bed of planks, in a pine coffin.

And suddenly he wanted some unscheduled diversion.

He was sitting alone in his quiet room.

He was reading the advertisements in *The New Time* very carefully. He was searching for something. He was comparing and choosing.

His pale face, which was beginning to waste away, showed signs of confusion and indecision. He picked up a pencil pensively. He placed the tip on the lampshade.

His hand was shaking. The pencil point was tapping away. He smiled. He thought:

"I'm getting old."

Again he lowered his eyes—at one time they had been always gay, now they were tired and indifferent; he turned his attentive, calm gaze to the pages of the newspaper.

Finally he chose one advertisement.

Some intelligent young lady, pretty and well brought up, finding herself in dire straits, was asking kind people to lend her fifty rubles: she was agreeable to all conditions. She requested that they write in care of general delivery, at the seventeenth postal division, claimant check number 205824.

Rezanov withdrew from a box a sheet of yellowish, rough

paper with uneven borders and the watermark, "Margarette Mill."

Smiling joylessly, he wrote:

Dear Madam,
I will give you the money you ask, though not as a loan and not as a gift, but for a task which I will now describe. I will write perforce succinctly—there is much one cannot say in a letter. But because, judging by your words, you are an intelligent woman, perhaps you will understand what, exactly, will be required of you. You are to present yourself to me as the image of my death—the more attractive, the better—and conduct yourself accordingly. If you are able to vary this happy game enough, then your earnings in the future may be enough for your subsistence. Are you in agreement? You are not terrified? Do you understand what is required of you? If you agree and are not afraid, and you understand, then write when and where I may meet you the first time. The best time for me is after five in the evening. Write to the general post office claimant, three rubles number 384384. I will pick up your letter on Thursday.

The brand-new three ruble note, with the banally beautiful 1905 design, crackled unpleasantly, like the starched dress of an empty-mouthed girl at confirmation. The numbers 384 were repeated twice. The coincidence seemed strange and significant.

He thought:

"What if?"

He smiled faintly.

"So be it."

He did not sign the letter. He sealed it. He took it himself and put it in the mailbox in order that it not lie about forgotten until morning, and so that it would arrive more quickly.

Then he returned home and thought of what she would be like when she came.

Emaciated, ugly, with a face grown brown from poverty and suffering, yellow teeth, a sparse, reddish mane of hair under a hat worn threadbare from the rain and wind, on which a feather and a bow flutter pitifully and comically?

Or very young, shy, quiet, with a seamstress's slender, needle-pricked fingers, a pale little face like wax, a large, lovable mouth?

Or would she come as a drunken prostitute, all painted up, beaten up, with a shrill voice and coarse manners?

Or a vulgar, provincial lady in an incredible outfit, with impossible manners, an unwashed neck, deserted by her husband and still uprooted?

Just what will she be like, my death? My death!

Or will she meet me in a dark passageway, and I will not see her and will only lower my wretched gold pieces into her cold hand?

On Thursday he went to the main post office. The summer day in the capital was dusty, hot, and noisy. Here and there they were repairing bridges, painting houses—and that was why it smelled so unpleasant. But still there was the usual cheerfulness and the signs of familiar restaurants looked festive and elegant.

He did not hurry. He drank beer at Leiner's. He met none of his acquaintances. Indeed, whom should he meet now? Except by chance.

It was close to four when he passed through the narrow opened doors into the post office's new glass-roofed hall. He recalled the old, bespattered, secluded corner, where they formerly gave out general delivery letters. Now even officials worry about good appearances.

He stopped by a little booth that sold paper and envelopes. The rotating display case showed him all the choice views of cloying vulgarity on the postcards.

"They buy these?"—he asked the salesgirl.

A pretty girl with a bored face, twitched her plump shoulders testily.

"What can I do for you?" she asked in a hostile voice. "Envelopes, paper, postcards."

He looked at her intently. He observed the little curls on her forehead, the porcelain color of her face, the blue pupils of her eyes. He said:

"No, I don't need anything."

And he walked on farther.

Directly across from the entrance, behind the two middle windows of a huge square enclosure, three girls were sitting, sorting letters. The recipients were standing on the outside. A stout lady with a wart on her nose asked for a letter under the name Ruslan-Zvonareva.

"Is your name Zvonareva?" asked the mail girl with a face the color of wheat bread, and walked away into the depths of the enclosure with the letters.

"Ruslan-Zvonareva," the lady with the wart said in a frightened half-whisper after her.

And when the wheaten mail girl returned to the little window with a packet of letters, the lady with the wart repeated:

"I have a double name, Ruslan-Zvonareva."

Next to her stood a red-haired gentleman with a bowler hat in his hand, looking with uneasy eyes at the letters which were being sorted by the second mail girl, the prettiest of the three and very proud of it. By all indications, the gentleman was expecting a "sensitive and frivolous" letter, and he was nervous and unattractive and pitiful.

The third girl was chubby, rosy, and had a wide and gentle face, thick chestnut hair pulled down on her forehead like a wide curtain; she was laughing to herself about something. She kept turning to the two others who were also smiling, and she laughed and said some snatches of words about something funny.

Rezanov silently held out his three ruble note to her. He looked at the girls. He was thinking how young, healthy, good looking they were. That is why they were chosen by the postal authorities who were concerned about the decent appearance of their establishment.

He recalled a recent polemic in the newspaper between the

postal director and some woman petitioner who had not gotten a position in the post office because she was skinny and unattractive. She was lethargic due to her shyness and poverty and undernourishment. And she was old—all of thirty-two years.

He closed his eyes—someone's face rose up—pale, haggard, frightened, eyes wide open, lips twitching nervously and timidly. Someone whispered so clearly and quietly:

"There's nothing to live for."

Someone answered, quietly and calmly:

"Don't live."

Rezanov opened his eyes. He looked with hatred at the chubby-faced girl who was searching for the letter with his number, tossing onto the table, one after the other, postcards and letters from the packet. And she was laughing all the while. So disgustingly, tiresomely.

Finally she held out a letter in a narrow stamped envelope. She threw the remaining letters aside.

"That's all there is."

"And all I need," said Rezanov in annoyance.

He stepped aside, and sat down on a bench by a column. He tore open the envelope. He was hurrying, but he was calm.

The even, calm handwriting was unexpectedly beautiful with its large, narrow letters and fine lines.

Dear Sir,
I agree. I am not afraid. I understand. Thursday, at six o'clock. Mikhailovsky Park, the path to the right of the entrance. A white dress. Your letter in the envelope in my right hand.
Your Death

The guard rang the bell. The hall was emptying. Rezanov went to the "Vienna" restaurant. He had dinner. He drank wine. He was hurrying.

He arrived at the park at five-thirty.

She was standing not far from the entrance, at the edge of the path under a tree. Her dress showed white against the dark green of the quiet park.

She was slender, pale, very quiet, and calm. She was looking at him intently as he walked up to her. Her eyes were gray, calm. They betrayed nothing. They were just attentive. In her face, which was not at all beautiful, there was an expression of clarity and submissiveness. The lips of her large mouth were smiling endearingly and sadly.

"Dear death," he said quietly.

He stood in front of her. Strangely agitated, he extended his hand to her.

She remained silent. She changed his letter to her left hand. She pressed his hand with her slender, cold, quiet hand.

He asked her:

"Have you been waiting for me long?"

She answered, slowly articulating each word, in a clear, lifelessly even, deathly calm voice:

"You didn't expect me. You thought that you would meet someone else."

And a coldness seemed to emanate from her. And the folds of her white dress were so quiet, so unmoving. Her simple straw hat with a white band, set high on her head, cast a yellow shadow on her tranquil face. Standing in front of Rezanov, she leaned over slightly and with the tip of her light umbrella, she drew a thin line in the sand, from left to right, between him and her.

He asked:

"Is it true that you agree to be my death?"

And her quiet answer was the same:

"I am your death."

He asked again, feeling a coldness in his body:

"Are you certain that you are not afraid to carry out such a gloomy role?"

She said:

"Death fears the living, and does not show itself to them so openly. You are perhaps the first one to see my face, the earthly, human face of your death."

He said:

"You master your role very quickly and too conscientiously. Tell me, what is your name?"

She smiled sadly and gently. She said:

"I am your death—white, quiet, serene. Hurry and breathe earth's air—your hours are numbered."

He frowned. He said:

"You are an intelligent lady, you find yourself in a difficult situation and ask for money. What brought you to such an extremity that you agreed to all conditions? And even to playing such a terrible game?"

She answered:

"I am hungry, sick, tired and sad."

He began to laugh. He said:

"First of all, rest a bit. Why are you standing? Sit on the bench."

They walked several steps. They sat down. She drew an intricate design in the sand.

He said:

"You are hungry—we'll eat, do you want to? We'll go somewhere and I'll feed you. I'll give you the amount of money that you asked for. Tell me, do you need anything else from me?"

She said:

"I will take from you everything that you can give—your money and your soul."

He shuddered. He began to laugh. He said:

"You play your role well."

She answered:

"I have come. My hour will soon come. I am waiting."

He pulled out a purse.

In the little middle compartment behind a metal clasp, lay the five golden coins which had been placed there earlier. He took them out.

She silently held out her narrow, pale hand—so quiet and calm—palm upward. Faint lines outlined a clear and simple design on her white, unmoving, open palm.

Five golden coins, jingling gently with a ringing sound, one against another fell into her cold, unfaltering palm. Her hand closed unhurriedly, her slender, long white fingers tightened—and she leisurely lowered the hand with the money to a slit hidden at the side of her white skirt.

And he was thinking:

"My wretched gold—my last gift—the meager earnings of a day-laborer—small payment for boundless labor—for you, my dear one."

Had he only thought that? Had he said it aloud? How clearly the words resounded! With what sadness his breast contracted!

And, full of sorrow, she was looking at him sideways, with her gray, attentive eyes, and she was smiling. Then she leaned over and quietly rustled the tip of her umbrella on the sand.

And she whispered:

"I have taken your money—I will take your soul. You gave me your money—you will give me your soul."

He said quietly:

"You took my money because I gave it to you. But how will you take my soul? And when will you take it?"

And she said:

"I will come to you at my hour, and I will take your soul. And you will give me your soul. You will give it because I am—your death, and you will not go away from me anywhere."

Anguish tormented him. He said, in a sharp voice, conquering his anguish and terror:

"You live in a rented room, you are looking for a position or work, your name is Maria or Anna. What is your name?"

And he shouted with savage spite:

"Tell me, what is your name!"

She repeated impassively:

"I am—your death."

So hopeless and merciless the words fell. He was shaking. He slumped. He askcd in a weak voice:

"You need my money because you are hungry and tired, but my soul, why do you need my soul?"

She answered:

"With your money I will buy bread and wine and I will eat and drink, and feed my hungry little dead ones. But afterwards, I will take out your soul and carry it carefully and place it on my shoulders and I will descend with it to a dark palace, where our invisible ruler resides, yours and mine, and I will give him your soul. And he will squeeze the juice out of your soul into a deep bowl, into which my quiet tears will also fall—and with the juice of your soul, mixed with my quiet tears, he will sprinkle the midnight stars."

Quietly, unhurriedly, word by word, the strange speech sounded like a formula of an obscure incantation.

And who was walking past, and what voices resounded nearby, and what carriages were rushing past, thundering over the outer roadway beyond the fence, and whether or not there was rapid, light-footed running or children's laughter and babbling—all this was concealed behind the magical shroud of the slow-moving speech. And as if hiding behind the waning smoke of incense, the resounding, varicolored, joyfully darkening day vanished.

And there was anguish and fatigue and indifference. He said quietly:

"If the trembling of my soul ascends to the stars, and in far-off worlds kindles an insatiable thirst and rapture of being, what is it to me? Rotting all the while, I will rot here, in a terrifying grave where for some purpose or other, indifferent people will bury me. What is there for me in the eloquence of your promises, what is it to me? What is it to me? Tell me."

She said, smiling gently:

"In the blessed passing there is eternal peace."

He repeated quietly:

"Eternal peace. And is this—a consolation?"

"I console with what I can," she said, smiling her same, unmoving, gentle smile.

Then he stood up and walked to the park's exit. He heard her light footsteps behind him.

He walked for a long time along the city streets and she walked behind him. Sometimes he quickened his pace in order to get away from her—and she walked more quickly, hurried, ran, lifting up the edge of her white dress with her slender fingers. Whenever he stopped, she would stand at a distance, examining the objects displayed in store windows. Sometimes he would turn around in vexation and walk straight towards her—and then she would hurriedly run across to the other side of the street or hide in doorways or under gateways.

And she followed him with her gray, calm, attentive eyes. She followed him persistently.

"I'll take a cab," he thought.

He was amazed that such a simple idea had not occurred to him earlier.

But he had barely begun to talk with the cabby when she drew near. She was standing very close by, and he felt a coldness and sadness emanating from her. And she was smiling.

He thought with annoyance:

"She'll get in with me. There's no way, on foot or otherwise, to get away from her."

The cabby was asking for sixty kopecks.

"Thirty kopecks," said Rezanov, and he quickly walked away.

The cabby was swearing.

Rezanov climbed to the third floor. He stopped by the door to his apartment. He rang. All the while he was listening to the quiet rustling of footsteps ascending the stairway. He rang a second time impatiently. Cold terror ran along his spine. He wanted to get in to his apartment before she got there, before she could see which door he entered—there were four doors on the landing.

But she was already approaching. Already near, her dress loomed white in the half-light of the stairway. And her gray eyes were looking attentively and closely into his frightened eyes as he, on entering the apartment, had glanced a last time at the stairway, hurriedly closing the door behind him.

He locked the door himself. The lock clanged so sharply. Then he stopped in the half-dark entry. He was looking at the door with anguished eyes. He sensed—actually saw through the suddenly transparent door—how she was standing outside the door, quiet, with a gentle smile on her dear lips and how she raised her clear, pale face in order to read and memorize his apartment number.

Then her quiet footsteps were heard descending the stairway. Rezanov entered his study.

"She's gone," someone seemed to say in a clear voice.

And another voice, hopeless and calm, seemed to answer: "She will return."

He waited. It was growing darker. Anguish tormented him. His thoughts were unclear and confused. His head was spinning. Shivers and fever were running through his body.

He thought:

"What is she doing? She has bought food, she has come home, and she is feeding her hungry little dead ones. That is what she called them—her little dead ones. How many of them are there? What are they like? Are they just as quiet as she is, my dear one, my death? Emaciated from malnutrition, whitelike, timorous. And unattractive, and with those same attentive eyes, just as dear as hers, my dear one, my white death."

"She is feeding her little dead ones. Then she will put them to bed. Then she will come here. Why?"

And suddenly curiosity flared up in him.

Of course she would come. Otherwise, why had she followed him home. But why would she come? How does she understand her task, this strange lady, who is ready to meet all conditions for money and even to walk among the dead?

But perhaps she is not a woman at all, but rather, genuine death? And would she come and take out his soul from this sinful and weak body?

He lay on the divan. He covered himself up with a blanket. He was shaking all over from an attack of cruel and sweet fever.

What strange ideas come to the mind! She is intelligent and conscientious. She took the money and she wants to earn it, she is playing her assigned role well.

But why is she so cold?

It is because she is poor, hungry, tired, sick.

She is tired from work. There is so much work for her.

> "I was haying all day,
> I am tired. I am sick."

She is walking, searching, hungry, sick. Her poor little dead ones are waiting, their hungry little mouths are open wide.

And he recalled her face—the earthly, human face of his death.

Such a familiar face. Kindred features.

In his memory, feature by feature, her face became clearer— the familiar, kindred, dear features.

Who is she, my white death? Is she not my sister?

> "I feel wretched—I am sick.
> Do help me, dear brother,"

And if she is my eternal sister, my white death—then what is it to me, that here, in this incarnation, she has come to me in the image of a person seeking something through an advertisement, of one who lives in a rented room!

I put my wretched money, my meager gift in her hand—hard cash in her cold hand. And she took my money with her cold hand, and she will take my soul. She will carry me off beneath the dark vaults—and the countenance of the Ruler will be revealed—my eternal countenance, and the Sovereign is—I. I summoned my soul to life, and I have commanded my death to come to me, to come for me.

And he waited.

It was night. The bell tinkled quietly. No one heard it. Rezanov hurriedly threw off the blanket. He walked to the entry, trying not to make any noise.

The lock jingled so sharply. The door opened—she was standing on the threshold.

He stepped back into the darkness of the entry. He asked, as if amazed:

"Is it you?"

And she said:

"I have come. It is my hour. It is time."

He locked the door behind her, and went to his bedroom through the unlighted rooms. He heard the light rustling of her feet behind him.

And in the darkness of his room, she clung to him and kissed him with a tender and innocent kiss.

"Who are you?" he asked.

She said:

"You called me and I have come. I'm not afraid and don't you be afraid. I will give you the last delight of life—the kiss of death—'and your death will be easy and sweeter than poison.'"

He asked:

"And you?"

She answered:

"I told you that I would go away with your soul along the only route which is before us."

"But your little dead ones?"

"I sent them ahead so that they could go before us, and open the doors for us."

"But how will you take out my soul?" he asked again.

And she pressed herself against him tenderly and whispered:

"The stiletto is sharp and it wounds sweetly."

And she clung to him and kissed him and caressed him. And almost as if she had stung him, she pricked him in the back of the neck with the poisoned stiletto. A sweet fire raced like a whirlwind through his veins—and he lay, already dead, in her embrace.

And she killed herself with the second prick of the poisoned point and fell dead onto his body.

In the Crowd

I

The ancient and renowned city of Mstislavl was celebrating the seven hundredth anniversary of its founding.

It was a city wealthy from industry and trade. Some of the factories and mills built there and in the surrounding area were renowned throughout all of Russia. The population had increased rapidly, particularly during recent years, and had reached an impressive figure. Many troops were stationed there. There were many workers, merchants and officials, students, and men of letters living there.

The town fathers had decided to celebrate the founding in grand style. They had invited dignitaries, called Paris and London, and Chukhloma and Medyn as well, and several other towns, but very selectively.

"You know, so that not just anyone can get in," explained the mayor, a young man of merchant origin, with a European education, and noted for the refined urbanity of his manners.

Then somehow they remembered that they had to call Moscow and Vienna, too. And so they sent invitations to these two cities also, but at a time when only two weeks remained before the celebration.

The literati and the students reproached the mayor for such inappropriate forgetfulness. The embarrassed mayor tried to justify himself:

"I was dog tired. Completely out of my mind. There's so much to do—you wouldn't believe. I'm seldom home nights—it's committee after committee."

Moscow did not take offense—we're birds of a feather, she said—and hastened to send a deputation with a congratulatory letter. Gay Vienna, however, limited herself to a postcard with congratulations. The postcard was artfully drawn: a naked boy in a top hat sitting astride a barrel and holding a goblet of beer in his raised hand. The beer was foaming luxuriously, the boy was smiling gaily and cunningly. He was round-faced and rosy, and the members of the city board found his smile fully appropriate to the festivities—gay and nicely German. And they found the whole drawing very stylish. Only they were not in complete accord as to the definition of its style: and said, "moderne," others, "rococo."

In a city that was unpaved, dusty, filthy, and dark—in a city where there were many nasty street urchins and few schools—in a city where, it happened, poor women gave birth on the streets—in a city where they tore down the old walls of a histori-cally famous fortress in order to get bricks to build new homes—in a city where by night, hooligans stormed the crowded streets, while in the outskirts, the residents' dwellings were robbed unim-peded under the very eyes of the nightwatchmen—in this half-wild city, they were arranging totally unnecessary celebrations and banquets for the distinguished guests and dignitaries arriving from all over, and they were spending money generously for this empty and stupid escapade, money that they did not have for schools and hospitals.

And for the simple people—it was impossible after all to leave them out—entertainment was being prepared on the town commons, in the area which was called, for some reason, Opa-likha. Booths were being built—one for the folk drama, another for fairytale performances, a third for the circus—a roller coaster was being set up, as were children's swings and poles for climbing contests. For the wandering clown business, they were buying a new flaxen beard, and it cost the town more than a silk one—really very artistically made.

They made gifts to be distributed among the people. They

intended to give each person a mug with the town's coat of arms and a small bundle: a kerchief with a view of Mstislavl, and in it, gingerbread and nuts. They laid in many thousand such mugs and kerchiefs with gingerbread and nuts. They were stockpiling them well in advance—and as a result, the gingerbread became stale and the nuts rotten.

A week before the day set for the people's public holiday, they set up tables and beer counters at Opalikha, and two platforms—the one for the public which charged, and the other for the distinguished guests.

They left narrow aisles between the counters so people could walk, one at a time, in turn, to the tables to get the gifts. The mayor had thought this up to maintain greater order. He was a wise and sensible young man.

On the eve of the holiday, they trucked in the gifts, put them in a shed, and locked them up.

The public, having heard about the amusements and the gifts, was coming in crowds from all over to the ancient and renowned city of Mstislavl, and people crossed themselves from a distance at the sight of the golden cupolas of its numerous churches. Rumor had it that there were all kinds of gifts and that in addition, there would be fountains of vodka at Opalikha, and you could drink as much as you wanted—even if you got dead drunk.

Many were coming from far away. And plenty early. Already on the eve of the holiday there were many strangers from far away loafing about. Most of them were peasants and there were many factory workers too. There were also those from the lower middle class from the neighboring towns. They came on foot, and some of them were driving.

And the celebration had already been going on for several days in the city. Flags waved on the houses. Garlands of greens were hung. Public prayers were celebrated. A military parade was held. Then there was a review of the fire brigade. There was a gay and noisy bazaar on the commercial square.

Many distinguished visitors, local and foreign, bureaucrats

and dignitaries, and many curious tourists had arrived. The local inhabitants came out onto the streets in crowds and gawked at the arriving guests. The distinguished foreigners were the subject of particulai atlention, and not, by the way, of a very friendly nature. People were trying to get rich: lodgings, food, goods— everything went up.

It was the eve of the public holiday. The city, as on all of these days, was ablaze with holiday lights. The municipal theater was set for a gala night and following it, a big ball in the governor's house.

But the crowd was piling up at Opalikha. And there was no supervision of it. The distribution of the gifts was set for ten in the morning, and the municipal authorities were convinced that no one would go to Opalikha before early morning. But before early morning meant at night, and still earlier meant in the evening. And from the evening on, the crowd had begun to gather at Opalikha, so that by midnight, in front of the sheds, which separated the public square from the reserved area, it had become crowded, noisy, and alarming.

Rumor had it that several hundred thousand had gathered. Even half a million.

II

On Nikolskaya Square, right by a precipice, stood the Udoevs' little house. Above the precipice, a garden was laid out, and from it a magnificent view unfolded onto the lower parts of the city, across to the other side of the river and the commercial district, and to the outlying regions.

From that altitude, everything was clear and seemed small, beautiful, and elegant. From there, the shallow, dirty Safat river looked like a narrow ribbon of shifting colors. The houses and commercial rows stood like toys; the carriages and people were moving peacefully, calmly, noiselessly, and aimlessly; a light, barely-visible dust kept rising; and the heavy thundering of the wagons drifted upward like the barely audible music of the underground.

Opposite the Udoev house, across the square, was the Treasury, a cheerless two-story building painted ochre. The head of the family, Matvey Fedorovich Udoev, worked there.

The fence around the Udoev house was drab and solid, there was a charming and cozy summer house in the garden, the lilac was sweet smelling, the fruit-bearing trees and the berry bushes held a promise of something delightful and sweet; the family of the old and respectable bureaucrat had organized a thrifty, sound life.

The Udoev children, Lesha, a student of fifteen, and his two sisters, Nadya and Katya, twenty and eighteen, had also decided to go to the festivities at Opalikha. That was why they were so gay and full of joyful excitement.

Lesha was a fair-skinned, risible, and industrious boy. He had no bright, distinctive marks: his teachers often mixed him up with some other pale and modest schoolboy. The girls were also modest, cheerful, and kind. Nadya, the older, was more lively fidgety, and at times, even mischievous. Katya, who was younger, was very demure, she loved to pray, especially in the monastery, and she went very easily from laughter to tears and from crying to laughter—and it was easy to hurt her feelings, but not difficult to comfort her and make her laugh.

Both the boy and the girls wanted very much to get a mug. They had already begged their parents beforehand to go to Opalikha.

They did not let them go to Opalikha willingly. Their mother grumbled. Their father remained silent. He did not care. However, he did not like it either.

Matvey Fedorovich Udoev was a silent, tall, pockmarked, indifferent person. He drank vodka, but a moderate amount and almost never quarreled with the household help. Domestic life passed him by. As did all life. . . .

It was passing by like a fleeting cloud, melting in a sky pierced by sunlight. . . . Like a tirelessly striding wanderer, past buildings he does not need. . . . Like the wind, blowing from a distant land. . . . Going past, going past, ever past. . . .

III

Lesha and both sisters were standing by the gate and looking at the passersby. It was noisy and crowded. People were walking, all dressed up, and it was obvious that they were strangers. They were walking mostly on one side—in the direction of Opalikha. The rumble among the crowd made the children vaguely uneasy.

Their neighbors, the Shutkins, approached: a young man, a boy, and two girls. They exchanged a few insignificant words, as people do who meet often and are used to one another.

"You going?" asked the older Shutkin.

"We're going, in the morning!" Lesha answered.

Without saying anything, Nadya and Katya smiled cheerfully and with a little embarrassment. The Shutkins began to laugh at something. They exchanged glances. They went on to their house.

"They want to go earlier than us," Nadya guessed.

"So let them," said Katya, and she became sad. The Shutkins' house stood next to the Udoevs' property. It was distinguished by its slovenly, dilapidated appearance.

The young Shutkins were all pretty much terrors and good-for-nothings. Sometimes they set out on daring pranks. Now and then, they incited the Udoev children to pranks, and quite often rather serious ones.

The Shutkins were dark-complexioned and brunette, like gypsies. The older brother worked as a clerk at the Justice of the Peace. He played a mean balalaika. His sisters, Elena and Natalya, loved to sing and dance. They did this with gusto. The younger brother, Kostya, was an awful bundle of mischief. He studied in a municipal school. They had threatened more than once to kick him out. He was still holding on somehow for the time being.

The Udoevs returned home. There was an awkward and uneasy mood. They could not sit quiet.

They had already decided to go early in the morning. But preparations were begun early in the evening. The lower the tired sun dipped, the more strongly the childrens' agitation and impatience grew. They all ran out to the gates to look, listen, and chat with the neighbors and passersby.

Nadya was the most agitated of all. She was very much afraid that they would be late. She said vexedly to her brother and sister:

"You'll oversleep, you'll oversleep for sure, I already have a feeling."

And she was wringing her slender, delicate fingers which was always a sign of great anxiety.

In answer to her, Katya smiled calmly and said reassuringly, "Don't worry, we won't be late."

"But we do have to sleep," Lesha said lazily.

And suddenly he felt lazy, and he thought that it would be unpleasant and useless to get up early and he didn't want to go. Nadya objected quickly and heatedly:

"Oh sure! Sleep. You don't have to sleep. I'm not going to sleep at all tonight."

"And you're not going to have supper?" Lesha asked in a teasing voice.

And suddenly it seemed to all of them that a long time had passed and supper was purposely not being served, and they began to worry. They looked often at the clock. They joined their father.

Nadya was grumbling:

"Why today, as if on purpose, has our clock stopped. We should've had supper a long time ago. It'll be no wonder if we oversleep tomorrow if dinner isn't served until midnight."

Their father said gloomily:

"What are you pestering me for? First one thing, then another."

And he looked at his children with an indiscernable look, as if he were seeing only that there were three of them. He took out his watch indifferently and showed it to them. It was still very early. They never sat down to supper so early.

In the meantime, the news came to the Udoev household from all directions that they were already gathering at Opalikha, they were going in crowds—that there was a crowd there already—a whole camp, with night lodgings, and all but tents.

And the children began to suspect that in the morning it would be late to start out for Opalikha—by then it would be reachable. And because of this, the mood in the Udoev house became excessively uneasy.

People were walking past the Udoev house. More and more people were passing by. In the crowd there were also the poorly dressed. There were many little boys. It was noisy, gay, and festive.

IV

Several persons came to a stop by the Udoevs' gates. One could hear animated conversation, arguing, laughter.

Lesha and his sisters once more ran out to the gates.

Standing in a small group were several peasant men and women. With them were several of the local lower middle class. They were conversing loudly, in an unfriendly tone, as if they were quarreling.

One of these, a middle-aged, bold woman with a sharp and sly face, dressed in a cotton print dress, bright-colored because of the festive elegance and noisy because of its starchy newness, with a pink kerchief on her oily, combed head, was talking to a tall middle-aged peasant woman:

"You should've put up at the inn."

An old peasant man was answering unhurriedly and pensively,

as if trying to find the exact words to express his significant and deep thoughts:

"Your yard keepers'll really cheat ya. They'll cheat ya, d'ya hear. You know, there's no way you can deal with them. Sure, they're glad. Those people aren't Christians. They're greedy for gain, y'hear. They'll really rip you off. They gotta yen to get rich ya know."

A good-natured little fellow, pale-faced and tow headed, with a perpetual smile on his plump lips and with gentle, clear blue eyes, said:

"There are good people, who'll let you stay for nothing."

Everyone looked at him mockingly. They burst out:

"There are, but not here."

"Go find some and let us know."

They were laughing, rejoicing maliciously for some reason, though apparently there was no basis for this joy at another's misfortune. The little fellow was grinning, casting looks around with his innocent eyes, and he was assuring them.

"But they let me. Really. A woman here let me."

"You're really smooth," said a red-headed and pock-marked peasant.

The two Shutkin sisters, Elena and Natalya, approached; they were very much like one another in every respect, so that it was strange to see that one of them was a redhead and the other a brunette. With them was their oldest brother. They were listening and smiling slyly, and today for some reason, it seemed that their smiles were nasty and that they themselves were unclean.

Winking at the Udoev sisters, the oldest Shutkin said.

"You getting up early tomorrow?"

"Yes," Lesha began speaking with animation—"we'll get up a little earlier, before sunrise, we'll get there before anybody."

And suddenly he remembered that there was no possible way of arriving before everyone and he became annoyed.

"Oh sure you'll get up early!" said Shutkin.

His sisters laughed insolently and slyly. And there was no understanding why or what they were laughing at. The oldest Shutkin said:

"What's going early! It'll be like last year when we went to the monastery for matins."

"What fun that was!" Elena shouted with laughter.

And it was obvious that both for her and her redheaded sister it didn't matter what they laughed about, and it didn't seem at all strange and indecent to mock even themselves.

Shutkin was recounting the story:

"That was last year. We went to bed early, without a light. We had a good sleep, got up. We didn't have a clock in those days, it was in hock for the simple reason that we had an excess of expenses above income. So we had to resort to getting a loan and pay twelve percent on it. So anyway, we took off. We walked and walked and finally got there. We see that everything's still locked. We think we've come too early. So we sat down on the bench by the gates of the holy cloister. The guard came up to us, asks with natural enough surprise: 'How come you've settled in here?' He says, 'Did it get boring at home, huh?' And we tell him real free and easy like—'We came for the matins; your monks,' we say, 'have overslept today.' And he says to us: 'You were fetched before dawn—y'see not long ago it was only the eleven o'clock bell was struck.' He says, 'Are you really going to wait?' He says, 'You should go on home.' So we listened to his intelligent advice and went home. That was a laugh."

And the Shutkins and Udoevs were laughing.

Just then the youngest Shutkin, Kostya, came running up, panting and sweating:

"I flew off to Opalikha and back already."

"What? How?" his family and the Udoevs were asking him.

Kostya, with a gleeful loud laugh said:

"There's a fantastic lot of peasants turned up. They've filled up the whole field completely."

"What oddballs they are!" Lesha said with a vexed laugh. "They won't start giving the things out until ten and they've gone in the evening."

The oldest Shutkin began to laugh and winked at his sisters.

"Who told you that?" he yelled. "It'll begin at two so the foreign guests can see. They're not used to going to bed early. And they get up late."

"No, that's not true, it begins at ten," Lesha objected hotly.

"No, at two, at two," all the Shutkins began to shout in one voice.

And it was immediately obvious by their insolent laughter and exchanged glances that they were lying.

"Well I'll find out for sure right now," said Lesha.

He ran off to the secretary of the town council whose house was not far away. He returned triumphant. He yelled from afar:—"At ten."

The Shutkins were chuckling and no longer argued.

"You thought that up on purpose," said Lesha, "so you could leave earlier, without us. What a bunch!"

Pakhomov, a thin and flighty schoolboy, ran by boisterously. He gave a hasty greeting to the Udoevs. The Shutkins looked at him in an unfriendly manner.

"Well, are you going?" he asked, and not waiting for an answer, said:

"We're off this evening. A lot are going this evening."

He hurriedly said good-by. He had looked at the Shutkins and wanted to greet them, but changed his mind and ran off. The Shutkins were looking maliciously after him. They were laughing. Their laughter seemed unpleasantly strange to the Udoevs—why this laughter?

"Sissy!" Kostya said scornfully.

Elena said maliciously and loudly:

"Little braggart! How does he know! He's lying."

The evening was so quiet and beautiful that the Shutkins'

unnecessarily coarse words rang out with a particularly sharp discord.

The sun had just begun to go down. The flaming reflection of its parting, purply-dead rays was still discernible on the clouds.

The evening was so beautiful, so peaceful. . . . But the dead Serpent's burning hot poison still gushed above the earth.

V

The Udoevs returned home. It was eerie and awkward, and they did not know what to do with themselves. Arguments and disputes flared up over every trifle. Restlessness gripped them all.

And Lesha suddenly became fidgety and uneasy like Nadya.

"We'll miss the boat," he said loudly and angrily.

As often happens, these insignificant words decided the business. Nadya said:

"So we'd better go this evening."

And everyone agreed with her and suddenly they were happy. Lesha suddenly flushed all over and shouted:

"Right! If we're going, let's go now."

All three ran to their father to ask.

"We've changed our minds and we're going this evening!" shouted Nadya, fidgeting in front of her father.

Their father maintained a gloomy silence.

"It's nothing to miss a night's sleep," Lesha was saying, as if trying to convince his father of something.

But their father remained silent and his face was as before— unmovingly gloomy.

The children left him. They ran to their mother. Their mother began to grumble.

"Papa gave his permission," Lesha shouted.

And the sisters laughed and chattered happily, loudly.

With a joyful squeal, all three ran about the house and garden. They were hurrying supper.

They remembered about the Shutkins. For some reason it was annoying to think about them. Lesha said to his sisters:

"Only let's not tell the Shutkins."

His sisters agreed.

"Just by ourselves," said Nadya, "To heck with them."

Katya frowned and drawled:

"What awful people."

And right away she began to laugh again.

At dinner the children ate hurriedly, though they did not want to eat and it was annoying that the elders were dawdling as if there was nothing special.

When they were finishing supper, their father suddenly fixed his gaze on the children and looked at them for a long time, so long, that they grew quiet under his gloomily indifferent look and he finally said:

"Knocking about with drunks—a great pleasure."

Nadya quickly blushed, and began to assure him:

"But there aren't any drunks. There aren't any drunks anywhere. Really it's odd, but just around our house today, the whole day, we didn't see any drunks. And that's amazing."

Katya was laughing happily and said:

"All they're thinking about is the gifts, and they don't want to drink. They're not up to it."

Finally supper was over.

They ran off to get dressed. The girls had wanted to dress up for the festivities. But their mother was decidedly against it.

"What for? Why? To knock around the peasants?" she was saying angrily.

And it was obvious by her whole alerted stance and her gray, insignificant face, that for no reason at all, she would not allow any wear and tear on a holiday dress.

The girls had to put on a simpler costume.

Finally they managed to get out of the house. They ran along the steep descent to the river. And suddenly, they saw the Shutkins just starting to come down.

They had to go together. It was annoying.

The Shutkins were angry, too. Neither they nor the others would get there first. The opportunity for boasting and mocking was lost.

The Shutkins had been inventing various gibes for the Udoevs. Several times, on the road, they almost got into an argument.

The evening was like the day, lively and noisy.

As always, the stars twinkled quietly above the city, so distant, so unnoticeable to the vacant look, and so close when one looks into their sky-blue surroundings.

The clear pale sky was darkening quickly, and it was a joy to look at the mystery which was immutably forming in it, opening the distant worlds of the night.

The bells sounded in the monastery; the evening service was coming to an end. The radiant and sad sounds were slowly spreading over the land. Hearing them, one wanted to sing and cry and to take off for somewhere.

And the heavens listened spellbound, listened spellbound to the radiant weeping of bronze—the tender, touching heavens. And the quiet little clouds, melting away, listened spellbound, they listened spellbound to the resonant weeping of bronze—the quiet, light little clouds.

And the air was flowing in a warmth-giving tenderness as from a multitude of joyous breaths.

And the touching tenderness of the high heavens and the quietly melting little clouds pressed against the children. And suddenly, the whole surrounding, and the bells' weeping, and the heavens, and the people—for an instant, everything began to glow and became music.

Everything became music for an instant, and the instant burned away and once more they became the objects and deceptions of the objective world.

The children were hurrying out of the city to the Opalikha valley.

But in the city it was crowded and noisy and there was an air of gaiety. Flags were waving above the houses. Holiday torches were burning in the streets, and here and there the nasty odor of tallow could be discerned.

The crowds were walking along the streets, along the descent and the embankment of the Safat River. Children were darting about and laughing in the crowd. And everything was ringing and gay as in a fairy tale and as it never is in everyday, gray life. And because of this, all the wild rumors people told, muffled by the general rumble, seemed to vibrate in the air and suddenly become possible.

Carriages were passing by with the guests of honor, the obliging faces of both the important men and the women were smiling at the crowd.

From the carriages one could hear the quiet, incomprehensible foreign speech and light laughter.

The Shutkins were looking at the wealthy people passing by with hostile eyes. Both evil and stupid thoughts sprang up in their minds.

And when they had already come out of the town, the oldest Shutkin said, grinning:

"Now'd be the time to set the town on fire. I'll tell you, it's a great idea."

His sisters and Kostya began to laugh.

Katya shivered, shook her little shoulders, and exclaimed uneasily:

"Why, how's it possible! What horrible things you're saying!"

"That'd really be some excitement!" agreed Kostya eagerly, jumping and squealing.

"Well if you were to lose everything in a fire," Nadya said with astonishment, "what would you have to be happy about!"

"Come on," Natalya objected, "what do we have worth burning. We wouldn't care."

Nadya looked at her. In the weak reflection of the smoky,

festive torches, her freckled face and red hair appeared flaming, and because her nostrils were quivering, it seemed that flames were running across her face.

VI

They reached Opalikha quickly, driven by a feverishly joyous agitation.

While they were still a long way off, the confused and menacing rumble of the human multitudes reached them. It inspired a terrible and sweet terror. They were running into the approaching darkness and gusts of night wind. People were walking, hurrying along with them; they were overtaken, then left behind. Grownups and small ones. Men, women, children, and old people. Mostly young people. And they were all equally agitated, and their voices rang out unevenly, and their laughter would rise up and then suddenly subside.

Beyond a bend in the road, the whole Opalikha valley opened up all at once, dark, terrifyingly noisy, disquieting.

Here and there bonfires were burning on the outskirts of Opalikha, and this made the field seem still darker.

One could see the flames of the bonfires and far beyond them. But one could see how they expired smokily, one after the other, there, in the distance of the smoky, noisy field. The crowd must have been extinguishing them with their feet, the coarse boots trampling their short-lived souls striving in the flames.

And an even more terrible and even sweeter terror gripped the Udoevs and began to flicker behind their shaking shoulders. But they tried not to appear afraid.

The Shutkins were delighted that there would be the crush, disorder, and commotion; for a long time afterwards they would be able to recount the curious and significant details of various incidents.

The Shutkin boy looked at the noisy, dark field, grinned stupidly, and said with an incomprehensible joy:

"They'll squash one of the weaklings for sure. You'll see."

But the Udoevs could not believe in the proximity of misfortune and death. This field where there was the noisy multitude—and death. It was not possible.

"—Yes, that's about it, they'll squash someone—" said one of the Shutkin sisters in a strangely unfamiliar voice.

And someone began to laugh coarsely and joylessly with dark laughter in the darkness.

"Well, yes!" Katya said indifferently.

For a moment it became boring. Because it was dark. Because of the flickering and uneven light of the bonfires. And they began to look and listen and they walked forward.

Judging by the faces illuminated by the bonfires—mostly the very young—and by their carefree voices and laughter, it seemed that everyone was very happy.

The noisy multitude of people was walking, standing, and sitting about the whole field.

Becoming more and more accustomed to this confused, troubled throng, the Udoevs became infected once more with the gaiety and good spirits of the crowd which had left behind the everyday human shelters and walls.

It became gay. Too gay.

The Shutkins walked off somewhere, and were no longer to be found. But the Udoevs kept meeting other acquaintances. They saw many of them. Snatches of gay conversation were tossed back and forth. They kept coming together and drifting apart again in the crowd.

They walked forward and perhaps to the side, and the field seemed endless. And it seemed so entertaining that different people kept turning up.

"Yes, it's really fun here. And you don't notice how the night passes," Nadya was saying nervously, giving an occasional yawn and huddling up her thin little shoulders.

And they walked for a long time, stopping, walking again, losing their way among the bonfires, listening to others' conversations, conversing themselves with total strangers.

In the beginning, it seemed that they were walking toward some kind of goal,—as if they were getting ever closer to it, and everything was defined and coherent, although submerged in the sweet frightfulness of the throng.

Later everything suddenly became fragmentary, and lost its coherency, and bits and pieces of unnecessary and strange impressions swarmed all around. . . .

VII

Everything became fragmentary and incoherent and it seemed that absurd and unnecessary objects were springing out of nothing. The absurd rose up unexpectedly from out of the stupid and hostile darkness.

In the middle of the field a ditch had been dug at one time for some reason. It had remained, and now—unnecessary and ugly, overgrown with prickly grass that was black in the darkness—it appeared for some reason terrible and strangely significant.

The children walked up to the edge of it. Two telegraph operators were sitting with their legs dangling in the ditch, talking. They were recalling their female acquaintances, and for some reason they were uttering unprintable words with great pleasure.

The Udoevs walked past the edge of the ditch. They saw a bridge of planks across it, with uneven railings. They walked across the bridge. The railing seemed flimsy, unsteady.

Lesha said warily,

"If you were pushed off here, you'd break a leg."

"But we'll go on a little further," Nadya said.

Her voice sounded uncertain and timid in the dark. It was strange not to be able to see how her lips moved as she spoke.

And again they were walking on, through the rumbling multitude, going from the circles lighted by the bonfires into pitch darkness,—and again the field seemed endless.

"So where are you going?"—one tipsy bum was arguing with another—"They'll squash you like a bedbug."

"Let 'em,"—his friend answered,—"So what's my life to me? If they squash me, no one'll cry over me."

They saw a well. It was covered with half-rotted boards. They were faintly surprised for some reason.

The tipsy peasant, shaking his disheveled long head, was staring into the well, and drawling:

"—e echh"

He ran away from the well, and shouted:

"Malanya!"

And he returned once more to the decrepit well structure walking with a drunk's tiny, faltering footsteps.

People looked. Laughed. Walked on by. They heard his drunken cries for a long time.

"I've got a knife put away," croaked the tall and scraggy bum.

His comrade, who was just as ragged and almost as tall answered in a sweet tenor:

"Me too."

"To be on the safe side," the hoarse voice of the first one was heard again.

And one could hear how the other one laughed.

Breathing in the sweetish smoke of damp wood, the children, with Lesha in front of his sisters, kept on walking in the unsteady darkness, in the nervously quivering bonfires' light.

They made believe that it was not so terrifying.

Again the field seemed endless, again they confused the bonfires, and because of the fatigue in their legs, they thought that they had been walking for a long time.

"We're going around in circles," said Lesha.

And their shared thought was expressed in those words. Katya felt sad, but Nadya, feigning gaiety, said,

"Never mind, we'll make it there."

Suddenly Lesha fell. His legs flashed upwards, his head was not visible. His sisters rushed to him. They helped to pull him out—it turned out that he had fallen headlong into some kind of unexpected pit.

"We have to get farther away from this place, it's dangerous here," said Nadya.

But later too, they stumbled more than once over the unevennesses of the ground.

VIII

"And the upper crust is going there, too," a vile tenor voice was heard next to the Udoevs.

One couldn't see who was speaking and who was laughing, sympathizing with the malicious words.

And the children understood that the whole crowd here was hostile, and alien through and through—incomprehensible and uncomprehending. And there, where the bonfires were burning, one could see faces scowling angrily, looking at the schoolboy and his sisters.

These hostile looks confused the children. It was impossible to understand why there was this hostility—where it originated.

Some strangers were looking sullenly, hostilely at the children passing by.

Now and then, cynical jokes could be heard. And because this was going on in the middle of an enormous crowd, and no one would think to stick up for anyone, the children began to feel terrified.

A drunken worker stood up from the bonfire and came up to the children.

"Mamzelle!"—he exclaimed. "I have the honor to greet you on this, our meeting. Delighted. And we may afford you every pleasure. We want to kiss."

He gave a lurch. He took off his cap. He hugged Katya. He kissed her right on the mouth.

Roaring laughter broke out in the crowd. Katya began to cry.

Lesha shouted something, threw himself at the drunk and pushed him away.

The drunk began to growl fiercely:

"What right do you have to push? So what if I want to kiss? What's so bad about that?"

His sisters grabbed Lesha by the arm. Quickly they led him into the darkness.

They were very frightened. The insult burned agonizingly.

They wanted to get away from this dark and unclean place. But they could not find the way. Again the bonfires' flames confused them, blinding their eyes, displaying a gloom blacker than gloom, and making everything incomprehensible and fragmentary.

Soon the bonfires began to go out. And the air's darkness became stable,—and the black night pressed close to the rumbling field, and became heavy with the noises and voices above it. Because they were not sleeping and were in the crowd, it seemed that this night was—significant, unique, and the last one.

IX

They had not been there very long yet and it had already become repulsive, sickening, terrifying.

In the darkness, an unnecessary, inappropriate, and therefore foul life was being created. People without a roof, far from their own comforts, were becoming drunk on the wild air of night's pitch darkness.

They had brought their own foul vodka and heavy beer and they drank the whole night long, and bellowed in their drunkenly hoarse voices. They ate stinking food. They sang obscene songs. They danced shamelessly. They laughed. Here and there one could hear ridiculous petty intrigues. A harmonica screeched vilely.

There was a bad odor everywhere, and everything was repulsive, dark and terrifying.

And now drunken and hoarse voices resounded everywhere.

Here and there men and women were embracing. Under one bush, two pairs of legs were sticking out—and from under the bush one could hear the intermittent, repulsive squeal of satisfied passion.

Here and there, in a few open places, people gathered in circles. Something was going on in the middle.

Some sort of repulsive, filthy little urchins broke into a wild cossack dance.

In another circle, a drunken old woman without a nose was doing a frenzied dance, shamelessly flapping her filthy torn skirt. Then she began to sing in a disgusting, nasal voice. The words of her song were just as shameless as her terrible face and her awful dance.

"Why have you got a knife?"—a policeman was sternly asking someone.

"I'm a working man," an insolent voice was heard, "I grabbed this tool just in case. I can give someone a jab."

Laughter resounded.

And here in this repulsive crowd, thrown into the vile revelry at the wrong time of their awakening life, the children were walking, and getting lost in the throng. The field appeared endless because they were circling around in a small area.

It was becoming even more difficult to make their way—everything had become more crowded all around.

It seemed that out of the blue, people kept rising up all around.

And suddenly a crowd gathered around the Udoevs. It became close. And all at once, it seemed that a heavy stuffiness was spreading and crawling towards their faces.

And a dark and strange coolness flowed from the dark sky. One wanted to look upwards to the fathomless heavens, to the cool stars.

Lesha was leaning on Nadya's shoulder. A momentary dream enveloped him. . . .

. . .He was flying in the blue sky, light as a free bird. . . .

Someone shoved him. Lesha awakened. In a sleepy voice, he said:

"I almost fell asleep. I even dreamed something."

"Don't you go to sleep now," Nadya said anxiously,—"we're still lost in the crowd."

"But I'd like to go to sleep," said Katya quietly and plaintively.

"I really hope we're not lost," Nadya was saying. She was trying to cheer up. She began to speak with animation:

"Let's put Lesha in the middle."

"Well, okay," said Lesha limply.

He was pale and strangely dull.

But his sisters put him between them. They were diverted by the fact that they were protecting him from the pushing. Until the crowd destroyed their order, confusedly pushing them in all directions.

"Well we're here, why don't they give out the stuff," a strangely happy and indifferent voice was heard.

And someone answered:

"Wait—in the morning the people will give out what's set up for distribution."

X

It was crowded and stifling, they wanted to get out of the crowd, out to the wide open spaces, to breathe fully.

But they could not get out. They were caught in the dark and faceless crowd—like a canoe caught in the reeds.

It was impossible now to pick out the road, to choose their own direction. They had to drag along together with the crowd,—and the crowd's movements were heavy and slow.

The Udoevs were moving along slowly in some direction. They thought they were going forward because everyone was walking in the same direction. But then suddenly the crowd was heavily and slowly moving backwards. Or it was slowly drawing to the side. And then it became totally incomprehensible in what direction one should go, where the goal was and where the exit was.

They caught sight of dark walls close by, a little to the side. They wanted to get to them for some reason. There seemed to be something familiar, reminiscent of home in them.

They said nothing to one another, but they began to push their way through to those dark walls.

And soon they were standing near one of the folk theaters.

It seemed that near the wall there was something familiar, protective—a kind of coziness—and therefore it was not so terrifying. The dark, upper part of the wall rose up, covering half of the sky, and because of this, the terrible impression of the uncontrolled, boundless crowd disappeared.

The children were standing, pressing up against the wall. They looked timidly at the gray, dim shapes of the people who were swaying about so nearby. And it was hot from the breathing of the nearby throng.

But a cold coolness from the heavens pressed down in gusts and it seemed that the suffocating earthly air was struggling with the heavenly coolness.

"It would be better if we could go home," Katya said plaintively. "It doesn't matter, we can't force our way through."

"Never mind, we'll wait a while," answered Lesha, trying to appear bright and cheerful.

Just then a heavy movement passed through the crowd—as if someone were elbowing his way to the wall, directly towards the children. They were pressed up against the wall,—and it became completely suffocating and difficult to breathe.

Then the crowd expanded with force and it seemed that the wall was shuddering and swaying—and two very pale students carrying a burden seemed to surface from out of the crowd.

They were carrying a little girl and she appeared to be lifeless. Her pale arms hung down as if dead, and her face with its tightly compressed lips and closed eyes was a dull blue.

The murmuring sound of voices was heard in the crowd:

"She's awfully weak, but she's pulling out of it."

"What are the parents doing?—Letting such a little one go!"

One could hear in the crowd's confused exchange of remarks, the desire to justify something that shouldn't have been—and it seemed that these people, for an instant, understood that they did not have to be there and crowd one another.

XI

Again the crowd began to move heavily and rudely. Severe jolts reverberated agonizingly in the body. Coarse boots kept treading on the childrens' lightly shod feet.

They could not hold their places against the wall. They were pushed aside, pressed back. They were squeezed into a crowded circle. Once more it became terrifying in the suffocating throng.

With effort, the children's heads were raised upwards, and their mouths greedily devoured the intermittent streams of the heavenly coolness, while their chests heaved in the dense and incomprehensible crush. Either they found themselves moving in some direction, or they were standing still. And now it was impossible to know whether or not much time had passed.

An excruciating thirst for open space tormented the children.

And thirst.

It had been sneaking up slowly for a long time now. Suddenly it announced itself with pitiful words.

"I want a drink,"—Lesha said.

And saying this, he felt that his lips had already been dry for a long time and the dryness in his mouth was uncomfortable and debilitating.

"Yes and me, too," said Katya, moving her parched, pale lips with effort.

Nadya remained silent. But one could tell by her face which had become pale and suddenly pinched looking, and by her dryly burning eyes, that thirst was tormenting her too.

Drink. Even if it were just a little sip of water, Water—holy, beloved, cool, fresh.

But there was no place to get any water.

And the coolness from the distant heavens was becoming even

more fleeting, vacillating, unsteady—it would gust into their hungrily opened mouths, and burn up.

Nadya hiccuped. She shivered slightly. Again she hiccuped.

She could not keep from it. Such excruciating hiccups in the closeness and stuffiness.

Lesha looked at Nadya in alarm. How pale she was!

"My God," said Nadya hiccuping. "What torment! Why did we come?"

Katya began to cry quietly. Quick little tears were falling, one after the other—and she could not stop the tears, and could not wipe them away—she could not lift her hands, the crush of the crowd was so great.

"What're you pushing for!"—a thin little voice squealed somewhere close by. "You're crushing me."

A hoarse, drunken bass answered maliciously:

"What? I'm crushing you? You don't like such manners? So go ahead and crush me. Here everybody's equal, God damn you."

"Oh, oh, they're crushing me," that same thin little voice began to squeal again.

"Don't squeal, you sniveler," croaked the fierce bass. "You'll go home later or be dragged. And you'll be without your guts, you pup."

A second later, there was a thin, shrill scream, without words, plaintive and pitiful. And in answer to it, a fierce shout:

"Don't scream!"

Then there was a repressed, thin wail.

Someone shouted:

"They've crushed a babe. Its little bones are crunching. Mother of Heaven!"

"Its little bones, the little bones crunched!" an old lady began to squeal.

Her voice sounded nearby, but she could not be seen beyond the crowd.

And then it seemed that she was screaming somewhere very

far away. Had they pushed her away from that place? Or had she suffocated?

The children were so crushed by the crowd that it was difficult to breathe. They exchanged remarks in a hoarse whisper. They could not turn around. They could look at one another only with difficulty.

And it was terrifying to look at one another, at the beloved faces, clouded by a leaden terror in the dim predawn twilight.

Nadya continued to hiccup, Katya hiccuped too.

A single desire was felt in that whole crowd, which was so terrifyingly and so absurdly compacted. The desire was excruciating and that was why it was still not recognized and that was why it was still more excruciating: to free oneself from that terrifying vise.

But there was no exit—and the fury was in full swing in the mad crowd, absurdly squeezed by its own will in that expansive field, under that expansive sky.

The people were now becoming like wild beasts, and they were looking at the children with the malice of wild beasts.

Hoarse, terrifying talk could be heard. Some indifferent, strangely calm person nearby was saying that there were already those who had been crushed to death.

"The little dead boy is standing upright, he's so squeezed in,"—a plaintive whisper was heard somewhere nearby—"he's all blue and so terrifying, and his head's dangling down."

"You hear, Nadya?" Katya asked in a whisper, "They say that over there a dead person is standing up all crushed."

"They're probably lying," whispered Nadya, "he's just fainted."

"But maybe it's true, too," said Lesha.

And terror resounded in his hoarse voice.

"It can't be," Nadya argued, "a dead person would fall down."

"Yes, but there's nowhere to fall to," Lesha answered.

Nadya became silent. Again the hiccups began to torment her.

A gray-haired, shaggy old woman, waving her arms above her head as if she were swimming, crawled out of the crowd straight towards the Udoevs. Howling frenziedly, she forced her way past them, and it was so crowded and difficult that it seemed that she was passing through like a nail.

Her frenzied howl, her excruciating appearance in the pale, dull, predawn haze, were like the specter of a bad dream. And from that time on, everything was lassitude and delirium in the consciousness of the suffocating children.

XII

Finally, after an excruciating and terrifying night it began to grow light rapidly.

A rapid, joyful, childishly gay dawn blazed up and began to laugh with the laughter of rosy little clouds. Golden sparkles blazed up in the hazy distance. And while the earth was still dark and grim, the sky was already blazing with joy, the universal joy of eternal exultation. And the people—all those people! They were still only people!. . .

The breathing of the great multitude of people formed a heavy steam which stretched from the dark earth, so sinful and burdened, to the illuminated heavens, blessed anew.

The night's coolness, curling up into the golden heaven's dreams, burnt up in the light clouds, in the glowing rays.

But the crowd, so strangely and unexpectedly illuminated from above by the serene glowing laughter,—this vast earthly crowd was pierced through with malice and terror.

It was moving heavily, rushing forward, and once again those who were arriving from the town stupidly and maliciously pressed those who were standing in front of them forward, on to the barns with the gifts.

Under the dawn's eternal gold, the wretched mugs' lackluster tin drew the people into the confusion and crush.

In the lassitude and delirium, grave thoughts crowded into the children's consciousness, into the dark consciousness of those suffocating, and each thought was terror and melancholy. Cruel perdition was drawing near. Their own perdition. The perdition of beloved ones. And whose is more painful?

As if awakening now and then, people began to yell and complain and beg.

Their hoarse voices flew upwards feebly—like a wounded bird with a broken wing—and fell pitifully and were drowned in the hollow rumble of the stupid crowd.

The sullen people's dimly severe looks were their answer.

Melancholy constricted their breathing and whispered evil, hopeless words.

And by now, there was no hope of getting away. The people were evil. Both evil and weak. They could not save anyone, they could not save themselves.

Prayers were heard everywhere, howls, groans—useless prayers.

And who could have been moved by the entreaties there, in that crowd?

They were not like people now—to the suffocating children it seemed that fierce demons were looking sullenly and laughing soundlessly from behind the human masks that were slipping off, rotting.

And the demonic masquerade stretched on excruciatingly. And it seemed that there would be no end to it—there would be no end to the boiling of this satanic cauldron.

XIII

The sun rose swiftly, a joyfully aroused, evil Dragon. There was the odor of the Serpent's hot breath. The evil Dragon ascended, burning off the last streams of coolness.

The crowd roused itself.

The rumble of voices was carried above the crowd.

Everything became distinct all around. It was as if the ancient masks had fallen, pulled off by an invisible hand.

Demonic malice was boiling all around, in the lassitude and delirium.

Fierce, satanic visages were visible everywhere. Dark mouths on dull faces were vomiting forth coarse words.

Lesha began to groan.

A red-haired devil, flashing his dry eyes, began to roar at him:

"You got here, so tough it out. We didn't ask you to come. Remember that, you dirty scum. We'll crush out your guts but good."

The raging Serpent enraged the people.

It seemed that the sun had risen swiftly and now suddenly it had become distant and merciless.

And it became so hot and stifling, and everyone was tormented by such a thirst.

Someone was sobbing.

Someone was praying pitifully:

"If there were only a little drop of water from the heavens!"

Katya was hiccuping.

Sometimes, some strangely and terrifyingly familiar faces came into sight. Like all the faces in this bestial crowd, they too were frozen in their terrible transfiguration.

It was even more terrifying to look at them than at the unfamiliar ones, because the bestiality of a familiar face was even more painful.

Lesha felt that someone was pressing on his shoulders. He pressed into the earth so heavily. Into the dark, cruel earth.

Someone was trying to climb upwards.

There were several intensely excruciating minutes. Then, for a brief instant, there was relief. Then the one who was climbing upwards, trod on Lesha's head with his boot. Lesha heard Nadya's quiet shriek.

Someone dark and corpulent walked over them to the side,

across shoulders and heads, and he was swaying strangely in the air.

Lesha raised his head to breathe in the air of the high open space. But it was hot up there.

The clear, triumphant, unattainably high heavens were shining, tenderly dotted by the mother of pearl of fleecy clouds on their western half.

A sea of triumphant light flowed from the sun which had just risen. And the sun was new, bright, majestic and fiercely indifferent. Forever indifferent. And all of its splendor sparkled above the rumble of the languor and delirium.

Someone was stamping heavily on Lesha's feet.

Katya was hiccuping heavily and excruciatingly.

"Stop it!" Lesha cried hoarsely.

Katya began to laugh loudly. The laughter together with the hiccups was strange and pitiful.

And the heavy, unbroken rumble of cries, groans, and squeals now floated above the whole breadth of the field.

And then the moments of mutual, senseless malice began.

People were beating one another as much as the crush would allow. They kicked one another with their feet. They bit one another. They grabbed one another by the throat and strangled one another.

The weaker ones were squeezed to the earth, and people were standing on them.

Cries and groans, prayers and curses, everything that Lesha heard he was repeating in a lifeless, suffocating voice, and like two dolls now, both sisters were babbling the same thing after him.

XIV

The prayers and groans suddenly became quiet and somnolent.

There was a short and strange half hour of calm, of languor, of fatigue without end, of a quiet, terrible delirium.

The rumbling of delirium floated above the crowd; it was a quiet rumbling, so oppressive, so terrible.

And now the delirium spread to everyone and the terrible consciousness of death barely glimmered to all three of them through the smoke of the delirium.

Both sisters were hiccuping heavily.

"You poor little angel!"—cried out someone nearby.

The morning drowsiness of the people half-crushed in the crowd was broken from time to time by wild cries of despair.

And again it became quiet and the terrible rumbling was floating above the crowd, but not ascending to the triumphant expanses, to the unmoving, evil Serpent of the heights.

Someone was hiccuping excruciatingly. It seemed that it was someone dying excruciatingly.

Lesha listened attentively and he understood that it was Nadya hiccuping.

With an effort, Lesha turned his head towards her.

Nadya's blue lips were opening and closing with a strange, mechanical movement. Her eyes were unseeing and her face took on a lackluster, deathlike hue.

XV

The languid period of calm flew by. And suddenly a storm of absurd rumblings and wails began to howl above the troubled crowd. Wild exclamations were beating the air.

It was obvious by the faces distorted with malice, that there were no people there. The devils had torn off their instantaneous masks and were rejoicing excruciatingly.

Several persons in the crowd suddenly went insane during these minutes. They were howling and roaring and screaming something absurd and terrible.

Wild death cries burst forth from under people's feet—there, on the ground, thrown down, knocked off their feet, they were unable to get up.

And these cries were shaking the souls of a few who had still remained people in the terrible crowd of devils in human form.

A ragged hooligan was standing next to his debauched and drunken girlfriend. They were looking at one another and speaking malicious words. The hooligan was moving his shoulder strangely.

He freed his arm through the effort of rabid malice. A knife glistened in his hand. The quick steel began to tremble with sharp laughter in the sun's bright rays.

The knife pierced the whore's body. She began to scream: "Goddamn you!"

She choked on her scream. She died.

The hooligan yelled. He bent down to her. He was gnawing at her red, fat cheek.

"They've crushed us completely, we'll die now," said Katya in a hoarse voice.

Lesha looked at her out of the corner of his eye, began to laugh senselessly and said loudly and distinctly:

"They've crushed Nadya. She's cold."

And large tears were streaming down his face, but his pale lips were smiling senselessly.

Katya was silent. Her face began to turn blue and her eyes dimmed.

Lesha was suffocating.

His feet stepped on something soft. A sharp stench was rising from the ground. Something, wheezing heavily, was turning over down below.

"It stinks,"—a strangely indifferent voice was saying behind Lesha. "They felled an old woman and crushed her stomach."

Katya's blue face drooped strangely, lifelessly.

Suddenly Lesha felt cold.

XVI

"It's six o'clock," someone said.

One could tell by the voice that a sturdy, calm person, who was not terrified at being in the crowd, was speaking.

"Four more hours to wait," a timid, choking voice answered him.

"Wait for what?"—someone bellowed maliciously in a rumbling voice.

"We'll all die for sure," a woman's deep voice answered calmly and quietly.

Someone began to yell desperately in a broken, half-childish shout:

"Brothers, we're sure to go on choking for a long time!"

An agitated rumbling rushed across the field like a noisy flock of frightened, black-winged birds. It rushed about, began to howl, and swayed back and forth. And the crowd rushed to meet it.

"It's time, brothers!" someone's shrill voice was bawling. "Keep your wits about you, the devils will take everything for themselves."

"Go, go!"—was buzzing around.

Now the whole crowd was moving swiftly and heavily.

And the unmoving, inclined faces of his sisters, cold and heavy on his shoulders, were looking at Lesha.

The mashed hairs of his beloved ones were tickling Lesha's pale cheeks.

Their feet were not taking steps. The crowd carried all three of them, both Lesha and his sisters.

"They're passing out the stuff!"—someone began to shout.

One could see how some little multicolored bundles were flying in the air and it appeared that it was not far away.

"For free!" an exhausted, gaunt peasant wheezed sullenly.

"Why'd you stop, go on!" the ones behind were yelling furiously at the ones in front.

"They aren't letting our people in, those damned guys ahead are sneaking in and we're stopped here, waiting," someone was bawling fiercely.

And rabid screams were coming from all over.

"Brothers, go on, no matter what!"

"Yeah, why look at the devil, grab him by the throat, throw him underfoot!"

"Go on, forward, what're you looking at."

"They're not giving it out, they're taking it themselves."

"O—oh, they crushed me!"

"Oh my God, my guts have come out."

"Choke on your own guts, you goddamned scum."

"Knife that Astrakhan bitch."

"Come on, don't hold back!" a fierce voice was roaring up ahead.

XVII

Everywhere around, fierce, despairing faces were threatening.

A heavy stream. And the same malice. . . .

A knife slashed a dress. And the body.

She began to howl. She died.

So terrifying.

The faces of his beloved ones, so strangely blue, look at him lifelessly. . . .

Someone is laughing. About what?. . .

The end is near. There are the barn walls already. . . .

In a hefty fellow's raised hand, a mug was shining dully in the golden sunlight. And his arm was raised strangely and unnaturally toward the sky, like a living staff.

Someone threw his head upwards. He knocked the mug down—so weakly was it held by a hand turned blue from the strain.

The mug fell slowly, heavily, describing an arc. It slid along someone's back.

The hefty fellow swore nastily.

He was red, sweaty, and the whites of his eyes, bulging from the strain, seemed huge.

He bent down after the mug with great effort. One could see his elbows moving.

Suddenly he drooped and gave a muffled scream.

Someone fell onto his bent back. Fell and cried out. Floundering, he crawled forward along the fallen man's back. Someone else from behind leaned on both of them with his stomach. All three sank. Their muffled cries were heard. The one on top raised up and appeared to be very tall. The crowd flowed together above those thrown down, and by its heavy settling, one could see how they were pressing the two crushed ones to the earth.

A robust peasant with a face reddened to a purplish blue, moving his elbows and shoulders, freed his right hand and stretched it forward. They squeezed him. His red hand was dangling strangely on someone else's shoulder, near a red kerchief.

The old woman in the red kerchief turned around, seized hold of the robust peasant's hand with her teeth. Her spite was incomprehensible.

Howling fiercely, the peasant pulled his hand away. He started to work his elbows despairingly. It seemed that he was growing.

They had pushed him upwards. He fell on some heads and under him, spiteful voices began to rumble. He raised up on his knees on someone's shoulders. He fell again.

Falling, getting up, falling again, getting on all fours, he forced his way forward, and the crowd under him was like a solid, uneven bridge, like a heavily moving glacier.

And now, many were pushing their way upwards with their elbows.

One could see several people awkwardly running across shoulders and heads to the roofs of the refreshment counters.

And many had already climbed up to the roofs.

XVIII

Two old women grappled. They were silent, sullen. One stuck her fingers in the other's mouth and tore her mouth. Blood was visible. A desperate scream was heard.

They were using knives in order to pave the way, and they

pushed the dead underfoot. Sometimes the murderer fell on the dead person and both drooped under the feet of the throng of fierce devils.

Many fell into the ravine. Others collapsed on top of them. In a short time, the ravine was filled up with people who were howling grievously and dying excruciatingly. And the devils were trampling them with their feet, shod in heavy boots.

The red-haired fellow in front of Lesha had long ago climbed upwards, working his elbows despairingly, pressing on his neighbors' shoulders. He was yelling something indistinct, and he was laughing hoarsely.

At first it was impossible to understand what he wanted and what was the matter with him. Suddenly, he began to rise up quickly and in a short time he had closed off from Lesha's eyes all that was in front.

His absurd cries were falling into the dull crowd from above in sharp, hissing lashes, and it was strange to hear his vile voice which seemed to be coming down from the sky. And then his words became clear.

And his words were—blasphemy and abuse, and foul swearing.

Then he suddenly collapsed and hit Lesha on the forehead with his heel.

But he began to rise up again immediately. He was on all fours. He seized hold of a half-crushed girl's brown braid. He stood up on someone's shoulders.

He was red-faced, red-haired, laughing, walking unevenly forward over shoulders and heads, stepping indiscriminately with his heavy boots.

He was walking slowly above the compressed crowd like a devil, howling terribly, and he disappeared in the distance.

And again it seemed to Lesha through the terrible languor and nausea and the crimson fog in his eyes, that someone enormous, with his head up to the sky—and even higher—a person or a

devil or a person-devil, was walking on the heads of those dying in
the suffocating crowd of people and disgorging terrible blasphemy onto them.

The crowd in front broke through into the narrow aisles between the wooden huts. One could hear cries, screams, and
groans coming from there. Caps and shreds of clothing flashed in
the air for some reason.

Someone's brown head banged against the sharp corner of a
booth several times, drooped, was carried forward in a rush, and
suddenly disappeared.

It seemed that more and more tall people were crowding
together between the booths. It was strange to see heads on an
equal plane with the roof of a booth. People were walking over
the bodies of the fallen.

The triumphant roar of the victors came from out of the
booths. Some multicolored rags appeared for a moment—something was being thrown through the air.

And Lesha and his sisters were shoved into one of the aisles
between the booths.

It was unbearably crowded there—it seemed to Lesha that all
of his bones had been broken. And the broken bodies of his sisters
were weighing on his shoulders terrifyingly.

But the narrow aisle came to an end.

Beyond the booth it became spacious, light, joyful.

"I'll die right now," thought Lesha, and he began to laugh.

For an instant, Lesha caught sight of someone's red, happy
face, and a person who was brandishing a small bundle above his
head.

And he fell.

Both sisters collapsed on him. They half covered him up with
their crumpled bodies.

Lesha could hear how they were running over him, inching
along his back.

The fierce blows of the devil's feet were reverberating painfully
in his whole body.

Someone's heel stepped on the back of his head.
There was an instantaneous sensation of nausca.
Death.

The
Queen of Kisses

How unreasonable and frivolous are woman's cunning desires, and to what strange and seductive consequences they lead; to which the story here offered, very edifying and totally authentic, will serve as an example: it is about a certain beautiful lady who wanted to be the queen of kisses and about what happened because of it.

In a renowned and ancient city lived a rich old merchant by the name of Balthazar. He was married to a beautiful young maiden—for the demon, powerful alike over young and over old, had presented the maiden's attractions to him in such a charming light, that the old man could not resist their fascination. Once married, he experienced no little regret: his advanced age did not allow him to revel in the voluptuousness of conjugal nights to full measure, and jealousy soon began to torment him. And not without reason: the young mistress Mafalda—as his wife was called—growing bored with the meager caresses of her aged spouse, was looking at the handsome youths with lust. Because of his business, Balthazar had to be away from home for days at a time, and it was only during holidays that he could be with Mafalda uninterruptedly. And for this reason Balthazar had appointed a reliable old woman, Barbara, who was supposed to keep constant watch on his wife.

Life became boring for the young and passionate Mafalda: not only was it now impossible for her to kiss one of the handsome youths, but even a fond glance stealthily directed at one of them incurred stern reproaches and merciless punishment from her husband; the shrewish, wicked Barbara informed him of everything.

Once, on a stifling summer day, when it was so hot that even the sun dozed heavily and lost itself in the sky and then did not know where it was supposed to go—the right or left—old Barbara dropped off to sleep. Young Mafalda took off all her unnecessary clothing, leaving on only what would have been absolutely necessary even in paradise, and she sat on the threshold of her room and looked with sad eyes at the shadowy garden surrounded by high walls. Of course there was no one from the outside in the garden and indeed there could not have been, because the one and only gate had been securely boarded up long ago and the only way to get into the garden was through the house—and in the house, the firmly locked outside doors allowed no one in. The captive young mistress's sad eyes saw no one. Only the sharp shadows lay motionless on the sand of the swept pathways, and the trees with their leaves faded from the intense heat languished in the motionless silence of their bewitched life, and the flowers gave off a heady and stimulating fragrance.

And suddenly someone called to Mafalda in a quiet, but distinct voice:

"So what is it that you want, Mafalda?"

She should have remained silent, she should have gone to her rooms, she should have blessed herself against this impure witchcraft; but no, Mafalda remained. Mafalda roused herself. Mafalda looked all around with curiosity. Mafalda smiled cunningly and asked in a whisper:

"Who's there?"

And not far from her, in the rose bushes, where it smelled so languorous and tender, someone began to laugh quietly, but with such a ringing and sweet laugh that Mafalda's heart froze from an incomprehensible joy. Here she had only just begun to whisper with the cunning tempter—and already she had fallen under the power of his foul spell.

And once more the mysterious guest began to speak, and his seductive words gave off an aroma:

"Mistress Mafalda, what do you care about my name? And I can't reveal myself to you. But do hurry and tell me what you wish and what you are yearning for and I'll grant you everything, charming lady."

"Why don't you want to reveal yourself to me?" asked the curious Mafalda.

"Mistress you are so lightly clad," the mysterious visitor answered Mafalda, "your black braids are thick and long, but still they don't completely cover your ravishing legs—and if I were to come out to you now, mistress, you would be ashamed."

"It doesn't matter, no one will see us, Barbara's asleep," Mafalda said.

But the sleep of wicked old women who guard pretty young girls is light. Barbara heard her name and awakened. She stood on the threshold next to her mistress, looked around suspiciously and asked:

"Mistress Mafalda, whom were you talking with just now? Who was with you in the garden?"

"Who is there for me to talk to?" Mafalda answered vexedly. "No one was here and indeed, who could get into the garden? Except maybe an evil spirit and what would I have to say to him? That's no great delight!"

But the old woman shook her head distrustfully and muttered:

"The young wives of old husbands are crafty. I have a feeling that someone was here: it doesn't smell like the devil here, but rather like a young cavalier in a velvet beret and a red cloak. Twirling his black moustache with one hand and resting his other hand at his side, around the handle of his sharp sword, he was standing there, behind the rose bushes, saying things that your husband will pay you for in hard cash."

Night fell, but it did not cool off. The black night was just as suffocating and gloomy as the day had been. Cruelly beaten by her husband because of wicked Barbara's denunciation, Mafalda cried for a long time and did not want to go to sleep. Next to her, on her spouse's couch, the venerable merchant Balthazar snored quietly—after having enjoyed his punished wife's forced caresses to the extent that his old man's prowess would allow.

And suddenly Mafalda heard above her that same temptingly sweet voice once more:

"Well, hurry up and tell me, Mafalda, what is it you want? Hurry, before your husband wakes up, before someone finds out that I'm here."

And without losing a minute now, Mafalda raised herself up on the pillows and turned a lusting look into the night's darkness:

"I want to be the queen of kisses."

The mysterious visitor started to laugh and everything became quiet again. But Mafalda sensed a change within herself. She still did not know what the change consisted of, but she was already joyful. And she slept sweetly and soundly and dreamed joyful and passionate dreams. Many handsome youths approached her, and showered her with such ardent kisses, the likes of which it seemed, no one had known either in heaven or on earth. And Mafalda dreamed that her strength was never-ending, and that she could kiss all the youths of that town and many other towns and bestow upon all of them ardent caresses to the point of exhaustion and death.

And morning came and a great thirst for kisses began to burn in Mafalda's body. Her husband had just barely left for his business. Mafalda threw off all her clothes and decided to go out into the street. Barbara began to shout frantically, summoning the servants, and wanted to detain her mistress in the house by force. But with a swift blow, Mafalda knocked her wicked overseer to the floor, pushed away all the servants with her elbows and fists, and ran naked out into the street, howling loudly:

"Handsome youths, I am going to the crossroads of your streets, naked and beautiful and thirsting for your embraces and ardent caresses—I, the great queen of kisses. All of you, the bold and youthful, come to me, take pleasure in my beauty and wild

daring, drain the drink of love in my embraces which is sweet
unto death itself and more powerful than death itself. Come to
me, to me—the queen of kisses."

Having heard Mafalda's shrilly ringing summons, the youths
of that city came running quickly from all over.

The youthful Mafalda's beauty, and more than this beauty, the
demonic fascination overflowing in her body, which was fearlessly and boldly bared before all, enflamed the desires of the
gathering youths.

The youthful Mafalda opened up her passionate arms to the
first one of them and sated him with the bliss of ardent kisses and
passionate caresses. She gave up her beautiful body to his desires,
stretched out right there on the street, on her lover's wide cloak
which had been hastily spread out. And they quickly took pleasure in fervent caresses before the eyes of the lusting crowd of
youths who were emitting howls of passion and mad jealousy.

But the first lover's embraces were scarcely broken, he had
scarcely bent down to beautiful Mafalda's feet in passion's languor, wishing for a short rest to restore love's furious ardor, when
they dragged him away from Mafalda. And the second youth
took possession of Mafalda's body and torrid caresses.

The dense crowd of lusting youths clustered together above
the two who were exchanging caresses on the hard stones of the
street.

"The ground is hard for them there," said someone sensible
and kind, "let's lay our cloaks down for them and also make ready
a splendid couch for ourselves when our turn comes to lie with
the queen of kisses."

And in an instant, a whole mountain of cloaks rose up between
the streets.

And one after another, the youths threw themselves into Mafalda's fathomless embraces and one after another, walked away
utterly exhausted, but beautiful Mafalda lay on the soft couch of
cloaks of all colors, from bright red to the deepest black, and she
embraced and kissed and groaned from boundless passion and

from the thirst for kisses that nothing could quench. She howled in a reedy voice and from far around, her voice was heard calling out:

"Youths of this town and other towns and villages near and far, all of you, come into my arms, take pleasure in my love, for I am—the queen of kisses, and my fondling is inexhaustible and my love is infinite and tireless even unto death."

The swift-winged rumor spread through the town about the frenzied Mafalda who was lying bare on the crossroads of the streets giving up her body to the fondlings of the youths. Husbands and wives, old men and venerable mistresses, and children came to the crossroad and made a wide circle around the tightly gathered crowd of those who were in a frenzy. And they raised a loud cry, and reproached the shameless ones, and commanded them to disperse, threatening them with all of the strength of parental power and the wrath of God and severe punishment of the municipal authorities. But the youths only answered them with the howls of their inflamed passion.

And Balthazar came and threw himself at his wife, howling furiously, showering blows and biting. But the youths did not let him get to Mafalda. The old man grew weak and, standing at a distance, tore at his clothes and gray hair.

The town's elders arrived and ordered the shameless mob to disperse. But the youths did not obey and continued to crowd around the beautiful and bare Mafalda. And the priests' entreaties had no effect on them.

And the shameful event lasted for a long time and now the day was turning into evening.

Then the guard was summoned. The soldiers fell upon the youths, severely beat many of them, others they managed to drive away. But then they caught sight of Mafalda's seductive body, though by now it was crumpled by the many caresses, and they heard her reedy, ringing howl:

"I am—the queen of kisses. Come to me, all of you who are thirsting for love's delightful consolations."

The soldiers forgot their duty. And in vain the elders exclaimed:

"Take this insane Mafalda and carry her to the home of her spouse, the venerable Balthazar!"

The soldiers, like the youths before them, surrounded Mafalda and thirsted for her embraces. But because they were coarse people and could not take turns like the courteous and modest local youths who were well brought up by pious parents, they began to fight and while one of them was embracing Mafalda, the others readied their weapons in order to decide by the might of the sword who should take pleasure in Mafalda's incomparable charms. And many were wounded and killed.

The elders did not know what to do. They gathered on the street near the place where the frenzied Mafalda was howling in the soldiers' embraces and showering them with tireless caresses.

An event which, in any other circumstances would have had to be considered terrible, came to the aid of the town's elders who were stricken by helpless anger and shame. One of the soldiers, young and weak—in comparison with the others—but no less passionate than they, could not wait for an opportunity to get near Mafalda's seductive body. He walked around the place where the delightful kisses resounded, where inexhaustible love gave his comrades a bliss incomparable to anything, and his comrades pushed him away from this beloved place and rudely laughed at him. And he lay on the hard stones of the bridge which were cold now, for a whole day had passed and the night's darkness was thickening above the town—he lay on the stones, covered his head with his cloak, and began to howl plaintively from the offense, and the shame, and his impotent desire. Inflamed with malice, he stealthily seized his dagger, and very quietly, like a snake, slithering in the grass, he crawled between the legs of the crowded soldiers. And he drew close to Mafalda. He felt her cold legs with his burning hands and he thrust his swift dagger into her trembling side.

A loud scream resounded and there was a broken wail. Mafalda lay dying in the arms of the soldier caressing her, and she was moaning more and more quietly. She began to wheeze. She died.

Spattered with her blood, the soldier raised up.

"Someone has knifed the queen of kisses!" he began to yell fiercely. "Someone wicked has prevented us from taking pleasure in the caresses which no one on earth had known because the queen of kisses came to us for the first time."

The soldiers were confused. And they were standing around the body.

Then the old men who were passionless from the length of years they had lived, came up and picked up Mafalda's body and carried it into the house to old Balthazar.

That very night, the young soldier who had killed Mafalda, entered her house. How it happened that no one noticed him and stopped him—I don't know.

He drew close to Mafalda's body which was lying on the bed—there still had not been a coffin made for the deceased— and he lay beside her on her red bedspread. And the dead Mafalda opened her cold arms for him and embraced him powerfully and until morning she answered his kisses with her kisses—cold and gratifying as death which comforts; and she answered his caresses with caresses dark and deep like death, like the eternal liberator from entanglements—death.

And when the sun rose and pierced the dusk of the quiet chamber with its burning rays, at this terrifying and languid hour, at dawn, the young warrior died in the embrace of the bare and dead Mafalda, queen of kisses, on her red cover. And breaking their embrace, the beautiful Mafalda smiled at him for the last time.

I know that unreasonable wives and maidens could be found who would call the fate of beautiful Mafalda, the queen of kisses, sweet and glorious—and one could find youths, so senseless as to envy the death of her last lover who was most affectionate to her. But you venerable, virtuous ladies who remove just your gloves for kisses, you, who so love the charms of the familiar hearth and the decency of your home, beware of frivolous desire, chase away the cunning tempter.

The Search

The pleasant in life is interwoven with the unpleasant. It is pleasant to be a student in the first grade—it makes for a certain standing in the world. But unpleasantnesses also occur in a first grader's life.

Day was breaking. People were walking, talking. Shura awakened and his first impression was that he felt something tearing. That was unpleasant. Something was crumpling under his side—and later there arose the more distinct impression of a torn and crumpled undershirt. It was torn under the arms and he could tell that the rip went almost to the very bottom.

Shura was annoyed. He remembered that just yesterday he had said to his mother:

"Mama, give me a clean undershirt; this undershirt has a little rip under the arms."

But his mother had answered:

"Wear it again tomorrow, Shurochka."

Shura frowned, as he loved to do when things didn't go his way, and said vexedly:

"Mama, it'll be all torn by tomorrow. So I'll have to go around like a ragamuffin!"

But his mother, not pausing in her work,—as if she had time to be sewing all the time!—said in a displeased voice:

"That's enough, Shurka, I don't have time for your goings on. What kind of fashion have you started—pestering your mother! I've already said that you could change tomorrow evening. If you got into less mischief, your clothes would be in one piece. They just burn up on you, you'll never have enough."

Shura wasn't a mischievous boy at all. He began to grumble:

"How can I get into less mischief? It's impossible. I don't get into much trouble. And if I do, then that's because it just has to be, there's no way out."

But his mother had not given him the shirt. And look what had happened! The shirt was torn all the way down to the hem. Now it would have to be thrown away. What a wasteful mother!

On the other side of the wall, he could hear his mother moving about busily, to get out of the house. Shura recalled that his mother had a good practice—one that meant long hours but good money. This was fine of course, but now his mother would leave and Shura would have to set off in a torn shirt—and what would it be like by evening?

Shura quickly jumped up, threw the blanket on the floor and ran to his mother, loudly banging along the cold floor with his bare feet. He cried out:

"Here, mama, just look! Didn't I tell you yesterday that you should give me a different shirt, but you didn't want to, and now look what's happened to it!"

His mother glanced angrily at Shura. She reddened with vexation. She began to grumble:

"Next you'll be running out naked. What a disgrace! You can't do a thing with such a spoiled child."

She took Shura by the shoulder and led him to her bedroom. Shura's heart skipped a beat. His mother said:

"You know that I'm in a hurry, but you still poke along. What a bother I have with you!"

But she had already seen that it was impossible to leave the boy in that shirt. She had to go to the closet, get a new shirt, one that had never been worn, because the others were still at the laundry and would not be brought back until evening.

Shura was happy. It pleased him to put on a new undershirt—it was so rough and cold and it was fun the way it tickled his skin.

While dressing, he laughed and fooled around, but his mother had absolutely no time to spend with him and she hurriedly left the house.

II

At school, as always, it was strange: fun and boring, lively and unnatural. It was fun during the break between classes, and boring during class itself.

The subjects which they had to study in class were strange and totally unnecessary: People who had died long ago and never done anything good, but whom for some reason one still had to remember after so many centuries, even though some of them had perhaps never existed; Verbs, which were conjugated with something; Nouns which were declined somewhere, but for which there was no living place in the living language; Figures, about which it was difficult to prove what was totally unnecessary to prove; and Many Other Things equally ridiculous and alien. And the one essential thing was lacking in all of this—there was no Link of Correlations, there was no direct answer to the eternal question: Why and Wherefore.

III

That morning, before prayers, Mitya Krynin came up to Shura in the hallway. He asked:

"Well, did you bring it?"

Shura remembered that yesterday he had promised to bring Krynin a little book of contemporary songs. He thrust his hand in his pocket—there was no book there. He said:

"Oh, I must have left it in my coat. I'll bring it right away."

He ran to the cloakroom. Just then the guard pressed on the buttons of the electric bells, and throughout the huge and boring school building, their sharp voices began to crackle. It was time to go to prayers—it was impossible to begin classes without them.

Shura rushed. He thrust his hand in a coat pocket and found

nothing, then he suddenly saw that it was someone else's coat, and he cried out angrily:

"Now that's something, I've got into someone else's coat."

And he began to search for his own.

Next to him a mocking laugh rang out. The unpleasant voice of the troublemaker Dutikov startled Shura by its unexpectedness. Dutikov, late for school and just coming in, yelled:

"Hey, brother, what are you doing getting into other people's pockets?"

Shura muttered angrily:

"What's it to you, Dutka? It's not your pocket."

He found the booklet and ran into the hall where the students were already at prayers, lined up in long rows according to height, so that the small ones stood at the front, closer to the icons, the taller ones behind, and in each row, the boys on the right were taller than those on the left. The teachers thought that one should pray according to height and in rows, otherwise nothing would come of it. In addition, boys were standing at the side who were good at singing church songs, and one of them each time they had to sing, would give a soft howl in various voices—which was called setting the pitch. They sang loudly, quickly, and without expression as if they were beating a drum. The student on duty read from the prayer book those prayers which were meant for reading rather than singing, and he read just as loudly and with the same lack of expression. In a word, everything was as it always was.

But after the prayers, there was an incident.

IV

Epifanov, a second grader, was missing his penknife and a silver ruble. The red-cheeked, chubby fellow discovered the theft and began to cry: the knife was a handsome one in a mother-of-pearl case, and the ruble was needed for the most pressing matters. He went to complain.

An investigation began.

Dutikov told how he had seen Shura Dolinin groping about in others' coatpockets in the cloakroom. Shura was called to the inspector's office.

The inspector, Sergey Ivanovich, fixed a suspicious gaze on the boy. It pleased the old teacher to think that here he was now, establishing the guilt of a little thief. Later there would be an emergency session of the Pedagogical Council, then the little thief would be expelled.

It would seem that there was nothing good in all of this. But the mischievous and disobedient little rascals had already given the old teacher a very rough time. With the malicious pleasure of a detective, he looked at the confused, blushing boy and slowly asked him questions:

"Why were you in the cloakroom during prayers?"

"It was before prayers, Sergey Ivanovich,"—Shura squeaked in a voice thin with fear.

"Let's assume that it was before prayers,"—the inspector agreed in an ironic tone of voice. "But I'm asking, 'why?'"

Shura explained why. The inspector continued:

"Let's assume it was for the booklet. Why were you getting into someone else's pocket?"

"By mistake," Shura said mournfully.

"A regrettable mistake," observed the inspector, nodding his head reproachfully. "Come on now, you'd better tell me, didn't you take the knife and ruble by mistake? By mistake, huh? Let's take a little look in your pockets."

Shura began to cry and said through his tears:

"I didn't steal anything."

The inspector smiled. It was pleasant to make the boy cry. The child's tears were so beautiful and dense rolling down the flushed cheeks and there were three distinct streams: two trickles of tears from one eye, and one from the other.

"If you're not guilty, why're you crying then?" the inspector said in a mocking tone. "I didn't say that you stole. I assume that you made a mistake. You took what came into your hand, then forgot. Let's have a little feel in your pockets."

Shura hurriedly pulled out of his pockets all that childish nonsense that little boys keep, then turned both pockets inside out.

"There's nothing," he said irritably.

The inspector looked at him inquisitively.

"But couldn't something have slipped behind your clothes? Maybe the knife fell into your boots, huh?"

The bell rang. The guard entered.

Shura was crying. And everything around swam in a pink fog, in the mad fainting feeling of humiliation. They turned Shura around, groping him, and searched him. They undressed him little by little: they made him take off his shoes and they shook them out; they pulled his stockings down too, just in case; they took off his belt, shirt and pants. They shook out and examined everything.

And a bright joy pierced through all of the agony of shame, through the insult of the humiliating and unnecessary rite: the ripped undershirt had remained at home and the brand new, brand clean undershirt rustled under the coarse hands of the zealous pedagogue.

Shura stood in just his undershirt and cried. Noisy voices and happy cries could be heard behind the door.

The door banged, someone small, flushed, and smiling entered hurriedly. And through his shame, and through his tears and through the joy over his new undershirt, Shura heard a voice that was either happy or embarrassed and panting slightly from running:

"It's found, Sergey Ivanovich. Epifanov himself had them. There was a hole in his pocket—the knife and ruble fell into his boot. He felt something uncomfortable and found them."

Then they suddenly became affectionate to Shura. They stroked his head, comforted him, and helped him to get dressed.

V

First he was crying, then laughing. At home he cried and laughed all over again. He told his mother. He complained:

"They undressed me completely. It would have been great if I'd been in that torn undershirt."

Later. . .and what about later? His mother went to see the inspector. She wanted to make a scene. Then she wanted to file a complaint against him. But on the street she recalled that her child was exempt from paying tuition. No scene came out of it. Besides, the inspector greeted her very amiably. He apologized profusely. So what more should there be?

The humiliating sensation of the search remained with the boy. Thus this sensation was engraved in him: he had been suspected of theft, searched, and ordered to stand half-naked, and turn around in the hands of an eager person. Embarrassing? But of course it was an experience, useful for life.

And his mother said, crying:

"Who knows—when you grow up there will be still other things. Anything can happen among people."

The
Red-Lipped Guest

I

I want now to tell about how, in our time, someone was saved—who though not very deserving, is nonetheless our brother—saved from the evil charms of nocturnal sorcery through the words of a chaste Youth. Power is sometimes given to Satan for days and hours—but He who was born in order to justify life and to dethrone death always conquers.

II

For Nikolai Arkadevich Vargolsky, this winter was difficult and languorous.

He strayed further and further away from all of his friends, relatives, and acquaintances. He was ever more willing to sit out the short, dark days and the long, black nights in the despondent splendor of his old private residence, and he restricted himself to short walks through the thoroughly cleaned avenues of the shady small garden in front of his house.

Nikolai Arkadevich did not even entertain anyone except for a recent acquaintance, Lydia Rothstein, a pale, beautiful young girl with terribly huge eyes and excessively bright lips.

In former times, Nikolai Arkadevich had loved all the attractions of a happy, dissipated life. He had loved fashionable company, shows, music, and sporting events. He frequented those places where everyone was usually to be found. He had a lively interest in everything that all those in his circle found interesting, in those things that were generally accepted as interesting. He was young, independent, wealthy, reasonably often in company and reasonably often alone, and free, cheerful, happy, and healthy.

But now suddenly all of this had changed in a strange and absurd way. Life's multicolored charm had lost its power over him. The diversity of impressions and sensations in a varied and cheerful life was forgotten. Nothing attracted him. He wanted nothing.

Everything that had formerly stood before his eyes as bright and lively, was screened now by the pale, terribly beautiful face of his red-lipped guest.

And he wanted only to look into the bottomless depths of these strange, greenish eyes that seemed lifeless and forever bewitched with quietude and mystery. And he wanted only to see this maddeningly scarlet smile on the pale face, to see this large, straightly-slit mouth with such bright lips; as if this mouth had just been slit and was still smoking with fresh blood. And he wanted only to go on listening to the quiet, evil words falling slowly from these strange and bewitching lips.

Everything that was beyond those walls became so boring! All this external, noisy life that he had lived until now seemed so tiresome and unnecessary.

A sluggish laziness was spreading through his body which formerly had been so hearty and joyous. His head began to ache frequently and to spin languidly—full of confused, mad noises and sounds. His face became pale as if Lydia Rothstein's brightly colored lips were drinking up his whole life.

III

How did it begin? It was somehow vague now and he recalled it with reluctance.

They had become acquainted somewhere, in the dusky, cold light of an autumn evening. It seems they had been talking about something unimportant. Nikolai Arkadevich was busy with something that day and distracted. She was pale, taciturn, and uninteresting. They spoke for a moment, no longer. They parted—and Nikolai Arkadevich forgot about her, as one always forgets about chance, unnecessary meetings.

IV

Several days passed. Nikolai Arkadevich was finishing his breakfast. He was told that a Miss Lydia Rothstein wanted to see him.

Nikolai Arkadevich was a bit surprised. The name meant nothing to him. He had forgotten completely. He frowned vexedly. He asked the servant:

"Who's that? Is she a petitioner? If so, I'm not at home."

The handsome young servant Victor, who took pains to imitate his master in manners and dress, smiled the same lazy and self-assured smile that was on Nikolai Arkadevich's clean-shaven, cold lips and said, with the same drawl as his master:

"She doesn't look like a petitioner. She's more like one of those stylized young ladies. You can meet them anywhere at the shore."

Now cheerfully smiling Nikolai Arkadevich asked:

"So why especially at the shore?"

Victor answered:

"Well, that sir is the way it seems to me. Judging by a general impression. The first impression almost never deceives one. Besides, I can't recall the likes of her from the city girls."

Nikolai Arkadevich asked, continuing to imagine just who this stylized Rothstein girl could be:

"What does she look like?"

Victor started to tell him:

"Her attire is black, Parisian, in the style of Tanagra, very elegant and expensive. Unusual perfume. Extremely pale face. Black hair styled after Cleo de Mérode. Her lips are such an impossibly scarlet color that it's just amazing to look at them. Besides, it's impossible to suppose that lipstick could have been used."

"Ah, that's who it is!"

Nikolai Arkadevich remembered. He became very animated. He said, almost joyfully:

"Fine. I'll go to her right away. Show her into the green drawing room and ask her to wait a minute."

He quickly finished his breakfast and proceeded to the room where his guest was waiting.

V

Lydia Rothstein was standing by the window. She was looking at the magnificent play of colors on the crimson-yellow autumn leaves which looked as if they had been scorched. Shapely, tall, all in elegant black, she was standing as quietly and calmly as if she were not alive. It seemed as if she were not breathing, that not one fold of her severe dress was moving.

From the side, the outline of her face was severe and delicate. Her face was just as calm and lifeless as her body, which was frozen in immobility. Only the excessive scarlet color of her lips was alive on the pale face.

These lips were smiling at something with cruel tenderness, and they were timidly rejoicing at something.

Hearing the distinct sound of Nikolai Arkadevich's footsteps along the cold parquet of this severely beautiful drawing room, in which the greenish malachite stone predominated, Lydia Rothstein turned to face Vargolsky.

Her excessively scarlet lips were smiling at something with tender cruelty, her lips of a beautiful vampire, and they were timidly rejoicing at something. Their joy was evil and conquering.

With a look that irresistibly took the soul into indissoluble captivity, she looked directly into the depths of Nikolai Arkadevich's eyes. And there was a strange confusion in him and an uncertainty, unusual for him, when he heard her first words, said in a golden, ringing voice.

VI

She said:

"I came to you, because it was essential. Essential for me and for you. More correctly, unavoidable. Our paths met. We must submissively accept that which must inevitably happen to us."

Nikolai Arkadevich, with his usual, almost mechanical courtesy, invited her to be seated.

The usual skepticism of a man of society and one who is very urbane suggested to him that his red-lipped guest was simply an individual who was in a state of exaltation, and that her words were high-flown and absurd. But in his soul he felt an invincible fascination being directed at him by the cold flickering of her overly calm, greenish eyes. And in his soul there was not that tranquillity which had been until now its permanent and natural condition in all kinds of circumstances in his life, even the most eccentric.

Lydia Rothstein sat down in an armchair offered her by Nikolai Arkadevich. Slowly removing her gloves, she took in the room with a lingering glance—its walls with the malachite columns,—its ceiling painted by some cunningly wise artist at the end of century before last,—its antique furniture: all of these charming things, in which there was combined the appeal of a clever antiquity and the slightly corrupt, refined taste of that distant epoch of powdered wigs, affected courtesy, and cold cruelty. The old house of the Vargolskys was a creation of that epoch.

VII

Lydia Rothstein spoke quietly:

"How charming all of this is that surrounds you here! This house has, of course, its own legends. Perhaps at night the ghosts of your ancestors walk about in here."

Nikolai Arkadevich answered:

"Yes, as a child I heard something of the kind. But I myself have never managed to see any ghosts here. People of our century are inclined to be skeptical. Ghosts are afraid to show themselves to us; we are too alive and too derisive."

Lydia asked:

"What do they have to fear?"

Nikolai Arkadevich answered, trying to maintain a light and joking tone:

"Electric light is harmful to them and our laughter is fatal to them."

Lydia repeated quietly:

"Electric light! The most terrifying ghosts for people are those that come in the daytime. In the daytime the way I came. Doesn't it really seem to you that I'm like one of those ghosts that comes during the day? I am so pale."

Nikolai Arkadevich said:

"That's becoming to you. You are charming."

He wanted to be slightly derisive. But against his will, his words sounded tender, like the words of love.

Lydia said:

"Perhaps I'll pass before you, like one of the ghosts of your old home, and I will disappear, banished by your skeptical smile, like those ghosts whom you have already banished. If you have banished them. Anyway, let's forget about them, those ghosts. I can only be with you today for a short time, but I must tell you many things. Or, perhaps, you don't want to hear me out?"

"Please, I am completely at your service," said Nikolai Arkadevich.

VIII

Lydia was silent for a while, and continued:

"My name is Lydia, but I prefer to be called Lilith. A dreamy youth called me that—one of those whom I loved. He died. He died as all have, whom I've loved. My love is fatal—and it is all right with me, because my love and my death are more joyful than life and sweeter than poison."

Nikolai Arkadevich remarked:

"If poison is sweet."

He was trying to smile lightly and jokingly, but his smile was pale and powerless.

With a cold, almost lifeless insistence, Lydia repeated her words:

"Sweeter than poison. Lilith's soul is in me, the lunar, cold soul of Eden's first maiden, Adam's first wife. The earthly, daily, coarse sun is hateful to me, to pale Lilith. I do not like daily life and its hideous achievements. I summon those whom I have loved to cold tranquillity. I summon them to the raptures of boundless and impossible love. I cover the hideous, savage world of daily existence with a shroud of dreams which are sweeter than the most aromatic of earth's fragrant banes. I cover this lackluster world with a bright, multicolored shroud before the eyes of my lovers. My embraces are strong, and my kisses are sweet. And, as a reward for the boundlessness and the impossibility of my consolations I ask of the one whom I will love, only a small gift, a meager gift. Only a drop of his hot blood for my veins which are growing cold, I ask of the one I have loved only a drop of blood."

The golden sounds of her speech, poisoned by the strange and terrifying desire, resounded with the charm of great sadness and boundless melancholy. In the cold depths of her eyes, a cold, green flame flared up—and the flickering of this flame bewitched and weakened Nikolai Arkadevich's will. He remained seated and kept silent, listening to his green-eyed, red-lipped guest's quiet words resounding like gold.

IX

And she said:

"Just one drop of blood. I will press my lips to my lover's body. Like a vampire come from the grave, I will bite with my eternally thirsting lips into the dear, hot spot between the throat and the shoulder, between the throat where life's breathing pulsates and the shoulder's white slope, where life's intense power slumbers. I will bite, bite into the sweet fruit of my lover and drink up a drop of his hot blood. One drop—or perhaps two, three or even four. Ah, my lover does not count! My lover would not regret giving all his blood—only that I, the cold one, should be revived by the hot pulsation of his own life,—only that I should not go away from him, that I not disappear, I, who am like a pale, lifeless ghost, disappearing before the early crow of the cock."

Trying to smile, Nikolai Arkadevich said:

"Everything you say is, of course, very interesting and original, but I don't understand what relationship I have to all of this."

But right away he felt the whole superfluity and untruth of his own pitiful answer. And that is why, as he was speaking, his voice was becoming more muffled and weaker, and he spoke the last words very quietly, almost in a whisper.

X

Lilith got up. She walked up to him. In her movements, there was not that impetuous passion with which earthly women pronounce their confessions.

Standing in front of Vargolsky, and looking directly into his eyes with the cold look of her terrifying eyes in which the green, dead fire was flickering, she said:

"I love you. I have chosen you, my lover."

Submitting to the golden sound of her voice, he got up from his place. And they were standing, one opposite the other—she, pale-faced, green-eyed, with excessively bright lips like a vampire, and completely cold, like one not alive, the lunar Lilith,—and he, bewitched and as if he had lost all of his will.

Lilith said:

"Love me, my lover. Better and more powerfully than you have loved your daily life, love me, your lunar, cold Lilith."

A moment of silence fell. It seemed then that not one word had been spoken.

And then Lilith asked him:

"My lover, do you love me? Do you?"

Vargolsky answered her quietly:

"I do love you."

And he felt his soul drowning in the green transparency of her quiet eyes.

And again Lilith asked him:

"My beloved, do you love me more powerfully than all of the charm and fascination of daily life, me, your lunar, your cold Lilith?"

Vargolsky answered her—and there was the coldness of great tranquillity in the sound of his quiet words:

"My lunar, my cold Lilith, I love you more powerfully than all the charms of daily life. And I renounce them now and reject them all, for your one cold kiss."

Lilith smiled joyfully, but her joyfully cold smile was insidious and evil. And Lilith asked:

"Will you give me a drop of your precious blood?"

Sensing that, in his soul, terror and rapture were springing up and interweaving in a wonderful struggle, Vargolsky said, reaching out his arms to her:

"I will give you, my Lilith, all of my blood because I love you boundlessly and forever."

And she clung to his lips in a long and languid kiss. A dark and languid self-oblivion overshadowed Vargolsky and he never could remember distinctly what happened to him later.

XI

From that day on, Lydia Rothstein visited Nikolai Arkadevich at indeterminate times, sometimes more often, sometimes less often, almost always unexpectedly, at a different hour, sometimes during the day, sometimes in the evening, sometimes late at night. Somehow she always managed to find him at home. And later, when he had almost completely cut himself off from people, this became easy.

These meetings with Lilith were always wrapped up in Vargolsky's consciousness with a thick shroud of strange oblivion that he found almost annoying. One thing he knew without a doubt—however strong Lilith's embraces were, however madly wild her kisses, their relationship continued to remain aloof from coarse, earthly achievements, and not once did this strange, red-lipped guest with the tender eyes and the apocryphal name, give herself to him.

When she was pressing to his shoulder, a light, sharp pain penetrated Vargolsky's whole body,—and then he experienced a sweetness and languor. Terrible sensations of intense heat and cold were alternating in his body—as if fever were striking him.

Lilith's intensely hot, hungry lips, the only living things in the cold of her body, were biting into his skin. Their kiss was like the cold fury of a sting. And it seemed to him then that his blood was oozing away, drop by drop.

XII

Lilith disappeared unnoticed.

For a long time after her departure, Vargolsky lay, immersed in languid debility, not thinking about anything, recalling nothing, not dreaming about anything. He wasn't even dreaming about or recalling Lilith then. The very features of her face were vague and indefinite in his memory.

Sometimes he thought about her afterwards, when that feeling of immobility into which her caresses had plunged him, passed by. He thought sometimes that she was not a person, but a vampire, sucking his blood, that she would destroy him, that he must protect himself from her. But these brief, sluggish thoughts did not ignite his weakened will. He did not care.

Sometimes he asked himself whether or not he loved Lilith. But, listening attentively to the dark voices of his soul, he did not find the answer to this question in them. And there was a cold, calm indifference in him. Whether he loved her or not—wasn't it all the same!

XIII

Nikolai Arkadevich's servant, Victor, was married. Once,

shortly before Christmastime, he came to Nikolai Arkadevich, not at the fixed time, and said to him:

"My wife, Natalya Ivanovna, was delivered the other day, and she asks you, Nikolai Arkadevich, to do us the great honor and favor of being godfather to our first-born son, our newborn babe, Nikolai."

Victor tried to maintain his usual calm, sedate tone, but at these last words, he remembered with all the acuteness of novelty that he was a father now, and he blushed from joy and pride and began to laugh with an unexpected, almost countrified simple-heartedness. But he immediately controlled himself and once more began to behave decorously and sedately. He said, with his usual dignity:

"And I, for my part, take the liberty of joining my wife's request. We'll consider it our great honor and we will be extremely glad."

Nikolai Arkadevich congratulated the happy father. He agreed right away,—not because he wanted to agree to it, but simply because sluggish indifference had already settled in him long ago.

And the strange thing was that this event, so apparently insignificant in his life, brought about an abrupt change in his relationship to Lilith and with a kind of unexpected force.

The very first time he saw the infant Nikolai, whom he had had to call his godson, he experienced a tender emotion for this weakly whimpering, red, wrinkled ball of flesh, wrapped in soft, neat diapers. The babe's eyes still could not fix on nearby objects, but there was an earthly soul joyously flickering in them; it had been created anew out of the dark, earthly languor, and it trembled with thirst for a new life.

Nikolai Arkadevich recalled the green, terrible little flames in the lifeless eyes of his pale guest with the excessively red lips. Suddenly his heart was wrung with horror and with a passionate melancholy for life that was noisy, joyous, many-colored, diverse.

XIV

When he returned home to the flickering quiet of his high chambers after the joyful christening ceremony, in which he had taken a small part, he again felt weak and indifferent to everything.

There, at Victor's, he had been reminded that today was Christmas Eve.

Just where would he meet the holiday? How would he pass it? For a long time now, for more than a month, he had stubbornly received no one and had himself not been to see anyone.

But over his cold indifference there now arose his godson's quietly gleaming little eyes, his weak whimper. And they reminded him of the Babe in the manger, and the star above the wondrous cave, and of the Magi bearing gifts. All that had been forgotten, that had been blown away by the cold breath of a dissipated, social life was called to mind again, and again it tormented his soul with a sweet presentiment of rapture.

Vargolsky took a book which he had not opened now for many years. He read through the touching, simple, and wise stories about the birth and childhood of Him who came to us to justify and gladden our poor, earthly, daily life, who was born in order to dethrone and conquer death.

His soul was trembling and tears came to his eyes.

Suddenly Vargolsky remembered the evil delusions of his insidious guest. How could he have given himself up to their deceitful fascination! When dear, innocent smiles blossom on earth, when children's dear, innocent eyes laugh and rejoice!

But of course, she, the lunar, lifeless, deceitful Lilith would come again. And she would bewitch him again with the charm of death's quietude!

But who could help? Who could save him?

The book fell weakly from Nikolai Arkadevich's hands. No prayer rose up in his weakened soul.

And how could he have begun to pray? To whom and about what?

How could he pray, if she, lunar, cold Lilith is already there, behind the door?

XV

Now he feels that she is standing there, behind the door, in a strange indecisiveness; and she lingers, hesitating on the threshold that is terrifying for him and her.

Her face is pale, as always. A cold flame is in her eyes. Her lips blossom with terrible brightness, like the fierce lips of a fugitive from the grave who has feasted upon hot blood, the lips of a vampire.

But Lilith overcame the fear which had stopped her for the first time at that threshold. With a movement quick as never before, she flung open the high door and entered. Her black dress gave off the terrible aroma of tuberose, the breath of fragrant, cold decay.

Lilith said:

"My beloved, here I am with you again. Greet me, love me, kiss me—grant me just one more drop of your precious blood."

Nikolai Arkadevich put out his arms towards her in a threatening and restraining movement. He made a terrible effort over himself in order to say:

"Go away, Lilith, go away. I do not love you, Lilith. Go away forever."

Lilith was laughing. The trembling of her excessively scarlet lips, doomed to languish in eternal thirst, was terrifying and pitiful. And she said:

"My dear, my beloved, you are ill. Who is speaking with your lips? You are saying things that you do not think, that you do not want to say. But I will take you in my embraces, I, your lunar Lilith. Again I will clasp you to my breast which breathes so calmly. Again I will press my scarlet, thirsting lips to your shoulder, I, your lunar, your cold Lilith."

Lilith slowly drew close to him. There was an irresistible charm in her laughing, scarlet lips. And the golden sound of her words was heard:

"Today I will cling to you with a final kiss. I will lead you away forever from the deceitful charms of life. In my embraces you will find now the blessed peace of eternal self-oblivion."

And she was drawing closer, slowly, irresistibly. Like fate. Like death.

XVI

Just when her extended hands were almost touching his shoulder, a wondrous light began to glow softly between them. A Youth in a white tunic stood between them. A wondrous light streamed from his head, as if it were radiating from his curly hair. His eyes were benevolent and stern and his face was beautiful.

The Youth raised his hand, pushed Lilith aside with authority and said to her:

"Wretched, cursed soul, eternally thirsting, cold, lunar Lilith, go away. The time has still not come, the period of waiting has not been fulfilled—go away, Lilith, go away. There is still not peace between you and the children of Eve,—go away, Lilith, go away. Disappear, Lilith, go away from here forever."

A light moan was heard and reedlike, quiet crying. Pale in the dusk of the half-lighted chamber, slowly fading away, Lilith quietly disappeared.

Brief moments passed—and then the wondrous Youth was no longer there, and everything was as always, ordinary, simple, in place. It was as if Lilith's evil appearance had been but a faint daydream of half sleep, and it was as if the wondrous Youth had not come.

Only an exultant joy was ringing and singing in the soul of the tormented, exhausted man. It was telling him that the pale, cold, lunar Lilith, evil enchantress with the excessive scarlet of her madly thirsting lips, would never return to him. Never!

The
Kiss of the Unborn

I

In the office of a large business firm, a bright young boy with close-cropped hair and two rows of tiny brass buttons on his tight jacket—it was dusty but didn't show it because it was gray—glanced through the door of the room where the five typists were at work, pounding away simultaneously on five noisily rattling machines, and taking hold of the lintel and swinging on one foot, he said to one of the girls:

"Nadezhda Alekseevna, Mrs. Kolymtseva wants you on the phone."

He ran off and his steps were inaudible on the gray mat extending down the narrow corridor. Nadezhda Alekseevna, a tall, shapely girl of about twenty-seven, with confident, quiet movements and with that profound look of tranquillity which is given only to those who have experienced difficult days, finished typing to the end of the line, stood up and unhurriedly walked downstairs to the room by the entry where the telephone was. She was thinking:

"What's happened now?"

She was now used to the fact that if her sister Tatyana Alekseevna wrote to her or phoned her, it was almost always because something had happened in the family: the children were sick, there was something unpleasant at her husband's work, some event in the school where the children went, or an acute attack of money troubles. Then Nadezhda Alekseevna would take a streetcar and set off for the outlying district of the city—to help, to console, to come to the rescue. Her sister was some ten years older than Nadezhda Alekseevna, she had been married for a long time; and although they lived in the same city, they did not see one another often.

In the cramped telephone booth, where for some reason it always smelled of tobacco, beer, and mice, Nadezhda Alekseevna took the receiver and said:

"Hello. Is it you Tanichka?"

She heard her sister's voice, tear-filled and agitated, just exactly as Nadezhda Alekseevna had expected it to be:

"Nadya, for God's sake, come right away. We've had a horrible misfortune, Seryozha is dead, he shot himself."

Not having had time to be frightened by this unexpected news about the death of her fifteen-year-old nephew Seryozha, Nadezhda Alekseevna somewhat confusedly and disjointedly said:

"Tanya, dear, what are you saying! How horrible! But why? When did it happen?"

And, neither expecting nor listening to the answer, she said hurriedly:

"I'll come right away, right away."

She threw down the receiver, even forgetting to put it on the hook, and quickly went to the supervisor to ask for leave due to family circumstances.

The supervisor allowed her to leave, although he made a dissatisfied face and growled:

"You know it's a very busy time before the holidays. All of you always have something urgent happening at the most inopportune time for us. Well, okay, go on if you have to, but just remember that the work's piling up."

II

Several minutes later, Nadezhda Alekseevna was already on the streetcar. She had to travel about twenty minutes. During that time, Nadezhda Alekseevna's thoughts turned again in that direction they always took at those moments in life, when life's all-too-frequent surprises, almost always unpleasant, destroyed the tedious flow of the days. But Nadezhda Alekseevna's feelings were vague and suppressed. Only from time to time the deep pity for her sister and for the boy suddenly caused her heart to contract painfully.

It was terrifying to think that this fifteen-year-old boy, who just the other day had come to Nadezhda Alekseevna and talked with her for a long time, this formerly cheerful schoolboy Serezha had suddenly shot himself. It was painful to think about how his mother would grieve and weep—she, who without this, was already wearied by a difficult and not very successful life. But perhaps there was something else more difficult and terrifying hanging over her life, that prevented Nadezhda Alekseevna from giving herself up to these feelings—and her heart, crowded with long-standing sorrow, was incapable of being sweetly exhausted by the torments of grief, pity, and terror. It was as if the source of assuaging tears was weighed down by a heavy stone—and only meager, occasional little tears welled up sometimes in her eyes whose usual expression was one of indifferent boredom.

Again her memory took Nadezhda Alekseevna back to that same passionate, flaming circle through which she had passed. She was remembering several years before, when she had lived those few days of self-oblivion and passion, of love, given without measure.

The bright summer days were like a holiday for Nadezhda Alekseevna. The heavens turned a joyful blue for her, above the wretched expanses of the Finnish countryside, and the summer rainshowers made amusing, happy noises. The odor of resin in the warm pine forest was more sweetly intoxicating than the fragrance of roses, which did not grow in that region that was so gloomy, but still gladdened the heart. The greenish-gray moss in the dark forest was like a sweet bed of bliss. The forest brook, streaming among the gray, awkwardly scattered stones, murmured so joyfully and sonorously, as if its transparent water were rushing straight for the fields of happy Arcady; and the coolness of those sonorous streams was delightful and joyful.

The happy days raced by so quickly for Nadezhda Alekseevna in the delightful ecstasy of being in love, and the final day came, but of course she did not know it was to be the final happy day. As always, everything about was cloudless and bright and artlessly delightful. As always, the vast shadow of the forest was cool and pensive, redolent with resin, and as always, the warm moss was joyfully tender underfoot. Only the birds had already ceased to sing—they had built their nests and were raising their young.

But there was a vague shadow on her beloved's face. It was because he had received an unpleasant letter that morning.

As he said himself:

"It's a terribly unpleasant letter. I am desperate. I won't be able to see you for several days!"

"Why?"—she asked.

And she still had no time to be sad. But he said:

"My father writes that mother is ill. I have to leave."

His father had written something quite different, but Nadezhda Alekseevna did not know about that. She still did not know that love can be deceived, that lips which have kissed, can tell a lie as well as the truth.

He said, embracing and kissing Nadezhda Alekseevna:

"There's nothing I can do; I have to go! What a bore! I'm sure it's nothing serious, but still I can't not go."

"Yes, of course," she said,—"if your mother is sick, then you must go! But write to me every day. I'll miss you so!"

She accompanied him, as always, to the large road at the edge of the forest, and then she walked home along the forest path, somewhat saddened, but convinced that he would soon return. But he did not return.

Nadezhda Alekseevna received several letters from him—they were strange letters. There was a touch of embarrassment in them, a sense of reticence, some kind of incomprehensible hints that frightened one. And these letters came less and less often. Nadezhda Alekseevna grew to suspect that he had ceased to love her. And suddenly she learned from strangers, in a chance conversation at the end of that summer, that he was already married.

"How is it that you didn't hear? Last week, right after the wedding, they took off for Nice."

"Yes, he's a lucky one—he caught a rich and beautiful wife."

"She had a big dowry?"

"I'll say! Her father. . . ."

She had already ceased listening to what the father had. She walked away.

She often thought back on everything that had happened afterward. She didn't want to remember—Nadezhda Alekseevna tried to drive away those memories, to stifle them in herself. It had been so difficult and demeaning, and so unavoidable then, during those first difficult days after she had learned about his marriage—and having sensed herself to be a mother there, among those dear places where she was still reminded of his caresses—having just felt the first movements of a new being, to be thinking already of its death. And to kill the unborn!

No one from home found out; Nadezhda Alekseevna thought up a plausible pretext for being away from home for two weeks. Somehow, with great difficulty, she got together the money needed to pay for a wicked deed. It was in some vile refuge that they had performed the terrible deed, the details of which she did not want to remember later, and she returned home, still half-sick, emaciated, pale, and weak, a pitiful heroism covering up her pain and terror.

Recollections about the details of this deed were persistent, but still Nadezhda Alekseevna was able somehow to deny them lasting power over her memory. She would recall everything quickly, hastily, then shudder from terror and loathing—and hasten to distract herself from those pictures with something.

But what was persistent and what Nadezhda Alekseevna could not and did not want to struggle with, was the dear and terrifying image of the unborn one, her child.

When Nadezhda Alekseevna was alone and sitting calmly with her eyes closed, a small child would come to her. It seemed to her that she could see how he was growing up. So lifelike were these sensations, that at times it seemed to her as if she were experiencing, year after year, day after day, all that a true mother of a living child does. At times it seemed to her that her breasts were full of milk. Later she shuddered when she heard the noise of some falling object—perhaps her child had hurt itself.

Sometimes Nadezhda Alekseevna wanted to have a talk with him, take him in her arms and caress him. She held out a hand to smooth the soft, golden-light hair of her son, but her hand met emptiness and she imagined that behind her back she heard the laughter of her child who had run off and hidden somewhere nearby.

She knew his face—it was her own child, even if he had not been born. She saw his face clearly—the dear and terrible combinations of her features with those of the one who had taken her love and discarded it, who had taken her soul and drained it and then forgotten it—his features, which in spite of everything, remained dear.

His happy, gray eyes are from his father. The fine little shells of his pink ears are from his mother. The soft outline of his lips and his chin are his father's. The rounded, delicate shoulders, similar to the shoulders of a young girl, are from his mother. The golden, slightly wavy hair is from his father. The endearing dimples on his rosy cheeks are from his mother.

Thus Nadezhda Alekseevna sorts out everything, both the little hands and feet, and recognizes everything. She knows everything. She recognizes his habits—how he holds his hands, how he crosses one leg over the other—he took this from his father, even though the unborn one had not seen his own father. He begins to laugh and looks askance, blushing tenderly and bashfully—this is from his mother, the unborn one took this from his mother.

It is sweet and painful. It is as if someone cruel and dear opened up a deep wound with a tender, pink little finger—it is so painful! But it is impossible to banish him.

"And I don't want to, I don't want to banish you, my unborn child. At least live, as you are able to. At least I will give you this life."

Only a life in dreams. He only exists in her. My dear, poor unborn one! You yourself do not rejoice, you yourself do not laugh for yourself, you yourself do not cry for yourself. You live, but there is no you. In the world of the living, among people and objects, there is no you. So alive, and dear, and bright—and there is no you.

"Oh what have I done with you!"

And Nadezhda Alekseevna was thinking:

"He's still little and doesn't know. When he grows up, he'll find out and compare himself with those who have been born, and he'll want a living life and he'll reproach his mother. Then I shall die."

She neither noticed nor considered that her thoughts would seem mad if they were to be judged by common sense, by that terrible and mad judge of our deeds. She did not consider that that small, unformed, wrinkled fetus which she had discarded, remained just that—an inanimate lump of matter, a dead substance to which the human spirit had not given animate form. No, for Nadezhda Alekseevna, her unborn one was alive and her heart suffered unending torment.

He was all light, in light clothes with little white hands and feet, clear, innocent eyes, a pure smile, and when he laughed, he laughed joyfully and sonorously. True, when she wanted to embrace him, he ran off and hid, but he did not run far away and he hid somewhere nearby. He ran off from her embraces, but on the other hand, he himself often threw his warm tender little arms around her neck, and pressed his delicate lips to her cheek—during those minutes when she was sitting quietly with her eyes closed. Only he never once kissed her directly on the lips.

"He will grow up and understand," thought Nadezhda

Alekseevna,—"he will grieve, turn away, leave forever. Then I shall die."

And now, sitting in the monotonously rumbling cramped streetcar, among bundled-up strangers with their holiday purchases in their laps, Nadezhda Alekseevna closed her eyes and once more saw her child. Once more she looked into his clear eyes, heard his light prattling—she was not paying attention to the words—and in this way she rode to the place where she had to get off.

III

Nadezhda Alekseevna stepped out of the streetcar and walked along the snowy streets past the low stone and wooden houses, past the gardens and fences of this distant suburb. She was walking alone. She ran into strangers—her dear and terrifying one was not with Nadezhda Alekseevna. And she was thinking:

"My sin is always with me and there is nowhere for me to go to escape it. Why then do I live? And here Seryozha has died."

She walked and there was a dull grief in her heart and she did not know how to answer this question for herself.

"Why am I living? But why should I die?"

And she was thinking:

"He is always with me, my little one. He is already growing up, he is eight years old and he must understand a great deal. Why then does he not get angry at me? Doesn't he really want to play with the little children here about, go sledding on the icy slopes? All the charm of our earthly life, everything that even I enjoyed so brightly, all of this charm, this perhaps deceptive, but so entrancing charm of life on this dear earth, in this best of all possible worlds, doesn't it entice him?"

Now, while Nadezhda Alekseevna was walking alone, along the strange, indifferent street, her thoughts did not remain long on herself and her child. She remembered her sister's family, where she was going: her sister's husband, overloaded with work, her sister who was always tired, the horde of little children, noisy, capricious, eternally demanding one thing or another, the wretched apartment, the lack of money. Her nephews and nieces whom Nadezhda Alekseevna loved. And the schoolboy who had shot himself, Seryozha.

Could one have expected this? He had been such a happy, smart boy.

But then Nadezhda Alekseevna remembered a conversation with Seryozha from last week. The boy had been sad and agitated. They were talking about something they had read in the Russian newspapers, no doubt something nightmarish. Seryozha was saying:

"It's awful at home and then you take the newspaper and all you see is terror and filth."

Nadezhda Alekseevna answered something which she herself didn't believe, only in order to distract the boy from his distressing thoughts. Seryozha smiled somberly and said:

"Aunt Nadya, just think how bad all of this is! Just think what's going on around us! Isn't it really terrifying if the best of men, and so old, flees his own house and dies somewhere! He only saw more clearly than any of us that terror in which we all live and he couldn't bear it. He left and died. It's terrifying!"

Then, after a period of silence, Seryozha spoke the words which had frightened Nadezhda Alekseevna at the time:

"Aunt Nadya, I'll tell you frankly because you are a dear and you'll understand me—I don't want at all to live in the middle of all that's going on now. I know that I'm just as weak as everyone else, but what can I do? I'll just be drawn into this vileness, bit by bit. Aunt Nadya, Nekrasov was right: 'It is good to die young.'"

Nadezhda Alekseevna was very frightened and talked with Seryozha for a long time. Finally, it seemed to her that he believed her. He smiled happily as he used to smile and said, in his former carefree tone:

"Okay. We'll live and we'll see. 'Progress advances and where it will end no one knows.'"

Seryozha loved to read, not Nadson and not Balmont, but Nekrasov.

And now there is no Seryozha, he shot himself. So he did not want to live and observe the majestic procession of progress. What is his mother doing now? Kissing his hands which have become waxen? Or is she smearing butter on bread for the little ones who have gone hungry since morning, frightened and tear-stained, so pitiful in their tattered little dresses and in their jackets with worn-out elbows? Or is she simply lying on the bed and crying, endlessly crying? She is fortunate, fortunate if she can cry! What in the world is sweeter than tears?

IV

Finally Nadezhda Alekseevna reached their house, climbed to the fifth floor, up the narrow stone stairway with its steep steps; she climbed quickly, almost ran, so that she was panting, and before ringing, she stopped to catch her breath. She was breathing heavily and she held on to the narrow iron strip of railing with her right hand in its warm, knitted glove and looked at the door.

The door was upholstered with felt and covered with oilcloth and this oilcloth was crisscrossed with narrow black stripes for decoration or strengthening. One of these stripes was torn in two and was hanging down, the oilcloth in this place was torn, and the gray felt protruded. And because of this, Nadezhda Alekseevna was suddenly sorry and pained for some reason. Her shoulders began to shake. She quickly covered her face with her hands and began to cry loudly. It was as if she had suddenly become weak; she quickly sat down on the top step, and cried for a long time, with her face covered. Abundant tears flowed from her closed eyes over the warm knitted gloves.

It was cold, quiet, half-dark on the stairway, and the tightly closed doors—three on one landing—were unmoving and mute. Nadezhda Alekseevna cried for a long time. Suddenly she heard the familiar, light steps. She froze in joyful anticipation. And he, her little one, embraced her neck and again clung to her cheek, moving aside with his little warm hand her hand in the knitted glove. He clung with his tender lips and said to her quietly:

"Why are you crying? You're not guilty!"

She was silent, and listened and did not dare to move and open her eyes for fear he might leave. Only her right hand, the one that he had moved aside, she let drop on her lap; and she covered her eyes with her left hand. And she tried to hold back her tears so as not to frighten him with her unattractive womanly weeping, the weeping of a wretched, earthly woman.

And he said to her again:

"You're not guilty of anything."

And again he began to kiss her cheek. And he said to her, repeating Seryozha's terrifying words:

"I don't want to live here. I thank you, dear mama."

And again he said:

"It's true, believe me, dear mama, I don't want to live."

These words which were so terrifying when Seryozha had said them, were terrifying because the one who said them had received the living form of a human being from a mysterious power and he should have preserved the treasure given to him and not destroyed it—now these same words, in the mouth of the unborn, were joyful for his mother. Ever so quietly, afraid to frighten him with the coarse sound of earthly words, she asked:

"Dear one, have you forgiven me?"

And he answered:

"You aren't guilty of anything. But if you wish, I forgive you."

And suddenly Nadezhda Alekseevna's heart was filled with a foreboding of unexpected joy. Still not daring to hope, still not knowing what would happen, slowly and timidly she extended her hands—and on her lap she felt him, her unborn one, and his hands lay on her shoulders and his lips pressed to her lips. She kissed him for a long while and it seemed to her that the bright eyes of her unborn one, bright as the sun of a benevolent world, looked directly into her eyes, but she dared not open them for fear she would die, having seen that which is forbidden man to see.

When the child relaxed his embrace, and the light footsteps were heard on the stairs, and her child had left, Nadezhda Alekseevna stood up, wiped away her tears, and rang the bell to her sister's apartment. She went to them, calm and happy, to give help to those exhausted from sadness.

The Lady in Bonds

A *Legend of the White Night*

At the house of a certain Muscovite patron of the arts (it is said that now patrons are found only in Moscow) there is a magnificent picture gallery, which after the death of the owner will become the property of the city, but which at present is little known and difficult to get at. In this gallery there hangs a superbly painted picture, strange in content, the work of a little known, though very talented, Russian artist. In the catalog, the picture is identified by the title, "A Legend of the White Night."

The painting depicts a young woman in an elegantly simple black dress, wearing a wide-brimmed black hat with a white feather. She is sitting on a bench in the garden which is about to burst into spring. The woman's face is beautiful, and its expression is enigmatic. In the uncertain, charmed light of the white night, which is entrancingly reproduced by the artist, it seems, at times, that the woman's smile is joyful, though sometimes this smile seems like a pale grimace of terror and despair.

Her hands are not visible—they are placed behind her back—and by the way the woman holds her shoulders, one would think that her hands were bound. Her feet are bare. They are very beautiful. One can see golden bracelets on them bound by a short, gold chain. The combination of the black dress and the white naked feet is beautiful yet strange.

This picture was painted several years ago by the young artist Andrey Pavlovich Kragaev after a strange white night, which the artist spent with the woman depicted in the picture, Irina Vladimirovna Omezhina, at her summer cottage near St. Petersburg.

It was at the end of May. The day had been warm and charmingly clear. Late in the morning, that is at the time when working people are getting ready to have lunch, Kragaev was called to the phone.

The familiar voice of a young woman said:

"It is I—Omezhina. Andrey Pavlovich, are you free tonight? I will expect you at my summer house at exactly two in the morning."

"Yes, Irina Vladimirovna, much obliged,"—Kragaev began.

But Omezhina interrupted him.

"So then, I'll expect you. At exactly two A.M."

And immediately she hung up the receiver. Omezhina's voice was unusually cold and flat, like the voice of a person preparing for something significant. This, plus the brevity of the conversation, greatly surprised Kragaev. He was accustomed to telephone conversations being prolonged, especially with women. Of course, Irina Vladimirovna was no exception to this. For her to say a few words and then hang up was unexpected and new—and it aroused his curiosity.

Kragaev decided to be punctual and to avoid any chance of being late. He ordered a car well in advance—he still did not have his own.

Although not particularly close to Omezhina, Kragaev knew her well enough. She was the widow of a wealthy landowner who had died suddenly several years before that spring. She had her own independent means. The summer cottage where she had invited Kragaev belonged to her.

There were strange rumors about her life with her husband. It was said that he beat her often and cruelly. People wondered why she, a well-to-do woman, should tolerate this and why she did not leave him.

They had no children. It was said that Omezhin was unable

to have children. And this seemed all the more strange:—why then, did she go on living with him?

It was exactly two o'clock by Kragaev's watch and was already becoming quite light when his car slowed down and drew up to the gate of Omezhina's suburban house, which he had had occasion to visit several times the previous summer.

Kragaev experienced a strange agitation.

"Will there be someone else, or am I the only one who was invited?" he thought. "It would be more pleasant to be alone with an attractive lady on this charming night. And I certainly had enough of all these people during the winter!"

There wasn't one carriage visible at the gates. It was completely quiet in the dark garden. There were no lights in the windows of the house.

"Shall I wait?" asked the driver.

"No, don't bother," Kragaev said resolutely, and he paid him.

The gate in the dark fence was partly open. Kragaev entered and closed the gate behind him. Glancing back for some reason, he noticed a key in the gate, and obeying some kind of unclear premonition, he locked it.

He walked quietly along the sandy paths to the house. A coolness came from the river, and somewhere in the bushes the first little birds were chirping weakly and uncertainly.

Suddenly the familiar voice, again as strangely flat and cold as in the morning, called to him:

"I am here, Andrey Pavlovich," said Omezhina.

Kragaev turned in the direction of the voice, and he saw his hostess on a bench in front of a flower bed.

She was sitting and smiling, looking at him. She was dressed exactly as he later depicted her in the picture: the same black dress of an elegantly simple cut with no adornments whatsoever; the same hat with the wide brim and the white feather; her hands were placed behind her back in the same way and they appeared to be bound; and on the damp, yellow sand of the path, one could see her tranquil white feet; and encircling her slender ankles, the gold of the two bracelets, secured with a golden chain, glimmered faintly.

Omezhina smiled with that same vague smile which Kragaev later transferred to the portrait, and she said to him:

"Hello, Andrey Pavlovich. I felt sure somehow that you would not fail to arrive at the appointed hour. Forgive me, I am unable to shake hands,—my hands are tightly bound."

Having noticed Kragaev's movement, she began to laugh joylessly and said:

"No, don't be alarmed,—you don't have to untie them. It has to be this way. That's how he wants it. It's his night again now. Sit here, next to me."

"Who is this 'he,' Irina Vladimirovna?" asked Kragaev with astonishment, but guardedly, as he sat down next to Omezhina.

"My husband," she answered calmly. "Today is the anniversary of his death. He died at this very hour—and every year on this night and at this hour, I give myself up to his power again. Every year he chooses someone into whom his soul enters. He comes to me and torments me for several hours. Until he becomes tired. Then he leaves and I am free until the next year. This year he has chosen you. I see you are astonished. You are ready to think that I am—mad."

"Pardon me, Irina Vladimirovna,"—Kragaev began.

Omezhina stopped him with a slight movement of her head and said:

"No, this is not—insanity. Listen, I'll tell you everything, and you will understand me. It's not possible that such a sensitive and responsive individual as you, such a beautiful and subtle artist, would not understand me."

When a person is told that he is subtle and sensitive, then of course he is prepared to understand everything that is wanted. And Kragaev felt that he was beginning to understand the spiritual condition of the young woman. It would have seemed appropriate as a sign of sympathy that he kiss her hand, and Kragaev would have gladly raised Omezhina's delicate little hand to his lips. But because it was awkward to do this, he limited himself to squeezing her elbow.

Omezhina answered him with a grateful nod of her head. Smiling strangely and uncertainly, so that it was impossible to know whether she was extremely happy or wanted to cry, she said:

"My husband was a weak and wicked man. I don't understand now why I loved him, why I didn't leave him. At first he tormented me timidly, then more openly and more wickedly with each year. He thought up all kinds of torments in order to torture me, but he soon settled on one of the most simple and ordinary tortures. I don't understand why I endured all of this. I didn't understand it then and I don't understand it now. Perhaps I was expecting something. Whatever it was, before that weak and wicked man, I was like a submissive slave."

And Omezhina began to tell Kragaev calmly and in detail, how her husband had tormented her. She spoke as if it were about someone else, as if it were not she that had endured all of this torture and mockery.

Kragaev listened to her with pity and indignation, but her voice was so quiet and flat and breathed such infectious evil, that suddenly Kragaev felt a wild desire to throw her on the ground and to beat her as her husband had beaten her. The longer she spoke and the more details he learned of that wicked torturing, the more clearly he felt within himself this growing, wicked desire. At first it seemed to him that what he felt was simply annoyance at the shameless openness with which she told him her agonizing tale—that it was her quiet, almost innocent, cynicism that was arousing in him this wild desire. But he soon understood that there was a deeper reason for this malicious feeling.

Or couldn't it actually be that the dead man's soul had become incarnate within him, the monstrous soul of a wicked, weak tormentor? He was terrified, but very soon he sensed how in his soul that momentarily sharp terror was dying and how in his soul, the wicked and petty poison of lust for torture flared up ever more commandingly.

Omezhina said:

"I endured it all. I didn't once complain to anyone. I didn't even grumble in my soul. But there was a spring day when I was just as weak as he. A desire for his death entered my soul. Whether the beatings which he gave me were particularly torturous, or whether it was the spring with its ghostly white nights that affected me—I do not know where this desire in me came from. It is so strange. I had never been wicked or weak. For several days I languished with this base desire. At night I sat by the window, looking at the quiet, vague light of the city's northern night, I wrung my hands with anguish and malice and thought wickedly and persistently: 'Die, you accursed one, die!' And so it happened that he did die suddenly, on that very day, at exactly two A.M. But I didn't kill him. Oh, don't think that I killed him!"

"Please, I think nothing of the kind," Kragaev said, but his voice sounded almost angry.

"He died on his own," Omezhina continued. "Or did I perhaps, send him to his grave by the strength of my wicked desire? Perhaps the human will is sometimes so powerful? I don't know. But I felt no repentance. My conscience was completely clear. And so it continued until the following spring. In the springtime, the clearer the nights became, the worse I felt. Anguish oppressed me more and more strongly. Finally, on the night of his death, he came to me and tormented me for a long time."

"So he did come!" said Kragaev with a sudden malicious delight.

"Of course you understand," said Omezhina,—"that this was not the deceased, coming from the graveyard. He was altogether too well-brought up and too urbane a man for such escapades. He was able to arrange it differently. He took possession of the will and spirit of a man who, like yourself, came to me on that night and tormented me cruelly and for a long time. When he went away and left me exhausted from torture, I cried like a little girl who had been unmercifully beaten. But my soul was calm and I didn't think about him again until the following spring. And now every year, when the white nights come, anguish begins to oppress me, and on the night of his death, my tormentor comes to me."

"Every year?" Kragaev asked in a voice choked with malice or agitation.

"Every year,"—said Omezhina,—"there is someone who visits me at this hour and each time it is as if my husband's soul were implanted into my chance tormentor. Then, after the night of torture, my anguish passes and I return to the world of the living. So it has been each year. This year he wanted it to be you. He wanted me to wait for you here, in this garden, in these clothes, with my hands bound, barefoot. And so I am obedient to his will. I sit and wait."

She looked at Kragaev and on her face was that complex expression which he later so artfully brought to his picture.

Kragaev stood up somehow too hurriedly. His face became very pale. Feeling a terrible malice within himself, he seized Omezhina by the shoulder and in a wild, hoarse voice, which he himself didn't recognize, he shouted:

"So it has been each year, and it will be no different with you now. Go!"

Omezhina stood up and began to cry. Kragaev, squeezing her shoulder, turned her towards the house. She walked after him submissively, shivering from the cold and from the dampness of the sand under her bare feet, hurrying and stumbling, feeling at each step the painful pulling of the golden chain and the jolts of the golden bracelets. And so they entered the house.

She Wore a Crown

In a most ordinary, modestly furnished room of a small Petersburg apartment building, a young woman, Elena Nikolaevna, was standing at the window, looking at the street.

There was nothing interesting there, on that noisy, dirty capital thoroughfare, and Elena Nikolaevna was not looking out the window because she wanted to see anything interesting. True, her son, who was due to return from school, would appear from behind the corner of the other cross street any minute, but Elena Nikolaevna certainly did not go to the window to wait for her son! She is so proudly confident of him and herself! He would come at his appointed hour, as always, as everything in life takes place at its appointed time.

Elena Nikolaevna stood there, proud, erect, with an expression on her beautiful, pale face, as if she were wearing a crown.

She stood there, recalling what had happened ten years ago, the year her husband died, with whom she had lived a very short time.

How terrifying death was! One bright day in early spring he had gone out of the house healthy and cheerful, but toward evening they brought his body back—he had perished under a streetcar. It had seemed to Elena Nikolaevna then that there was no more happiness in life for her. She would have died from grief, except that her small son bound her to life, and the dreams she knew from childhood comforted her with time. And how difficult it became to live, how little money there was!

During the summer, Elena Nikolaevna lived in the country
with her son and her younger sister. And now today she recalled
again, with amazing distinctness, that clear summer morning
when such a joyful, strange and seemingly insignificant event
had taken place, and this astonishing clarity descended to her
soul, illuminating her whole life. That astonishing morning,
after which, her whole life, Elena Nikolaevna felt so proud, so
calm, as if she had become the queen of a great and glorious land.

That morning, so memorable to her had begun with a vague
sadness, like every morning of that summer, filled with her tears.

Having done quickly with her few household chores, Elena
had gone to the forest, to be further away from people.

She loved to go into the depths of the forest and to dream
there, or sometimes cry, and recall past happiness.

There was a lovely little glade there—its grass was soft and
moist, the sky above it, high and clear. The moist, tender northern grass, and the pale, lovely, northern sky. Everything in
harmony with her sadness.

Elena had come and stood beside a gray stone in the middle of
the little glade, looking straight ahead with her clear, blue
eyes—her dreams carried her far away. If someone were to
approach her now and call:

"Elena, what are you dreaming about?"

Elena would shudder and forget her sweet dream; in an instant
the many-hued swarm of reveries would shatter; and not for
anything would Elena tell what she had been dreaming.

And really, what business was it of others, what she dreamt
about! They wouldn't understand anyway. . . .What would they
care about these princesses of a dreamy land, with their radiant
faces, their clear eyes, in their shining clothes—these princesses
who come to her and console her!

Elena is standing in a quiet meadow. There is sadness in
Elena's blue eyes. Her arms are crossed on her breast. The sun,
high above her head, warms her slender shoulders from behind,
it plays above her light brown braids like a golden halo. Elena is

daydreaming. And suddenly she hears voices and laughter. There are three radiant maidens, three forest princesses in front of her. Their clothes are white, like Elena's; their eyes are blue, like Elena's; their braids are light brown, like Elena's. On their heads are crowns—flower garlands of many colors. Their slender arms are open like Elena's, and the lovely sun kisses their slender shoulders, like Elena's shoulders. Their slender, slightly suntanned feet bathe in the damp grass, like Elena's feet.

Three forest sisters laugh and come up to Elena and say: "How lovely!"

"She stands and the sun makes her hair golden."

"She stands like a queen."

Sadness and joy are strangely mixed in Elena's head. Elena extends her slight, shapely arms to them, and speaks in a joyfully ringing voice:

"—Greetings, dear sisters, princesses of the forest!"

Elena's voice rings, it rings like a little golden bell,—the forest princesses' light laughter rings, it rings, it pours forth in golden bells.

And the forest princesses say to Elena:

"We are princesses, but who are you?"

"Are you not the queen of this place?"

Elena smiles sadly and answers:

"—How could I be a queen! I have no golden wreath, and my heart is sad because my loved one is dead. No one will crown me."

The sisters are no longer laughing. And Elena hears the quiet voice of the oldest forest princess:

"—Why this earthly sadness! Your loved one died, but is he not really always with you? Your heart is grieving, but does it not have the strength to triumph and rejoice? And does not your will raise you on high?"

And they ask Elena:

"And would you like to be our queen here?"

"I would like to"—says Elena.

And she shivers from joy and joyful little tears glisten in Elena's blue eyes.

And again that forest princess asks:

"—But will you be worthy of your crown?"

Elena trembles from an extraordinary terror and says: "I will be worthy of my crown."

And that princess says to Elena: "Always stand before fate as pure and brave as you are standing before us, and look people directly in the eye. Triumph over sadness, do not fear life, and do not tremble before death. Drive away from yourself slavish thoughts and base feelings, and should you be in poverty and in forced labor and in captivity—be proud and free, dear sister."

Elena trembles and says: "And in slavery I shall be free."

"We crown you"—the princess says.

"We crown you, we crown you"—repeat the others.

They pick golden and white flowers: with their white hands they quickly weave a fragrant crown, the forest queen's flower crown.

And thus Elena is crowned, and the forest princesses link arms and do a quiet dance around her—they have enclosed Elena in the circle of their joyful whirling.

Faster, faster—their light clothes curl around them, their graceful, dancing feet are interwoven with the damp grass. They have enclosed, encircled and carried Elena away into their rapid whirling of rapture—they have carried Elena away from sadness, from life, timidly and dully grieving.

And time was burning up, and the day was melting, and the flaming sadness was transformed into joy, and Elena's heart languished with rapture.

The forest princesses kiss Elena and run off.

"Farewell, dear queen!"

"Farewell, dear sisters," Elena answers them.

They disappeared behind the trees; Elena was left alone.
She walks home, proud, wearing a crown.
She told no one at home about what had happened to her in
the woods. But she grew so proud and radiant, that her little sister
Irochka, who was easily given to laughter, said:
"Elena is shining today like a birthday child."
Elena did not tell anyone at home, but she needed to tell
someone.
Toward evening, Elena went to visit a little boy, Pavlik, who
was soon to die. Elena loved him because he was always serene
and because he would remain serene forever. Sometimes at night
Elena awakened with a feeling of acute pity for Pavlik—she
awakened to cry about the young boy who was soon to die. And
in her heart there was a strange mixture of pity for her late
husband, for herself, orphaned at an early age, and for the young
boy who was soon to die.
Pavlik was sitting alone in a high summer house above a
ravine, and he was watching the quietly flaming sunset. He saw
Elena and smiled,—he was always glad when Elena came. He
loved her because she never told him untruths, and she did not
comfort him as the others did. Pavlik knew that he would die
soon, and there would be only two who would long remember
him—his own mother and dear Elena Nikolaevna.
Elena told Pavlik what had happened to her that morning in
the forest. Pavlik closed his eyes, he became pensive. Then he
smiled joyfully, and said:
"I am happy, my forest queen. I always knew that you were free
and pure. You see every one who can say 'I' should be the master
on earth. The ruler of the earth is—man."
Then Pavlik peered at three girls who were passing below,
under the ravine, and he said to Elena:
"Look, there are your dear forest princesses walking this way."
Elena looked and recognized them and her heart contracted
with sudden anguish. Three girls! They have on the very same

white dresses as this morning and their eyes are blue and the braids are brown and the arms shapely, but there are no longer any wreaths, but rather, they have white hats on their heads. They are ordinary girls, vacationing girls!

They were hidden for a moment behind the bushes and then came back into view, and turned upwards, walking along a narrow path past the summer house where Pavlik sits with Elena. They nod to Pavlik tenderly, and they have recognized Elena.

"Greetings, dear queen!"

"Sisters!"—Elena exclaims joyfully.

And Elena was gladdened forever. And the joy of a crowned life appeared to her in everyday life. She would carry her queenly pride and her exalted dignity through all the ordeals of a poor, wretched life.

And now after many years, here she was, standing before the window, dressed in a poor, worn dress, waiting for her son, and she whispers, recalling the day of her coronation:

"Man—is the ruler of the earth."